Mister Blue Sky

James Dargan

Published by Danny Boy Books, 2013.

Mister Blue Sky
Copyright © 2013 by James Dargan
Published by Danny Boy Books
Book cover picture courtesy of WikiCommons

Also by James Dargan

A Bayside City Book
Dead Soprano
Purple Haze
Red Magic
Honey Bee
Killer Toast
Tiger Dawn
Bullet City

A Napoleon Clancy Book
Lenin's Ghost
Napoleon Clancy

A Neo-Noir Crime Thriller
Pig Killer
Gun Smoke
Butcher Boy
Fat Cat
Fat Cat & Gun Smoke: Two Neo-Noir Crime Thrillers

Napoleon Clancy Books
Spaghetti Junction
Cuyahoga Blues
Dublin Murder Mystery
Spanish Poodle

Standalone
God and the Lonely Emperor
In the Dole-Drums

1: At New Wembley with Tears in Me Eyes

2011

The final whistle's just gone and I'm chuffed like. We've just won a cup final. At last, after all these years – and I aiyn't talkin' about none of them Mickey Mouse competitions like the Leyland DAF Cup - we've finally won summat. It's hard for me to describe what I'm feelin' right now, as winnin' at Wembley Stadium's unbelievable. Okay, it aiyn't the proper Wembley, it's New Wembley, but it's *still* Wembley. I think I'm gonna cry in a minute. Well, I wanna anyway.

But that's summat else. Just bein' here brings it all back. Ya, know, how it was and stuff. What I wanna do is tell ya about what happened to me and why it happened to me. It dayn't matter if ya think I'm a knob or summat. Ya probably will think that anyway, but I'm gonna leave all that for ya to decide.

Even though it was a long time ago now, I still remember what happened in all the little details. I suppose ya can say I was a bit stupid and selfish and stuff, but that was the way it happened and there aiyn't nothin' I can do about it other than tell ya the truth.

2: Some Villa Scumbag and a Bombshell

1985

Life's a bit like Subutteo really: sometimes ya win, sometimes ya draw, but mostly – and I mean this – ya end up treadin' on the little players barefoot and it hurts to fuck.

It all started with a scrap in a city-centre booza. I aiyn't sayin' I'm scared shitless, but I'm a bit worried at any comeback from it, especially when I heard he's one of the top boys from the C Crew, Vile's 'supposed' main firm. He was slaggin' off me team, ya see, and I wasn't gonna put it with that. One thing led to another and it kicked off big time. He's a big, hard cunt in his early forties as far as I can remember. I've promised meself not to go for a tot in town now, just to be on the safe side, at least for a while.

Nah, let me say it another way: it was a little scuffle - well, I landed a lucky punch in before I legged it for me life along with a mate.

Apart from that little run in, though, the music and the fashion and the atmosphere are spot on like – so was the Birmingham City–Leeds United rumble at St Andrews in May on the last day of last season. I wasn't there, mind ya – at the match, that is - but a mate was, Alan Irving, and he got a right good kickin' or so that's what he told me.

These are the Thatcher years, and bein' honest with ya Brum aiyn't much to look at really – it's all concrete and stuff and the fuckin' Bullring's an embarrassment. Lads can be lads but there aiyn't no fuckin' jobs to be had and we're all pissed off about that.

What I just told ya's bollocks though, ya know, about the music at least: there aiyn't no fuckin' music culture at all. I mean, come on, if Duran Duran and UB-fuckin'-40 are all we've got, we're definitely in for it. Now Manchester – there's a place for music: they've got New Order, The Smiths, The Fall – and they had that bloke Ian Curtis too before he killed himself, the silly cunt.

Yeah, but Brum... it aiyn't got much. Nothin' apart from dole queues as long as the eye can fuckin' see and, not countin' me own bird, the ugliest slags known to man.

Oh, yeah, and the football... Tellin' ya the truth, I aiyn't a hooligan anyway. I like the culture, the talk, ya know, the 'exteriors', but when it comes to really mixin' it, well, that's another thing. I aiyn't sayin' I aiyn't never scrapped, but not like some of me mates have.

Me best mate, Nobby, hates footy with a passion and aiyn't got no idea what's really goin' on with the hooligans and their reputation that's bin followin' the game round like a dark fuckin' shadow for more than a decade. He's a good lad, if ya know what I mean, as least comparin' him to some of the other clowns I hang round with. He stops me really gettin' into the terrace culture and gettin' meself a nice little police record.

Music's what Nobby loves. Yeah, and it's Nobby who got me into The Smiths last year when their first record came out and Morrissey was leadin' 'em in his own daffodil revolution. We listened to their first album for hours over cans of lager and fags. But it's their second effort, this year's *Meat is Murder*, that's really put 'em in the big league of music legends as far as I'm concerned. A modern masterpiece, it shows how music – I mean the alternative type – should be played.

Well, it's this band that's the backdrop to our lives at the minute.

Most, ya know, especially Thatcher's posh shower down in Cockneyland, are all well up their own arses and think lads like us are just wasters, but all we're askin' for is a fuckin' stable job and a decent wage. The twats can only write bad things about us in them poxy fuckin' newspapers like *The Times* and *The Observer*, rags I never read.

I live at home with me mom and dad, ya know. It's comfortable that way – there's no washin' or ironin' or cleanin'' to do. Pretty cushty, really, and seein' as I'm on the dole, me only alternative.

I met the love of me life this year at a friend's house-party. There weren't no sparks at first between me and Lynsey - it happened sorta quick like a bit later on – it was Saint Patrick's Day in a city-centre pub where we met for a second time by accident. I only went there coz Nobby's Irish and he sorta forced me to go.

Me family's English and proud of the fact, so the Irish piss me off a bit even though, like I said, Nobby's a Paddy. Lynsey too, but she's fit and I have to just grin and bear it. I wanted to get me end away and was pissed outta me tree and with all me Dutch courage I went over and gave her a snog. Funnily enough, I dayn't even get blown out and a fuckin' slap on the face as woulda loadsa blokes in the same situation. We started spendin' loadsa time together. It was great at the beginnin': Friday and Saturday nights we'd be in the pub with Nobby and a couple of the other lads, but somehow I always ended up back at Lynsey's. She's got her own gaff, ya see – well, not her own, she rents it – she's loaded compared to me and is also two years older at twenty three.

I have to say I love the older woman – most of 'em are slags, mind ya, but I like the dabble now and again. Nobby and I used to bet each other for a sky-diver to see who could pull the oldest minger. Nobby usually won as his standards are lower than a British Railways carriage toilet. He once pulled an old bastard in a Sparkhill nightclub and brought her back to his gaff, an adventure which ended with him gettin' the crabs.

After that little escapade he's more careful when out on the pull.

It pisses him off a bit now that I dayn't chase after skirt like we used to after I met Lynsey, though I always have to remind him of '83 – I hardly saw the twat at all that summer and what was he doin'? He was only shacked up with some bird called 'Vicky', well till they had a massive argument and split up. He was knockin' on me front door a few hours later and we were smokin' draw down the local park.

Before The Smiths came onto the scene I dunno who I'd listened to – nothin' worth talkin' about, probably. I'd always liked music, I suppose, but nothin' had ever stirred me like The Smiths. Not that there hadn't bin no good stuff before they appeared, it was just I dayn't know about it. Nobby loved 'em more than I did, though. By the time I met Lynsey, Nobby had already sin 'em loadsa times up and down the country – he's a real madhead for 'em. I aiyn't sin 'em yet, but I wanna – it's just since I lost me job any dough I've got I spend it on the football.

Me and Lynsey have just celebrated six months together. But it aiyn't as happy as all that. There's always summat that fucks everythin' up.

Only medicine can help, but I dayn't see the fuckin' NHS doin' much to save her. When I told Nobby over a pint at our local he was sound like. I aiyn't ashamed to say it really touched me the way he was. All right, Nobby talked wearin' his rose-tinted glasses even though I knew next to nothin' about the illness other than it was a nasty killer.

I aiyn't never bin the religious kind. Me Church of England upbringin' aiyn't helped me there, I suppose. Lynsey's a Catholic, and a practisin' one too. I aiyn't never understood what all the fuckin' fuss is about over the Mass: it seems a complete waste of time to me and I even took the piss outta the Church a few times and Lynsey didn't like that.

She went to the Queen Elizabeth for tests. I didn't know at the time coz the Blues were playin' Southampton away in a First Division match. We lost the game one-nil. I was more pissed off than usual coz we'd lost to 'em at The Dell only five days before three-nil in a League Cup third-round replay. The season's bin a disaster and we've lost most of our matches and are near the bottom of the table.

When I got back to Brum the match faded into insignificance.

The doctors say it's leukaemia, and the most aggressive type too, though I dayn't remember the name of it, but the name dayn't matter anyway – leukaemia's enough, LEU-KAEM-IA, coz I understand that. It means 'deadly' and fuckin' 'life-threatenin'.

She was feelin' slightly unwell all summer: weakness and hot flushes and fatigue. She even took time off work in the council. Nobody knew about it, though - she kept it all hush like – she didn't wanna worry nobody, she says now. Well, after I came back from the South Coast I went straight to her parents' gaff to find her there in the livin' room cryin' her eyes out along with her old lady. They told me everythin'. She was goin' into hospital right away to start induction chemotherapy or summat. Her bags were beside her and packed. That was the 16th November. I remember her old man and the proper fuckin' stare he gave me like some loony bastard from a mental hospital. I knew he wanted it to be me, but it wasn't and it aiyn't. She's his only daughter and he loves her, I suppose. He's got two sons as well, but I remember Lynsey tellin' me once he's a right hard prick with 'em. Lynsey always gets away with murder.

"It's the Irishman – he just loves his daughters," she said to me one day about it.

She has to find a bone marrow donor, coz the doctors believe the chemo aiyn't gonna decrease the leukaemia cells or summat. All that doctor lingo flies right over me head. Word's already gone round from her old schoolmates to people she works with, and posters in every pub from Billesley Common to Small Heath. I did me thing too, I suppose: I got Matty Jackson, one of me terrace mates, to contact one of the top boys in the Zulus in the hope of gettin' a donor drive started at St Andrews. Unluckily, the bloke who Matty contacted - a real aggressive sort from all accounts who earned his stripes in many a ruck against other firms for the Apex Boys in the '70s - refuses to lift a fuckin' finger as far as I know, sayin' Lynsey's old man did a foreigner on his uncle's roof last summer and made a right dog's bollocks of it. He accuses Christy - Lynsey's old man - of goin' back on his word when he refused to repair it. It's a small world. I'm relieved, mind ya – I dayn't wanna owe some yob who's a nob a favour, a favour I know I'd have to repay someday in me own blood or summat. I aiyn't told her parents nothin' about it. Best to keep it hush, I think.

Listenin' to the depressin' Smiths aiyn't helpin' the situation, either, but I can't help meself. They're part of me and part of Lynsey. Their music's a symbol of our love - only Lynsey dayn't know about it. She's more into Wham, Duran Duran, ABC, and Scritti Politti. That stuff's all fuckin' crap to me but probably better music to listen to in a time of crisis. I mean there's either what she likes or what? King? Depeche Mode? Madonna? Although Gahan and his group are all right, they dayn't really hit the spot like Stephen and the jingly compositions of Johnny-the-god. Just as well I'm a stubborn cunt. There are a shitload of songs I listen to, some for no other reason than I like 'em - others coz I always see me lynsey's face when I listen to 'em. *That Joke isn't Funny Anymore* and *Well I Wonder* are like that. It's bad, really – I'm givin' meself extra grief listenin' to 'em. Most of the casuals on the terraces, dressed to the bloody nines in their designer Ralph Lauren and Pierre Cardin gear, would laugh their heads off if they sussed it.

Most of the older ones are still in their late '70s time warp of Two-Tone and Coventry's favourite sons, The Specials. I know such blokes - hard as nails most of 'em but I wouldn't call none of 'em me mates, though every Saturday we share the same tribal emotions on the stands at St Andrews and round the country, and in some ways, though I dayn't like to admit it, I suppose they are me brothers, at least from August to May for ninety minutes on a Saturday afternoon. Nah, I aiyn't one of them yobs anyhow – I actually like watchin' the footy on the pitch, even if at times it is takin' the piss.

But we have had some good players in our history, and a few exceptional ones. Trevor Francis - Britain's first one-million-quid player – bein' one of 'em. What a legend he was – shame we had to flog him off in the end.

When Lynsey went into hospital, I went with her. The chemo's gonna be hard and is gonna make her feel like shit.

The NHS is nothin' to write home about, either, like I said. It's underfunded and on its last fuckin' legs. It's like English footy in a way: the grounds - like the hospitals - are fallin' to pieces. Some hospitals aiyn't had a proper do up in fifty years. The grounds too. When Valley Parade caught fire on the last day of last season - and on the same day as our ruck with Leeds – it was only coz the wooden terracin' was so flammable it was takin' the piss. There was no investment, ya know what I mean? It was a tragic day for English football. Later in May, the Liverpool fans went berserk at the Heysel stadium, beginnin' what's a European ban for all English clubs. Not that it means much to Birmingham City, mind ya. Nah, ya can't compare us - we're light years away in football terms to them Scally cunts. We aiyn't never enjoyed no glorious mid-week nights under floodlights in Europe, except for a few Fair's Cup matches in the '50s and '60s, matches that most die-hard Bluenoses dayn't remember much about anyway.

But I drifted off again, like I always do. Yeah, but goin' back to the hospitals – which is the most important thing in the end when it comes down to it. Lynsey's ward is pissin' me off as well: Eight beds and fulla Pakis and it stinks like an Alum Rock curry house. I aiyn't gonna complain about it, though, as most of the doctors are Pakis too. One of 'em, a Doctor Khan with a snobby, public schoolboy accent, had the fuckin' cheek to stop me eatin' Monster Munch over Lynsey's bed the other day, when the fuckin' Pakis beside us had brought chicken samosas and pakoras with 'em and were eatin' 'em like there was no tomorra.

I aiyn't no racist, or that's how I like people to see me, though maybe a couple of years back I was a bit like. I know the difference between a Pakistani, an Indian and a Bangladeshi. I aiyn't ignorant, though I know lads who are. We Bluenoses are some of the most racist in the country yet it's funny that our firm, the Zulus, is one of the most ethnically mixed: Blacks of Jamaican and West Indian descent mainly, though there are a few Pakis, though most of 'em go unseen. The Pakis are pretty good scrapers, too, when they wanna be: knife merchants who aiyn't afraid to mix it. I know a few personally – sound lads, they are. They dayn't spend a lotta time in the boozas, especially the Pakistanis as they aiyn't allowed a tot, but they enjoy a scuffle now and again. The few that do drink, the Sikhs, are well up for it even after half a fuckin' shandy. Can't handle the drink at all that lot, and they're like fuckin' girls when they're pissed.

I have to say the Pakis in Brum suffer from a shit loada stick. Name callin' every day, as well as the occasional beatin'. From time to time I often call 'em names meself – even once to a brother of Sanjiv on New Street. Sanjiv's a lad I know from St Andrews, and when I saw his brother later on the same day in a Small Heath pub I went red-faced with shame, ya know what I mean. I explained meself to Sanjiv and his brother let me off.

I hate political correctness with a passion and it seems to becomin' more and more common these days. Racist name callin' is just a natural part of the landscape. I know enough lads who use the word 'Paki' and aiyn't really racists. This is our lingo and we dayn't think twice about it.

Lynsey's first full day in hospital was bad for us all. There were tests for this and that and for everythin' else. At the end of it I went home, knackered, where I cried. It was like at me grandad's funeral a few years before.

I lost me grandad and now I think I'm gonna lose Lynsey too.

Nah, it can't be like that. I can't give up hope, ya know what I mean? Nah, I aiyn't gonna let it happen like... Just as I said, nah, it just aiyn't gonna happen... I'm sure of it... There aiyn't no way.

3: Dreams of some Casual and The Gunners Away

I've got an interview for a job Lynsey arranged for me on the bins a few weeks ago. At the time I was chuffed but climbin' outta bed and even thinkin' about goin' is makin' me feel sick. I dayn't have no choice, though: I'm skint and owe people dough - me old lady for starters: she's doin' her nut as I aiyn't paid her no housekeep in ages.

It turns out to be a bad two minutes:

"Why do you want the job, Mr Acheson?" the interviewer asks me, sittin' behind his desk, the double of Bernard Mannin', just a bit fatter and not funny.

"Coz I wanna better meself, ya twat... Why d'ya think... I need a job and there aiyn't many of them cunts around at the minute..."

I dayn't get the job. It's no tragedy, mind ya – I already have one of them things eyeballin' me.

In the afternoon I go to the hospital again with grapes under me arm. I dunno why I took 'em other than the fact I've always sin 'em on the patients' bedside tables in the American sitcom, *St Elsewhere*, which me mom loves. I wanted to bring her a couple of Rowntree's Yorkies and some Cadbury's crème eggs, though I wasn't sure how well that woulda gone down with the nurses.

When I get there she dayn't look too smart. I stay the whole day but she's outta the game for most of it. Not bein' family I have to fuck off at eight in the evenin'. Just before I leave, luckily, she wakes up and we talk for a few minutes, but it aiyn't the same with half her family round the bed.

And there's the strange thing to that too. Yeah, her family. They're shifty and Irish. I dayn't like 'em and judgin' by their attitude they feel the same about me.

I'm at Nobby's by nine and we talk, drink and smoke draw half the night – I end up crashin' at his in the end after I pass out.

The next mornin' I get me arse off his uncomfortable settee well after eleven. Nobby calls a sicky as he's as hungover as meself. Me mouth's dry as fuck, so after checkin' that there's fuck all in his fridge, I go to the Paki shop to get meself summat there. With me last fiver in me pocket I buy a can of Irn-Bru, a packet of sausage and a thick-sliced loaf.

Over breaky we talk:

"I can get ya a job if ya wanna?" Nobby says. I've let Lynsey down already with the job in the council. I feel a rush of guilt.

Nobby works in a factory on a lathe. He calls himself an engineer, but ya have to have a degree to be one of them. Nobby aiyn't even got a CSE to his name. He's bin in the job since he was sixteen – it's off one of them shitty YTS schemes that everybody in the country's takin' the piss outta. It's the most borin', mind-numbin' work known to man. But still, a fact's a fact: Nobby's got a job and I aiyn't.

"So, can ya try and get me there?" I ask, slurpin' me tea.

"I'll ask the gaffer."

I've bin a prat, really: jobs are like gold dust: three- million-odd people on the dole and I'm bein' a fussy cunt. Like Nobby, I dayn't have no qualifications from school, so that aiyn't gonna get me very far. All me mates left comp in 1980 like meself with fuck all. We thought we were clever cunts but I'm startin' to have me doubts.

The only good thing with bein' on the rock-and-roll is I've got a shitload of time to visit Lynsey in the hospital.

"Nah, fuck it, Nob – I couldn't handle that lathe all day doin' me head in... And anyway, I dayn't think I'd be good at it."

"What d'ya mean 'ya wouldn't be good at it'?" Nobby asks, pissed off, "a monkey as blind as ten Mogoos could do what I do."

"Nah, I can't be arsed."

"Ya havin' a laugh, aiyn't ya. Dayn't be pissin' around... D'ya want me to ask the gaffer or not?"

"Nah, just fuck it."

4: Porn and Ya Wrong Crap Ex-Arsenal Keeper Bob Wilson

Lynsey's gettin' worse: they aiyn't found a bone marrow donor but we still aiyn't given up hope. Although she's chirpy at times, she's gettin' weaker. They've pumped so many shitty cocktails into her body she dunno if she's comin' or goin'.

After visitin' the hospital more times than I can remember this week, I need cheerin' up. It's Friday – but I aiyn't in no mood to head down the booza. Nobby wants to watch a porno he got from a mate at work. Feelin' a bit guilty, I tell him no. Half an hour later, though, I give in and for the rest of the evenin' we 'enjoy' watchin' skinny little white bastards – all John Holmes lookalikes with stupid tashes - enjoyin' anal with countless big-tittied darlings.

Only I still feel guilty. How can I watch it knowin' Lynsey's sufferin'. Well, I know the answer: like any lad, sex is sex and I aiyn't gettin' none at the minute so I might as well.

"I'd love a wank now," Nobby says, takin' the cassette from the video recorder. A ham shank's as far from me mind as givin' Denis Thatcher a blowjob. I dayn't need to hear what Nobby wants. And anyway, I'm thinkin' of the Liverpool match at home tomorra, and I dayn't have the dough for it.

I leave Nobby's twenty minutes later, thinkin' all the way home how I can get some cash for the game. By the time I close me eyes and am almost asleep, I still dunno what to do.

Goodnight sweetheart.

I roll outta bed the next mornin' late as usual, go downstairs in only me kegs to see what's to eat. The house and the fridge are empty and I'm starvin'. I have beans on toast. After that I go into the livin' room and switch on the telly, only for Max Headroom to be on the box. I turn over to BBC One and *Football Focus* has just started with Bob Wilson. He's goin' on about the Liverpool match and, like always, the pundits dayn't give us a fuckin' chance. That pisses me off – it's like that with the cunts from the BBC and Central television with their football prejudices: the Midland's clubs dayn't exist for 'em, except for maybe Clough's Forest. It's the north and south and the bit in the middle they dayn't give a shit about.

I go back upstairs and get dressed, brush me teeth, have a shit, then leave for the QE again. When I get there she's sleepin'. They've sedated her coz she was in pain. After spendin' the day at her bedside, I leave the hospital at eight. When I get home me old lady tells me that Nobby's phoned and that he wants me to ring him back. I think it's about the job again, so I phone him but he dayn't pick up, probably already on his fifth jar down the pub.

"Mom, got a couple of quid to lend us?" I ask, hopin'.

"Piss off, ya already owe me fifty... and what about me housekeep?"

It's a quiet night in then.

Lynsey's family's treatin' me like shit. I reckon it's all coz I aiyn't a Catholic and a Paddy or summat. That's me guess, anyway. I'm doin' me nut about it – did I invent all the cancers and leukaemias and everythin' else that's bad in the world? Sorry, but nah. It aiyn't *my* fault. I love their Lynz, and I guess they're jealous of it.

Yeah, but I'm tryin' to suss 'em out, but it's difficult – what do they want from me?

I listen to the whole *Meat is Murder* album about five times waitin' for Nobby to ring and thinkin' over the loss against Dalglish's men and Lynsey's family. He dayn't ring back in the end and I just doze off, thinkin' what coulda bin if Liverpool didn't have Alan Hansen and Ian Rush.

5: Me Old Lady's cookin', Saviour of the British Car Industry and a Black Eye

I wake up early to the smell of me old lady's fry-up. I run downstairs like an Ethiopian at dinner time and throw meself onto the chair at the table. She dishes up. Me old man's still in bed - he always has a lie in on a Sunday, as every other mornin' – includin' Saturdays – he's up at five for work at Rover. I worked there for a few days last year and I fuckin' hated the place. Me old man got me in like, but I couldn't hack it. Assembly line work's a waste of time. Me dad went ape shit when I walked out half-way through a shift on me second or third day, I dayn't remember exactly – let him down, he still says. But I aiyn't gonna put meself through that crap for nobody. If them blokes wanna work there, then let 'em, but I just can't be arsed. Me old man likes the work, mind ya. He tells me the monotony's comfortin' – thick twat, he is. 'Comfortin', what does that mean?

I never wanna be like me dad and Nobby and all the others. They can support the heart and soul of British fuckin' industry willingly if they wanna, but that aiyn't me.

After breakfast I'm back down the hospital for the millionth time (only jokin'). On the way, though, I call for Nobby but he dayn't answer the door, so I suppose he must be pissed up from last night and dead to the world or shacked up somewhere with a bird havin' his little prick nibbled to pieces big time.

I get to the QE at twelve. This time I'm loaded with apples and oranges and a small box of Milk Tray, spendin' almost the last of me dough. I give Lynz the chocolates normally, and there's no climbin' mountains, jumpin' canyons and dodgin' Dobermans to get 'em to her.

"I hope those chocolates aren't for whom I think they're for," the nurse on duty asks as I'm walkin' into the ward.

"Nah, love," I say, grinnin' and lyin' through me teeth.

She smiles and lets me in.

She's awake. She woke up an hour ago and is still groggy. Her old man's with her and they're talkin'.

"How ya feelin', Lynz?" I ask, me smile as long as a copper's truncheon.

"Not bad," she answers. I know it aiyn't true. Her old man looks at me. I suss it that he aiyn't pleased to see me. I've interrupted 'em. He leaves soon after the doctor comes round for his daily check up on her. He dayn't feel comfortable with me. The air – ya know, he couldn't breathe, or at least that woulda bin his excuse if he'd had to make one.

"Feel better today, Lynsey?" the doctor asks.

"I'm knackered, doctor."

"It's normal. That's what the medication does to you. Don't worry about it too much."

I stand back as he examines her.

"Everything's fine," he says.

Fuckin' lyin' cunt, I think – she's almost dyin' and all he can do is put his dirty fuckin' hands all over her and play the nice bloke.

The doctor leaves and we're on our tod for over an hour till Lynsey's old lady arrives with her youngest brother, Noel.

She's really up for talkin'. Nah, it's just the opposite. The drugs she's on take all her energy. A zombie with its mouth gagged is better conversation. But I know the story – it's okay, as long as I can be near her that's enough.

I go home depressed.

I'm in me room and listenin' to The Smiths again. I love self-torture.

There's a knock on me bedroom door: Nobby walks in with a shiner over his right eye. It's a beauty.

"What the fuck happened to ya?" I ask, risin' from the bed.

"I got jumped by two cunts in town last night," he answers, angry.

I sense some pride in his voice. He has a battle scar and wants everybody to know about it.

"Where exactly?"

"Outside one of them fuckin' pubs on Corporation Street."

"Which one? There are loads down there."

"Dunno. I dayn't remember."

I'm thinkin' to meself if it's the same one where I nearly got laid out by that Villa scumbag. Nobby aiyn't got no idea I was on Corporation Street. And anyway, I wanna keep it all hush – it's a bit embarrassin'

"Ya know it's a fuckin' Villa pub, dayn't ya?"

"What is?" he asks.

"Ya were probably in one of them Villa bars."

The truth is it aiyn't really – there's a mixture, and on a Friday and Saturday night ya get the boys from both sets of hooligans drinkin' up and down that part of the City Centre, though at the minute – at least since the May tear up with Leeds - many of the top boys from the Zulus are on the run from the Old Bill, who've set up an investigation or summat on Steelhouse Lane, and coz of it town's lackin' the real buzz that's bin around over the last couple of seasons between the two clubs. And anyway, the Zulus' work's bein' taken over by the Junior Business Bovver boys at the minute, teenagers really, but little cunts ready for a bang off in the name of their club, Birmingham City F.C. They're doin' what the Zulu's did before with The Apex. It's survival of the fittest like, Darwin without all that scientific bollocks.

If a bloke on the street asks me about all this, I can blag him a good line that I know all the ins and outs of what's happenin' on the terraces, but the reality is summat else. Okay, I know a few top lads from the manor, bin nicked once for swearin' at a black copper for summat I dayn't wanna repeat, and bin witness to when the Vile got turned over by the Zulus on one occasion as well as a few things at away matches, yet most of the time when trouble comes me way, I'm usually the one leggin' it.

Nobby dayn't give a flyin' fuck about football and a booza's a booza to him. The place I nearly got done over in aiyn't exactly a kangaroo court, either – far from the dives in Lozells and Handsworth in that respect – but with the Vile drinkin' there trouble's always a possibility.

It's hard to define what the terms 'Blues pub' and 'Villa pub' mean anyway, coz in the past it was all about territory and stuff. Us lot are mainly in the south and east of the City. Villa in the north and west. In town, though, nothin' is so clearly cut, and when there's any aggro it's usually footy related.

"D'ya smack one of the cunts?" I ask, burnin' with anger and shadow-boxin' like I'm doin' Rocky in a game of charades.

"How Daz, I couldn't see a thing?"

"So ya didn't see their faces?"

"Nah."

"Were they Villa?"

"Dunno."

For the rest of the evenin' we listen to The Smiths and talk. Nobby asks me about Lynsey and he leaves at eleven. I go straight to bed.

6: I'm Quite Intelligent Really

I get up and go downstairs, switch on the telly and watch the mornin' news. Ronald Reagan's met the week before with the new Russian leader, Mikhail Gorbachev, in Geneva, and one of them analyst blokes is givin' it loads, sayin' how it will change the Cold War. I'm sat on me sofa like, scratchin' me balls and pickin' me nose, and I dayn't even know what the Cold War is – it could be two Eskimos havin' a snowball fight for all I care, coz really I dayn't give a shit. I'm a total ignorant cunt like that. Maybe it's hard for lads like meself to appreciate how hard governments are workin' for us, the scumbags wasters in Birmingham: the blokes and young lads who aiyn't got no idea why they're livin' other than to get pissed and start a brawl in a booza, or if not that to give the verbals to some poor bloke for no other reason than to piss 'em off. Maybe summat a little more interestin' like vandalisin' a phone box or muggin' an old cunt of their poxy fuckin' pension. It aiyn't everyone, but there are a few like that – more than a few, in fact.

So many things have happened or are happenin' now in the world: The Iran- Iraq War, the Indian Bhopal Chemical Disaster – even the Falklands War... Ya see, I'm only crankin' ya up – I aiyn't that stupid really.

British people are some of the most ignorant on the planet: brain-washed by the news and by all them shitty soaps such as *Coronation Street* and *Brookside*, that sorta create a shit-for-brains mentality. I've bin sucked in big time meself.

"I hope ya gonna get off ya arse sometime today and get on down the blasted Jobcentre?" It's me old lady.

And that is the word I really hate: the 'Jobcentre'. For the unemployed it offers hope, or some would say, tries to offer it. For me it's a hard decision choosin' what's worse: the Vile or the Jobcentre? It's a hard one. Thousands hold onto some hope - welcomed by the orange, white and black sign above the door – but quickly lose it as it turns into distrust and bitterness.

Signin' on's an experience too. I find the twats' incompetence and lack of respect for us claimants beyond a joke. Ya just a number. Bein' on time for ya appointment's a waste of time as well – a sixty-minute wait aiyn't uncommon. Most of the knobs who work there are fuckin' ignorant cunts who dayn't have no respect for the jobless. They dayn't give a shit if ya find a job or not – it's just about statistics and goals for them. A tick here in this box, a tick there in that one. Forms, forms and more forms. Queues of people – some to sign on, others seekin' help in findin' a low paid job as a cleaner or some other work that pays piss poor. Most of us - but especially the old bastards - know we dayn't have a Bob Hope in findin' summat even half-decent. They're always askin' the same, pointless questions put to ya by the sad, bespectacled, middle-aged civil servant, usually in a worse mental state than the unemployed he or she's supposed to be helpin'. Years of robot-like repetition has made their lives unbearable.

7: Bloke from the Black Stuff

"Are you currently seeking work, Mr Acheson?"

"Yeah."

"Where?"

"In factories, mostly."

"Would you consider doing other kinds of work?"

"Yeah."

"We have a vacancy for a security guard on a building site in Nechells... would you be interested in that?"

"Nah."

"Why, Mr Acheson?"

"Them twelve-hour shifts are killers."

"You do realise you've an obligation to the State to be actively seeking work at all times; anything against this could jeopardize your unemployment benefit."

There he is, given it loads, usin' his fancy words with me, tryin' to make me feel as gormless as he looks.

"Are ya threatenin' me?" I ask him.

"No," he replies calmly, rubbin' his chin. "You could lose your benefits with an attitude like that, Mr Acheson."

He's lookin' for a smack, but though I'm stupid, I aiyn't that fuckin' stupid.

"What d'ya mean?" I say, me eyes fixed on him like a mad-headed Rottweiler.

"I'm just telling you how it is, Mr Acheson," he goes on in his borin' voice, typical of ya state careerist. "Maybe you need some help preparing your CV for potential employers? We're running a training course soon on returning to work.

He hands me a shiny leaflet: he's scored a victory, or so he thinks, judgin' by the wanker-like smirk on his face.

"How many trees did ya bosses down in London cut down to make this shite?" I say, before scrunchin' the leaflet up in me jacket pocket. It's gonna end up in the bin outside.

I get up from me seat. Just as I'm about to leave, four big bastards – brickies or labourers if their cement-covered boots are anythin' to go by – come in. They seem real hard cunts and a bit dodgy lookin', Paddies maybe, coz two of 'em are ginger like. It's clear they're here to sign on. The staff behind their desks, too afraid they'll get chinned if they happen to say fuck all, just look on with a nod of the head to show they aiyn't happy with the blokes' behaviour. They know they're doin' casual work - such takin' the piss outta the staff in the Jobcentre's common practice, ya know, but most of 'em turn a blind eye to it.

The Pakis are the worst, though. Maybe they can run a cornershop or a takeaway, but they're fuckin' useless at doin' any real graft. Most of 'em dayn't speak a word of fuckin' English too. They aiyn't used to gettin' off their lazy arses. Them who can't cook or dayn't have the dough for a business are in for a rude awakenin' on the shop floor or on the buildin' site. The majority – and this is all bad news for the government - find themselves in the Jobcentre, either lookin' for summat easy or a way into education or full-time trainin', that way they dayn't have to exert themselves too much. They get away with murder as well: the Jobcentre staff hand 'em out leaflets in every fuckin' language under the sun, but when a mate of mine, Paul Dell, needed help fillin' in an application form for a job some time ago, coz he's a thick twat and couldn't do it himself, the fuckers didn't give him the time of day.

8: Still Dreamin' of Arsenal at Highbury

On Saturday we're playin' Arsenal away. I desperately wanna go but I'm skint. I've got exactly fifty five pence in me pocket, and that aiyn't even gonna get me to the other side of town and back, never mind north London. If I wanna go, I'm gonna have to get the dough quick like. With a return Intercity train fare, entry into Highbury and enough lose change for a couple of pissy London lagers and a pie and chips, I reckon I'm gonna need around twenty quid. A small fuckin' fortune to me.

The old lady's off limits and me old man's a fuckin' tight cunt. To top it all off, Nobby's skint too – he's just bought himself a new record player from Curry's. I aiyn't got many options really. I'm gonna have to earn it if I wanna go, but how am I gonna get the money?

I aiyn't got no idea at the minute.

I walk out of the poxy Jobcentre fumin' like all the other times in me life. I've wasted an hour for nothin' on waitin' in the queue and then for some dick to gimme a lesson on me life like I was back in school.

It takes a few hours wanderin' round before I get a whiff of an idea on how to get some dough: a few weeks ago in me local, a mate from school, John Raynor, promised me a couple of weeks casual – cash in hand like – if I wanted at a scrapyard in Sparkbrook. It aiyn't ideal work, but I wanna go to the Arsenal game at any cost.

"I need that job, mate?" I ask John. His face is black from oil and grease and dirt – the best Justin Fashanu impression I've sin all day.

"Wait there a minute," he says.

He disappears into the portacabin office: Thirty seconds later, a tall, skinny bloke in his mid-fifties comes out, followin' John.

"This is Darren, Dave?" John tells him.

We shake hands. Fuck, he's a scrawny lookin' bastard.

"Sow, afta a bit a casual, ay yow?" he says in his Black-Country accent.

Just what I dayn't need: a fuckin' Yam-Yam. God knows where he's from? West Brom, Wolverhampton, Walsall – they're all the same to me, like north Birmingham, it's bandit country.

"Tow quid an hour, all riowt? I'll need yow here tomorra at eight. Dow't be late."

So, I've got a job – well, not a 'job', but summat at least to keep me goin' for a few days, and I'll be able to go to London.

9: Billy-no-Mates Amongst the Fenians

Straight after the 'interview' I go to the hospital. Like yesterday, she's sleepin' her head off. Her whole family's round the bed lookin' like it's her funeral or summat. I feel like a stranger who's crashed a private party, ya know, and maybe I have.

"How is she?" I ask, lookin' at Lynsey's old lady. She looks at me like a right cunt – it's a stupid question to ask.

"What d'yer think, yer feckin' gobshite, she's poorly sick like," her old man says.

I stand there in shock. I haven't sin this much hostility since we last played the Vile. And I still stand there. I think I'm gonna get a reaction of some kind from 'em – but nothin'. Why am I here with 'em - here, in the family sanctuary, invadin' their privacy?

Just then, Lynsey opens her eyes. She looks round slowly, determined like, at the people round her bed. At first she dunno who we are coz she's bleary-eyed from kip, then her mom says 'Lynz' in her squeaky, high-pitched Dublin accent. Her daughter smiles. One by one they kiss her.

She looks round the ward again, then she catches a glimpse of me, behind her family, at the back, almost out of sight, Mr Fuckin' Nobody. She smiles at me and I smile at her. For some funny reason it takes me back – and there's only one time in me life that compares to it:

The first match of the 1970-'71 season at St Andrews. We were playin' QPR and it was me first ever game. Me uncle Des took me. Both teams were then in the Second Division. We won the game two-one – I dayn't remember who scored, though. We came ninth that season, so it wasn't the best like. Yet the match - well, the crowd, the emotion on display on the terraces by both sets of supporters - is summat I've never forgotten. The memories in some way are like I was there and I wasn't it was so magical. The players – even now – seem legendary and outta this world, their blue strips movin' like lightin' across the pitch. I remember snippets, only snippets, and the roar of the crowd twice as me team scored. Me uncle, huge hands and all, liftin' me up in celebration at the end when the whistle blew for full time and the mass exodus through the turnstiles as he grabbed me arm.

"Come here, Daz," Lynsey says in a faint voice.

I go up to her, all the time lookin' at her parents lookin' at me lookin' at their only daughter. What do they want from me? I lean over the bed and kiss her gently on the lips. She's connected to a drip and a thousand other fuckin' medical devices.

"I love ya," she whispers in me ear. It's great to hear.

"I love ya too," I say.

"Can ya leave us?" She says to her old lady but meant for everyone.

They look really pissed off and ready to kick the shit outta me.

"Why, yea' don't want us to stay?" her mom asks.

"I wanna talk to Darren on me own, that's all."

"Well, if that's what yer want," her mom replies, sighin'.

They all leave the ward one by one, sayin' goodbye and kissin' her.

We're alone. I pull up the chair her old man was sittin' on and move as close to Lynsey as I can.

"How've ya bin?" she asks me, before plantin' a kiss on me lips. I try to put me tongue down her throat for a sly snog: I'm as horny as fuck and me blood vessels in me dick are gaggin' for a shag. She pulls away.

"Not in hospital, ya twat," she says with a laugh, before screamin' out in pain.

"What's wrong?" I ask.

Silly fuckin' me again. I know what's up – she's got bastard leukaemia.

"Me back hurts."

"D'ya want me to go and get the nurse?"

"Nah," she says after a moment.

"I got some work... it aiyn't great but it'll do for the time bein'," I say.

"Where?"

"In a scrapyard. It's only casual like."

She smiles, then her eyes start to close by themselves.

"What about the council job on the bins... did ya go for the interview?"

Fightin', she tries to keep her eyes open, though she can't.

"Tired and weak... tired..."

She falls asleep again. I go for the nurse.

"It's the drugs, sir – nothing to worry about," the nurse, a right hot piece, says kindly, tryin' to calm me.

I stay with her till her old lady comes back at four. At that point I trap. I have to get an early night: work tomorra.

I spend the night alone in me room and finish off a bottle of White Lightning. I think I'll be okay and won't have a problem gettin' me arse outta bed in the mornin'.

10: A Job at Last and Fruit machines

Anyway, some silly cunts never learn and I'm fifteen minutes late for work on me first day. Yam-Yam aiyn't pleased with me as ya can imagine:

"First day and late – that's just fuckin' bostin, that is, mate," he says.

"Sorry, mate," I say, when really I couldn't give a fuckin' monkey's.

"Where were yow?" he asks.

"I overslept." He looks at me like he's got no greater enemy in the world. "What d'ya want me to do about it?" I go on cheekily. Arsenal, Arsenal's playin' continuous in me head like an irritation – nah, not an irritation, I'm talkin' to one of them, but *irritatin'*. I have to go there, and the job's me only hope of makin' it.

"Come with mey," he orders.

I follow the twat to the back end of the scrapyard.

"I want yow tow put them exhaust pipes from the mowtas intow two big piles."

"What for?"

"Coz I'm the fuckin' gaffer and I'm tellin' yow tow," he says, aggravated.

Without further argument – the Arsenal bell's ringin' again – I get down to the most pointless task I've ever done in me life. It makes completely no sense, but if the gaffer's mug enough to pay me a couple of quid for the pleasure, I aiyn't gonna be stupid enough to turn it down. It takes till lunchtime.

"How was the mornin'?" John asks me over a cuppa.

"Gis a sarnie, mate?" Me old lady forgot to make me some and I'm fuckin' starved. John gives me one – only cheese and onion but it'll do. "I had a right job to do," I say, complainin' and chompin' at the same time. "It's fuckin' thin-sliced, John... How can these slices fill ya up?"

"They dayn't have no thick-sliced in the shop."

"For fuck's sake."

"So, Daz, what were ya doin' this mornin'? Were ya round the back? I dayn't see ya at all."

"Yeah, pilin' up some shitty exhausts for no fuckin' reason."

"Cunt... them things are." John begins to laugh, before goin' on: "The gaffer's bin tryin' for over a week to get me to do 'em – totally forgot..."

"So I'm the skivvy now, am I?"

"Ya said ya wanted some casual, not me."

Lunch is over quickly and the sarnie John gave me hardly fills the gap. The rest of the day me stomach's rumblin' to fuck.

After lunch I'm on a general clean-up and just makin' meself look busy – skivin' in other words.

At the end of the day I get me dough cash in hand, as we agreed, and then I fuck off. There aiyn't no way I can go straight to the hospital the way I look and smell, so I go home, have a bath, eat me tea and then leave.

When I get there at half six, her family's round her again, some of 'em I dunno. There are also a few of her old school mates. It's a case of two's company, three's a crowd. The hospital's policy on visitors is relatively strict like: no more than four at a time till eight in the evenin', though in more serious cases – as Lynsey's is – the doctors make exceptions, though when ya got three or four of these 'exceptions' in an eight-bed ward at any one time, especially durin' the evenings, it's like bein' at the Ibrox Stadium crush back in '63. All in all it's like a riot free-for-all.

Lynsey's sleepin', but her family get some good news regardin' the donor and they all have smiles on their faces. Her chemo's gonna continue for some time. If then the leukaemia cells or summat like that are still causin' havoc, then consolidation chemotherapy will go ahead, and if that fails a bone marrow transplant as a last resort. As she's sleepin' – and coz the sense of claustrophobia's pissin' me off – I get me arse outta there.

Happy at the news, and coz I've got a bitta dough in me pocket, I wanna spend some of it in celebration. I call Nobby when I get home. As usual, he dayn't pick up the phone. I decide to see if he's down our local. Being a Tuesday, I dayn't wanna drink – at least not a session.

The Lounge's almost empty like it always is on a Tuesday night, apart from a couple in the corner, and Charlie, the local barfly, talkin' to the newish barmaid, Tina.

"Have ya sin Nobby, Charlie?" I ask.

"Nah."

"A lager, please," I say to Tina.

She's lookin' sexy, but not as hot as she was on her first night a couple of Saturdays ago. I was in a bad mood that night after returnin' from the home game against Newcastle United, which we lost fuckin' one-nil. Walkin' in the Lounge after the match and seein' a wicked bird put the smile right back on me face. I spent the whole night chattin' her up. I'm still a young lad and the world's fulla young, sexy birds, so why not try to pull her.

I sit in the corner, promisin' meself I'll only have the one, lookin' at Tina, the slag who blew me out.

"Are ya goin' down on Saturday, Daz?" Charlie asks from the bar.

"Hope so, mate."

"Who ya goin' down with?"

"Dunno."

I finish me pint and buy a second – this is me last, I promise meself.

An hour's past – the last ten of which I've bin starin' at me empty pint glass, thinkin' whether or not I'm goin' to the bar again.

Nobby walks into the Lounge.

"Where the fuck have ya bin?" I say.

"Next door with Jason and Scott."

I never go into the Bar: it's fulla dickheads and troublemakers and gettin' a couple of pence off a pint's hardly worth the trouble.

"That's fuckin' great – I've bin waitin' ages and I even phoned ya earlier."

"I was out – I went straight to the bookies after work... Ya wanna pint?" he asks me, walkin' up to the bar.

"Nah, I'm off now."

"*Already?*"

"Yeah, I can't be fuckin' late again for work tomorra."

"So ya started that job then in the council?"

"Nah, it's a different one – only casual like... In a scrapyard."

"Two pints, Tina love," Nobby says with a great smirk on his face. I look at him and know I aiyn't gonna go home well until after the bell rings for last orders.

We sit down by the fruit machines. As well as his love for The Smiths, Nobby's other passion's gamblin'. Though he aiyn't that addicted, he does spend quite a bitta time down the bookies on a flutter and in the pubs on the fruit machines. The one-armed bandits are a real fuckin' irritation when it comes to me best mate. Sometimes, though it aiyn't always, he's glued to the thing with all its flashin' lights and Fisherprice children's activity centre noises. It's a real head-doer but there aiyn't much I can do about it – a passion's a passion.

Nobby's lookin' at it: the lights are pullin' him in.

"Dayn't even think about playin' now, ya cunt?" I warn him.

Nobby pulls out some change from his pocket.

"Tina, has it paid out tonight?" he asks.

"Nah," she says.

He gets up and puts ten pence in the slot. Plonk. He presses the start button and the fruits start spinnin', disappearin' into a blur of colours. And then he presses the hold buttons, each one randomly. They stop: one, two, three, four. All the fruits are different: a lemon, a strawberry, a banana, an orange – he's lost and I piss meself, happy with the outcome. It's a mug's game, anyway.

"Bastard!" he shouts "It should be payin' out now."

"Well, it aiyn't, so sit the fuck down."

He sits down. We talk about Lynsey:

"How is she?"

"Come with me tomorra to the hospital and ya gonna find out?"

We agree to meet outside the main entrance at the QE at six after work the next day.

"How's the new job then?"

"Hardly a job, is it? It's just a bitta casual for a week or two."

"Are ya goin' down to London on Saturday?"

"Fuckin' hope so, mate. I should have the dough, I just hope me old lady dayn't go on at me for some housekeep before then."

"I told ya ages ago to get outta there and rent ya own gaff," he says, smilin'.

He's always takin' the piss outta me for livin' at home.

"Yeah, I'm probably gonna soon," I say, not connectin' no urgency to the words, "but ya know it's so fuckin' easy at home – no washin' or cookin' or anythin'."

"Better sooner than later, mate," he replies.

Nobby's eye still has the tracin' of bruisin' on it.

"How's the eye now?"

"All right."

"It'd be nice to get the fuckers, wouldn't it?" I say.

"Yeah, but there aiyn't much chance of that happenin'."

"Ah, ya never know."

We roll outta the pub at half eleven. I get home, undress, set me alarm clock for seven and fall asleep like a new born babbee.

11: Two Fingers for the Bus Conductor

Fuckin' miraculously I get up on time and make it to work with a couple of minutes spare. I buy a copy of *The Sun* on the way and begin readin' it under the shelter of the bus stop. It's pissin' down. Like always, I start with the back page for the footy news. I only read the shitty tabloids, papers that most with half a brain wouldn't wipe their shitty arses with. I love *The Sun* coz it has the best stuff on the football, and when it comes down to it, what else is important to a lad like me other than that?

I'm like all of 'em - Charlie the barfly, Tina, the blokes in the St Andrews Spion Kop and the Railway End – who all get their knowledge on the world from this rag. It's workin'-class and shite, but every mornin' without fail - bar Sunday when me old man buys *The News of the World* together with its brainless supplements - I buy meself a copy.

I'm on the top deck of the bus readin' me paper. It's one of them horrible, pale yellow and navy blue numbers from the '70s West Midlands Travel still have runnin' the inner-city routes, while the newer buses serve the posh wankers in Sutton Coldfield, Edgbaston and Solihull. I'm pissed off anyway: I've sat on some wet chewin' gum that some spiteful cunt put down on purpose for a dick like me and I can't get it off me jeans. That's made worse when the ticket inspector gets on.

"Ticket, please," he says.

I didn't notice him climbin' the stairs, as I have me face buried in me paper.

"What?" I say, lookin' up to him.

"Your ticket?"

I look quickly for the ticket every passenger gets from the driver once ya've popped in ya exact money fare into the slot by the cabin. I've thrown it away again. I look under me seat and around me feet.

"I had it... I dunno where it is?"

"That's what they all say, mate."

The ticket inspector tutts as he pulls out his fine book from his small, leather satchel.

"Ya can put that fuckin' thing away for starters, coz I aiyn't payin' no fine, ya hear?"

"You have to – *no ticket, no ride.*"

"I had a ticket – fifteen pence... I just lost it."

"It's not *my* problem, mate."

Now I'm pissed off – who does the cunt think he is? The bus comes to a standstill at a bus stop and, without thinkin' too much about it, I leg it down the stairs to the open doors, even knockin' an old bastard to the side in the process. I run off, givin' it loads and me two fingers to the bus as it moves away.

I realise I've left me paper on the bus, and the stop where I get off is still three away from me intended, but luckily I make it through the gates with a bitta time to spare.

12: Them Arabs and a Clash of Interests

"Learned yow fuckin' lesson, did yow? Yam-Yam says to me as I come strollin' in.

He gets me doin' more of the same cleanin' as the day before which lasts till late in the mornin'. At lunchtime I go to the chippy and buy meself a saveloy and chips, eatin' 'em back at the portacabin with John.

"What d'ya think about that highjackin' last week then, Daz?" John asks.

"What highjackin'?"

"It's all over the papers – fuckin' loada people killed and all."

"Where?" I ask.

"Err... it says here in Malta," John replies, scannin' the paper.

I aiyn't really interested what's goin' on in Hall Green, never mind in Malta.

"That's interestin'," I comment, raisin' me eyebrows.

"Tragic... them fuckin' Arabs again... I tell ya what, mate... them cunts'll be the ruin of all of us, I tell ya... The Pakis here need to fuck off to where they came from for starters."

"I'm goin' to the Arsenal game on Saturday," I say to change the subject.

"Lucky cunt," John says. He's put down the paper and starts drinkin' his tea and eatin' his sandwiches.

"Why dayn't ya come?"

"I can't."

"Why?"

"Some people have to work."

"Take the day off then?"

"I can't... and anyway, I'm seein' me daughter after one, and I can't let her down again... I missed the last meetin' coz I had a fuck-off hangover and couldn't make it."

And it's like that – teenage parenthood. John got his bird up the duff when she was fifteen and he was sixteen. They split up some time after that, though, and he sees his daughter every other Saturday. Teenage pregnancies in Britain are reachin' epic proportions if the statistics by the Government are anythin' to go by and it's gettin' outta hand like: Ya can't walk down no fuckin' high street or estate without seein' a seventeen-year-old girl with a fag in her mouth and pushin' around a pram or two.

"Look at this," John says, handin' me the paper, "at the bottom, there on page six.

I take a look: RONALD REAGAN $3M FOR LIFE STORY. I read the first paragraph and then I stop.

"So what?" I say.

Ronald Reagan means nothin' to me – sure, I know he's the president of America like, but apart from that nothin' else.

"Well, I bet ya'd like that much for ya fuckin' life story?"

I stare at John for a second while I gather me thoughts. I put another chip in me mouth.

"I dayn't give a shit really, mate," I say.

"Well, I'd sell me story for a tenner."

"Yeah, that's coz it aiyn't worth no more," I answer real sarcastic like.

"Ya think so?" John replies, smirkin'.

"D'ya think here we all live such interestin' lives? I mean come on, look at us: who the fuck would wanna write about our fuckin' lives?"

"I would."

"Then ya the only one."

"I dayn't think so, mate."

"Listen, I wouldn't give ya the steam off me piss for it... And that's the end of the conversation."

We finish our lunch and have a fag. I've run outta smokes and John crashes me one, though he aiyn't happy as he's only got a couple left himself.

The rest of the afternoon I do more cleanin' and sort out wing mirrors and windscreen wipers. Dull work, but Arsenal's on me mind so I have to put up with it.

"Twenty Benson, please mate." I say to Paki Pete, owner of the local newsagent's round the corner from where I live.

"Got none. Sorry," Paki Pete says.

"It's the third time, Pete. When ya gettin' some in?"

Paki Pete shrugs his shoulders.

"Okay, Embassy," I say in hope.

"Sold outta them too."

"Fuckin' hell... Okay, twenty Rothmans then," I say, rollin' me eyes.

I fuckin' hate Rothmans with a passion but what else am I gonna do... smoke Silk Cut? Them fags are for fannies and it's more like breathin' fresh air with every drag. Nah, I wanna die – the fags with the filters take the piss. I take a Curly-Wurly, pay and leave the rank smell of sweat and curry powder behind in the shop. I'll buy me Bensons somewhere else.

Although I hate 'em, I also love the Paki shops, as they're open 365 days of the year - even Christmas Day - and they sell more exotic stuff than in the shops owned by white people. I tried me first packet of Bombay mix from Paki Pete's, and I can still remember the taste. Sometimes, though, they try to rip ya off: a penny here, forty pence there – it all adds up if ya think about it, and this is what I dayn't like about 'em.

I'm already washed and changed and on me way to the hospital. I get the number 11, that palava of a bus route – it goes on for three hours or summat from start to finish, at least that's what I heard. Me trip, luckily, is shorter than that and I keep me ticket in me pocket just in case one of them fuckin' idiots gets on again.

I spend the journey – all fifteen minutes – smokin' and drinkin' a can of Carling. On the back of the seat in front of me own there's graffiti: In thick black, permanent marker, someone's written: IF YOU WANT SEX CALL TASHA ON... and the number. Next to it, scratched in with what was probably a penknife or summat like that: FUCK YOU VILE. Underneath it in red pen: BCFC – BASTARDS CUNTS FUCKERS... Nothin' is written for the last C. Only a thick Villa wanker could write that, I think, smilin' to meself.

We meet outside the hospital. As usual, Nobby's late – like he's late for everythin' – but not by five minutes, it's more like twenty.

"Where the fuck have ya bin? I ask, throwin' down me half-smoked cigarette on the ground.

"Sorry, it was the bus."

We go in together to see Lynsey. Her family's there, and as I'm with me best mate they treat us all right. She's sleepin', so we can't speak to her.

"How's she bin?" I ask her old lady.

"The doctors want to operate immediately."

"Why?"

"It's too aggressive."

"And the chemo?" I ask.

"Well, it's just makin' her weaker, like, really, that's all."

I dayn't wanna go into the medical bullshit with her, as I aiyn't got no idea what's goin' on. All I know is the operation is a matter of life and death.

"Who's the donor?"

"It's all confidential... the person doesn't want be identified and all, like."

I kiss Lynsey goodnight and we leave.

"What did her old lady say?" Nobby asks as we're waitin' at the bus stop.

"She's gonna have an operation."

"When?"

"They dunno yet."

"In a few days, I suppose."

"Could be."

"And what are ya gonna do about the match in London?"

There is that thing now, and I've only just realised it too. Maybe I'll leave the game, but I really wanna go. There's a choice – it seems simple but it aiyn't to me. I love me Lynsey and I love me footy.

Coz I'm mixed up and confused, I head straight home. Nobby asks me to go down the pub for a swift one but I aiyn't in the mood for that.

On Thursday mornin' I find meself doin' what I've bin doin' for the last two days. There's no fuckin' glory in this job and I'm startin' to realise it.

In the afternoon I get to do summat a little more interestin': helpin' Yam Yam strip down engines of some new cars which arrived earlier in the week. Now this aiyn't bad graft, I have to say, though ya do have to get ya hands and face dirty. It takes the best part of three hours till we knock off at five, and this is enough time for me to find out a little bit about me gaffer:

"So, where are ya from, Dave?"

"Wolverhamptun."

"Are ya a Wolves supporter?"

"That's a fuckin' daft question, aiyn't it... Ahr, I am"

The Wolves are strugglin' in the Third Division and if he has anythin' to be proud of it's in their history now. I complain about bein' a Blues supporter – maybe I dayn't have nothin' to complain about really.

"Yow Villa?" he asks.

"Ya fuckin' jokin' now, mate, aiyn't ya?

"Ay, yow a Bluenose, like that other twat?"

"Yeah. What's wrong with that?" I'm bein' defensive now: me team means a lot to me.

"Well, ay, there aiyn't much rioght with it... Yow must be barmy supportin' 'em?"

I leave the cunt to soup in his old gold blood juices and go home. It's becomin' a habit now – the hospital's waitin' for me again.

When I get there I quickly find out to me annoyance that Lynsey's operation is gonna be on Saturday mornin'. This clashes with me plans for Arsenal and I'm well pissed off. I try to hide it from Lynsey when I see her. She's bin moved to a smaller ward with four beds. It's more comfortable for her, which is great like.

She's sittin' up and has a smile on her face.

"How are ya, bab?" I ask.

She's drowsy from the drugs and her voice is weak.

"They're operatin' on Saturday," she answers.

"I know."

I'm gonna have to make a big decision: two loves are competin' with each other and it can't end a nil-nil fuckin' draw.

"Will ya stay with me, Darren?"

"Of course I will, bab."

She falls asleep.

Her parents, who are here as usual, are on edge – and quite rightly: this operation's important. That's it, plain and simple. If it aiyn't gonna be successful, she's gonna die, or she *could* die. Yeah, that aiyn't great but what else are we gonna do about it? Whatever time we've got left, I want it to be special.

However, the Arsenal match's comin' and I dunno if I should stay in Brum on Saturday.

I leave the hospital soon after Lynsey falls asleep and, not feelin' like goin' home, I go down to the pub for a tot or two and a bit of relaxed conversation.

13: Little and Large

"Daz!" It's Mickey Platt and Danny Dunford, two mates from the football who happened to go to the same school as me but were in a different year. "Come here, ya cunt," Mickey says. They're both at the bar.

Mickey's the confident one. A small lad of twenty-four with a dark, handsome face - ya typical casual dressed up to the nines in designer clobber. Danny, his old school mate, is a big aggressive fucker at nearly eighteen stone that aiyn't just fat. He can look after himself with his fists like any heavyweight bruiser and is always lookin' for a row. Mickey's the brain and Danny's the brawn. They're each other's foil. I usually go to away matches with 'em and always feel safe in their company, as well as bein' able to have a laugh with 'em, though recently Danny's started to get on me tits a bit. Mickey was once in with some of the big boys from the Zulus a few years back, but he decided not to get too involved with such a crowd in the end, which is a good thing, really. They're independent in that respect, but with me we're the terrible threesome, alone and only lookin' out for our own backs.

We're similar and we click, I think – they like goin' to the matches, and if a ruck comes their way they aiyn't the type of blokes to shy away from it and scarper. Or that's how I think they are.

"Sorry to hear about ya bird, Daz," Mickey says.

"Yeah, thanks... she's havin' an op on Saturday so we're hopin' everythin' is gonna be all right."

"Get the pints in, Danny," Mickey orders his big mate.

We stand at the bar and drink.

"Tina aiyn't workin' tonight, Daz?" Danny asks.

"Dunno, mate."

"So, Daz, ya comin' with us down to London on Saturday?" Mickey asks.

"Yeah, too right I am," I say. It's like all me problems have disappeared and the words I say are from some other bloke's gob. What would Lynsey's family think of me?

"What time are we leavin'?" I ask.

"We'll get the nine o'clock from New Street... that'll give us a few hours in London before the match to fuck around and have a few jars," Mickey says.

We dayn't wanna go with the main group of supporters on the Football Special train with the 'scarf brigade', a negative term for the real footy fans given to 'em by the casuals, the proper football hooligans, who prefer to travel on the InterCity trains, made famous by West Ham's ICF, or Inter City Firm. We'd look too outta place there and the Old Bill would be watchin' us. Nah, it's the InterCity train – that way we're gonna attract much less attention. Bein' decked out in Fila clobber aiyn't gonna work – we'll have to go incognito: a normal sweater and jacket – no logos. Same with the trainers: the branded ones we'll have to ditch and leave in the wardrobe at home – normal shoes only. In the crowd with the 'respectables' we are gonna be invisible to the Pigs.

"Listen, lads, I've gotta shoot off," I say, downin' me pint.

"Nah, stay," Mickey begs.

"Can't, work in the mornin' and I'm savin' me dough for the trip."

I leave confused again, and in two minds whether to go. I've already told 'em I would – why, I think to meself, when I know there's summat more important goin' on the same fuckin' day? There's always the chance Lynsey's op will be postponed - then I'll be able to go down to London guilt-free, but that looks unlikely at the minute.

Me sleep's crazy and I wake up loadsa times. I aiyn't got no time left to decide and it's killin' me.

14: Why You Have to Have a Licence to Drive a Forklift

Red-eyed and knackered, I go to work. I'm thinkin' it's gonna be me last day, yet in the back of me mind I hope Yam Yam offers me another week. John said there's a chance and I'm countin' on it anyway. I dayn't wanna go back down the fuckin' Jobcentre to them cunts who are about as useful as hair gel is to Kojak.

The plan's to go to Lynsey again in the evenin' before headin' off down the pub to see Nobby. For once, I wanna persuade me best mate to come down to London with me, Mickey and Danny, though I suppose he won't wanna. The Smiths are playin' in Ireland on a three-tour date of Dublin, Dundalk and Belfast in February, and coz Nobby has family in Ireland he wants to go and see 'em. All his dough will go on the trip.

When I get to the yard Yam Yam's in a right fuckin' mood: John's pissed him off coz he accidentally drove the forklift into the side of the portacabin, dentin' it in the process and nearly decapitatin' Sid, the machine operator, when he tried to jump into the cabin to stop the fucker – the forks just missin' his bonce by an inch.

Sid tells me the story a bit later that Yam Yam comes out screamin', runnin' outta the office holdin' his 'Who Shot JR?' mug of steamin' hot tea. He then said that John was sayin' he couldn't stop the bastard coz the fuckin' brakes were fucked on the thing.

"Fuckin' late again, ay yow?"

I look at me watch.

"It's only a couple of minutes past, for fuck's sake. Lay off a bit."

"Okay, now problem, but I'll dock it from yow fuckin' wages."

I say nothin'. I can do the day, get me dough for Arsenal, and never have to see the prick again.

"What d'ya want me to do?" I ask all calm.

"Take the fuckin' wheel caps over there and bring 'em over to the red container next to the skip for starters."

I do what he tells me without complainin'. The match's a little over twenty hours away and I'm excited – and so I should be: we're playin' the Gunners, a side packed with talent and one with a great history in English football.

I spend the whole Friday thinkin' about Lynsey – even at lunchtime over crusty cheese and onion cobs made by me old lady. Me mind's nowhere else.

"Hey, Daz, look at the melons on that?" John says, turnin' *The Sun* round to the page-three spread. It's Samantha Fox. Her tits, big and firm and all natural, dominate the page. I dayn't really care, though. I stare into space in the hope a plan saves me. But it aiyn't no good daydreamin', a fact's a fact: tomorra Lynsey's gonna be in the operatin' theatre and I'll be at the away end of Highbury shoutin' for me team at the top of me lungs... If I let it happen.

Everythin' is in me hands.

The rest of the afternoon I take it easy: Yam Yam's left Sid in charge as he's had to go and pick up his brother from Willenhall coz his car broke down or summat. I aiyn't gonna kill meself now that the gaffer's away.

"Hey, John, what time's the gaffer back?" I ask.

I'm busy sweepin' the office floor while John's repairin' the hole in the side of the portacabin made by the forklift.

"Dunno... ya might be lucky if he gets back at all."

"What d'ya mean?" I'm worried now.

"Sometimes when he pisses off in the middle of the day he just dayn't bother comin' back."

"Well, that's just fuckin' great, that is."

"Yeah, he probably aiyn't gonna be back today."

"But he's gotta pay me."

"Can't help ya there, mate."

"Fuck, I need that dough for the match tomorra."

"He'll pay ya on Monday if he aiyn't back."

"But I can't wait till Monday."

"Sorry, mate."

That's takin' the fuckin' piss. I'm short and I need the gaffer to pay me.

"Who's lockin' up today?" I ask.

"Sid."

"What time?"

"At six if the gaffer aiyn't back."

"I'll have to stay behind and wait for him then."

"Well, good luck, mate, but I wouldn't count on it."

Five o'clock comes and it should be knockin' off time for me. John goes home and I stay behind with Sid in the hope Yam Yam comes back. I pass the time readin' Sid's copy of *The Star* in the office.

It's five to six and still no sign of the gaffer.

"Listen, son, I'm lockin' up in five so ya better start makin' a move. I dunno what ya gonna do... Dave probably aiyn't comin' back... looks like he went straight home."

"Well, that's just fuckin' great, that is, aiyn't it?" I say as I get up from the chair.

"What about me wages?"

"Dunno, son."

"Am I in next week or what?"

"Ya'll have to ask the gaffer, coz I dunno."

"How can I ask him if he aiyn't here?"

"Dunno, son."

It seems as if Lynsey's playin' a trick on me. Yeah, she's right there, in her hospital bed, pissin' herself now, I can see it. She knows all right, and tomorra, by hook or by crook, she wants me to be there. Maybe me team can win without me. It's her magic, the feminine touch of insecurity that's doin' it for her.

Sid snaps the padlock shut to the yard and all me positives thoughts leave me. It's a reality: tomorra I'll be in Brum.

"Anyway, mate," Sid begins, "I hope to see ya on Monday... but ya'll have to get in touch with the gaffer, like I said – ya best bet would be to turn up on Monday mornin', there's plenty of work anyway."

"Some good news then," I say with a sigh.

"Ya know I only have about nine hundred days left before I retire?"

"Are ya countin' workin' days and weekends too?" I ask.

"Ah, I dunno."

"Well, ya a lucky fucker in any case."

And then, as if by a miracle, an old, brown Bedford van pulls up outside the gates of the yard. It's the gaffer. He gets outta the van with his usual face on him. What's wrong, I think. He aiyn't in no physical pain, but he looks like he's givin' birth to a sumo through a straw.

"Still fuckin here, ay yow?" are his first words.

"Well, yeah, I'm waitin' for me wages."

"Fuck me, that's bostin' and it figures."

"Well, I'm off," Sid says, before walkin' off casual like.

Yam Yam takes out a great wod of notes from his pocket: there must be a small fortune in his hand, enough to buy me a season ticket anyway and admission to every away game five times over.

"What happened to ya brother in Willenhall?" I ask, half takin' the piss.

"Bleeder's fan belt on his mowta snapped."

"D'ya fix it like?"

"Now I dayn't. I had to buy him another one... There yow gow," he says, siftin' through the wod, "that's what I owe yow... I've got another week or two if yow wanit?"

"Yeah, great."

I walk off with a big smile on me face.

"And down't be fuckin' late on Monday."

I'm goin' to the Arsenal match. Lynsey aiyn't such a voodoo witch after all.

On the way home I see Alan Irving, me mate who got a beatin' against Leeds back in May, on the bus. He's sittin' on the top deck at the back. This place is where all the black druggies smoke draw or ya aggressive sorts are pissed up and lookin' for a row, so I usually avoid it like the plague, and always at night. Alan's sprawled out between the aisles. He's decked out in a black Lacoste cardigan and a pair of white Adidas Samba – addin' his elegant blonde mullet to the mix and he's an A1 casual.

"Ah, Daz!" he calls out.

I sit down next to him.

"Nice gear, where d'ya get it from?" I ask.

"Ya mean the cardigan like?" Alan says proudly.

I touch the cardigan, not in a gay way, just to feel the quality.

"Yeah?"

"Ya aiyn't gonna believe it, but it's robbed."

"Where d'ya rob it from?"

"Nah, I didn't, a cousin of mine went to Brussels in May for the Final and taxed it there."

"Ya got a Scouse cousin?" I ask wide-eyed.

"Nah, ya cunt... He went to Brussels to cause some trouble with them Wops, dayn't he... but he's from Birmingham... well, Solihull."

"Did he get into the ground, Heysel like?"

"He didn't wanna... he wasn't interested in that."

"Well, did he find any Italians?"

"Nah... not in the end... But a few of 'em smashed the display window to a designer shop and robbed the fuckin' lot."

"So, what, there's a lotta decent clobber in Europe, abroad like?"

"Fuckin' loads, mate... And it's all top-quality stuff."

"Have ya got summat to sell?"

"Ya fuckin' jokin', mate... Anythin' I got I'm wearin' meself."

"Well, I have to give it to ya, ya look well decent, mate," I say.

Though I aiyn't no clothes horse, I aiyn't too badly dressed meself usually. I've got a couple of Fila t-shirts and a Ben Sherman jacket that I found and bought for ten pence in a charity shop on King's Heath High Street some time ago, but keepin' up with blokes like Alan aiyn't cheap.

"So, how are ya?" Alan asks.

"Not bad, mate, not bad."

"Are ya goin' down to London tomorra?"

"Fuck, yeah," I say.

Alan takes out his box of fags: they're Silk Cut.

"D'ya wanna fag?" he asks.

"Can't smoke them shite, mate." I take out me own packet of Bensons. "These are smokes."

"Yeah, I'm goin' too... Can't fuckin' wait."

"Yeah, I'm well up for it."

"Better fuckin' win."

"I wish they'd fuck off that Charlie Nicholas."

"Why?" Alan asks, puzzled.

"He'll probably score on us tomorra."

"Ah, fuck him... we're gonna win."

"Hope so, mate."

"Who are ya goin' down with?"

"Mickey Platt and Danny Dunford."

"Ah, how's Mickey, anyway?"

"Sound, mate."

"Are ya goin' on the train?"

"Yeah. The nine o'clock from New Street."

"The Football Special, aiyn't it?"

"Nah, it's the InterCity... How ya gettin' down there?" I then ask.

"Four of us in Martin Fowler's car."

"Fuck, I went to primary school with that fucker... Does he still hang round with Richie Venables?"

"He's goin' with us too."

"I aiyn't sin him for ages."

"I heard ya had a bitta trouble in town with one of the Vile lot?" Alan asks after a moment.

"Where d'ya hear about that?"

"The word gets round, mate."

It's strange like, I thought I kept that quiet. Musta bin pissed one night and let it out.

"Well, that's bin and gone... But dayn't worry, I'll get the cunt."

"What exactly happened?"

"Ah, fuckin' shoutin' his mouth off, he was."

"About what?"

"Summat about our lot can't fight and that we're gonna be relegated this season or summat... Maybe not, though... Ah, fuck knows, I dayn't remember."

"Did ya lamp the cunt?"

"Yeah."

We both light our fags and smoke in silence for a moment.

"Oh, yeah... heard about ya bird, mate... Sorry to hear it... How is she now?" Alan asks.

"She's got fuckin' leukaemia or cancer or summat... but she's got an op tomorra."

"*When?*"

"Tomorra."

Alan looks at me all serious. And he keeps lookin' at me. The stare aiyn't friendly and I dunno what's up till I think about it.

"Are ya fuckin' jokin'?" Alan says.

"Nah, it's tomorra."

"Fuck me, mate, I know footy's important, but come on... be reasonable."

Alan's old lady died a few years back from breast cancer, so he knows what it's like to lose somebody close.

"What's the matter, mate?" I ask, though I've already sussed it.

"Ya should be here and not fuckin' off."

I dayn't need some bloke tellin' me what's right and what's wrong.

"But why?" I ask.

"It's ya bird, that's 'what for'... Ya should be takin' this more serious."

"What's the point hangin' round the hospital – I'll only be waitin' and wastin' me time?"

"Fuck me, Daz... This is me stop... Ya a cunt... Just remember," he says, gettin' up, "a match's a fuckin' match... ya'll never get a second chance with somebody after they've gone, remember that... I know."

Alan gets off the bus. It's food for thought. I've got a choice.

"What's for tea, mom?"

"Ya dad's bringin' fish and chips home after work... And by the way, where's me housekeep?"

I take out a new, crispy twenty from me pocket.

"There ya go," I say, handin' it to her, chuffed like.

"But that aiyn't everythin'."

"Ya'll get the rest next week."

"Remember, I aiyn't counted this week's and last week's in that."

I sigh, resigned to the fact I'll forever be owin' people dough, before goin' upstairs for a bath and a night out for a couple of tots.

"How's Lynsey doin'?" me mom asks as we sit in the livin' room watchin' the news and chompin' on our fish and chips.

"She's havin' an op."

"When?" me old man asks, smotherin' his chips in vinegar.

I dunno what to say: I dayn't need a lecture from 'em as well.

"Err... next week, sometime next week..."

I leave the house after six. It takes me twenty minutes to get to the QE. I'm gettin' tired of it now – not coz of Lynsey, but coz of her family. I know they'll be there again, I can count on that, but I have to at least try and make an effort for Lynsey's sake.

I walk into the ward and, as always, the usual suspects are there, crowded round her bed, surroundin' Lynsey in a shell of love and protection. Me presence goes unnoticed at first, and they dayn't even turn their heads – I'm a no-man, invisible like. She's sleepin', surprise-surprise, coz the doctors have heavily sedated her again.

So much for a conversation.

"The operation's tomorra, yeah?" I ask.

"Half ten in the mornin'" Noel, Lynsey's brother, says.

"You'll be there, I hope?" her old man asks. His tone is unfriendly. He dayn't even look at me when he says it.

I say goodbye to Lynsey, even though I know she probably dayn't even hear it, kiss her on the cheek and leave.

At the number 11 bus stop outside the hospital I have plenty of time to think about what I'm gonna do. I've lied to me parents and lied to Lynsey's parents too. Tomorra they expect me to be there, ready and waitin', bitin' me nails while me bird goes under the knife.

15: Mad Men in Blue and a Change of Perspective

The pub, The Bantam Cock and Darren's local, was bursting with the rumpus of Friday night people three thick at the bar trying to get served. It was as crowded as it could ever be. When Darren walked in the jukebox was screaming out Simple Mind's *Someone Somewhere in Summertime*. Nobby was at the bar, tightly trapped between 'barstool' Charlie and two blokes in British Gas overalls who he'd never seen before. Tina was working along with Arthur aka 'Bagpuss', the pub landlord, as all the locals thought he looked like the BBC children's television programme character.

"Hey, Nobby!" Darren called out.

Nobby turned around:

"What?"

Jim Kerr's voice and the racket of a hundred-odd Brummie gobs talking at the same time wasn't going to get you heard. Darren gesticulated, lifting an invisible pint to his mouth; Nobby instinctively knew the sign and its significance, like all the thousands of other regulars around the country – Friday and Saturday nights were special: it was about talking to your mates, pulling a minger if you had the bottle and generally getting as pissed as your budget would allow. Simple.

"Fuck me, Nob, it's heavin' in here tonight."

Nobby was already tanked up: he finished at one on a Friday and had been on an all-dayer.

"Dunno, mate," he replied. There was a bit of totty in the corner and Nobby clocked them immediately. "Follow me, Daz."

They homed in but the birds were having none of it:

"Piss off," one of the three said.

"Ladies, ladies, ya breakin' me heart... Where are ya from girls?" Nobby was persistent.

"None of ya business," the blonde said. She was well hot and Nobby was gagging for it. "And anyway, why d'ya wanna know?"

"*Don't* encourage him, Sue," her mate said, not half-bad herself with short, dark hair.

"We're all from Erdington," the blonde answered.

And that was the thing, you see, to Darren at least. Brummie girls were great until they opened their mouths, and then everything went downhill. I suppose Darren thought it wasn't their fault, though someone had to be blamed in the end. Darren's Lynsey was different, she was your classier type - at least that was what he believed - and light years ahead of the three he was now looking at in terms of refinement.

"Ya jokin'," Darren commented to himself. They weren't supposed to hear but they did.

"And what's the matter with that?" the last of the three said aggressively. She was ugly and fat.

"Nah, I was just sayin'," Darren replied.

He hated Erdington and Erdington birds – it was Villa land and full of slags and dogs.

"So, ladies, what brings ya up to this neck of the woods?" Nobby asked, trying to use his natural charm to impress them.

"Well, we're goin' to Moseley later for a party," the blonde said.

"A house party?"

"Yeah, a twenty-first."

"Maybe ya girls need an escort – what d'ya say, Daz?"

The song *Frankie* by Sister Sledge broke out from the jukebox and the girls started singing together. They sounded like cats being tortured, but that didn't stop them:

"Hey Frankie, do you remember me? Frankie... do you remember me... Frankie..."

"Great voices, ladies," Darren imparted, totally lying to them, of course.

After a moment Nobby realised he had about as much chance pulling them as he had of becoming The Smith's next bassist, so he left them alone to sing to themselves and end up in the bed of some other unlucky bloke.

"Shit," Nobby said.

"Ya win some, ya lose some, mate – ya dunno know that yet?" Darren commented.

"course I do."

The smoke in the Lounge was like a London fog and it was difficult to breathe. Nobody seemed to mind, though - as long as the beer kept flowing, they could've choked to death.

"Get in the jars, Daz," Nobby ordered as he polished off yet another pint.

"Ya look wrecked, Nob, are ya sure?"

"It's ya round... get the fuckers in."

Darren fought his way through the throng of inebriated bodies, some more willing than others to give up their space and let him pass. Most of the punters he knew, but because they were so drunk, many didn't recognise him through the pea-soup miasma and their own alcohol-laced vision.

"Fuck me," Nobby said. The voice of Jim Kerr rang out again, this time to the song *Don't You Forget About Me.*

"What?" Darren asked.

"Simple Minds again."

"So?"

"Who the fuck keeps puttin' this shite on?"

Nobby's musical tastes were strictly reserved for The Smiths, Joy Division and New Order - anything outside these three he saw as bad taste. It was a Manchester thing, you see – he thought the New Romanticism of Scotland's finest belonged in some other place. Darren didn't entirely agree, but he usually let it go, so as not to cause an argument, though tonight he was in a different mood.

"Come on, Nob, they aiyn't that bad, d'ya know what I mean like?."

Nobby was angry now, and the alcohol wasn't helping the situation.

"What are ya on, Daz?"

"They aiyn't that fuckin' bad... I mean, come on, that's all I'm sayin'."

"Ya fulla shit."

And how was Darren to know? He was a casual into designer gear and the match on a Saturday afternoon. The music was just a sidetrack for him, something to take his mind off the stresses of being a Birmingham City supporter; but for Nobby music was something else, otherworldly and unexplainable, especially to a part-time musicateer like Darren.

"Nob, listen," Darren went on, adamant he was going to have his say, "I aiyn't sayin' they're the best, but they aiyn't that bad... what about the *New Gold Dream* album... I mean, it's a fuckin' classic."

"Nah, if *they* were good, they aiyn't no more."

"Why's that?"

"Any band that associates itself with a shitty Hollywood-effort of a film is askin' for trouble – it's artistic suicide."

The Smiths were artists incarnate for Nobby, and would never sell themselves to Hollywood.

Nobby was slurring his words and was making little sense.

"Just let it go, Nob."

"What time are ya off tomorra?" Nobby asked after a moment.

"Nine."

"And ya aiyn't stayin' at home with Lynsey?"

"Fuck me, Nob, dayn't *you* start now."

"I aiyn't." He knew he'd touched and nerve and wanted to carry on riling him. "But come on, mate, ya now ya should be stayin' – do I have to tell ya?"

Darren was about to walk out when in walked Mickey and Danny. They nodded to each other and they went to the bar.

"All right, lads," Mickey said.

"Aiyn't sin ya in here for ages," Nobby said to Mickey.

"Ah, ya know, bin busy... and anyway, judgin' by the music I won't be in here much longer."

"*See*," Nobby said to Darren, "it's shite - even Mickey agrees."

"So, the jukebox's over there... Go over and put yaself summat on," Darren said. He'd had enough of the criticism.

"Dayn't worry, I'm gonna," Mickey replied. He went over to the jukebox and put twenty pence into the slot, coming back with a smile on his face.

"What d'ya put on?" Nobby asked, he was a music man and thought he was the only one amongst them able to give a critical assessment on the tunes Mickey had picked. "Well, what?" he said again, waiting for the answer.

"Patience, lads."

"The Jam, I bet," Nobby continued.

More than the New Romanticism that had exploded in Britain with the likes of Spandau Ballet, Ultravox and a plethora of other bands, Nobby hated the Modes, those disenfranchised lot made famous by the 1979 film *Quadrophenia,* Mickey's all-time favourite. Mickey was all about style, taste, looking good all the time for the ladies and the terrace culture. Together they were all interwoven, making a culture cool to the kid next door. This was why Nobby didn't like him – he was jealous, though he was too proud to say it openly. For him The Smiths were the complete opposite of the Modes and everything Mickey respected.

"Chill out, Nob," Darren said.

"Yeah, I knew it... ya put them cunts on, dayn't ya?" Nobby was now fuming but Darren didn't know why:

"It's only fuckin' music, Nob, forget about it."

"Listen, I put the money in so it's up to me what I want. If ya so pissed off about it go and put ya own music on," Mickey said.

He would've if he'd had any money left, but he was skint as always.

"Right, lads," Danny said, rubbin' his hands together, "are ya ready for tomorra?"

"I aiyn't goin'," Nobby said.

"I know ya aiyn't goin', I was talkin' to Daz... *Daz*, are ya?"

"Fuck yeah," he answered.

"Yeah, and we're gonna win," said Mickey.

They all hoped so but none of them really believed it. They were playing the mighty Arsenal, pride of the capital, so what chance did they have?

"Let's fuck some Gooners up tomorra, lads." It was Danny again. When he said it his eyes came alive and it was the possibility of violence that triggered it.

It was clear that Danny meant it. Darren didn't want to; he'd had enough going on in his life without the added burden of a possible scrap with some apoplectic fucking Cockneys and a possible run in with the Law.

"I thought we were just gonna piss around a bit down there, d'ya know what I mean like? Nothin' too brutal. Just some drinkin' and laughin', ya know?" Darren said.

"Ya fuckin' jokin', mate... I guarantee ya if I dayn't see no Gooners, I'll definitely pan a few Pakis," Danny said.

Danny was a bloke with a real psychopathic nature at heart who hated the immigrants. Once, on the way home from an all dayer in a pub in Digbeth, Danny had given some sixteen-year-old Bangladeshi boy such a battering, he ended up breaking the poor lad's arm and getting himself a suspended prison sentence and a criminal record for GBH. He never learned his lesson.

"Nah, I aiyn't interested in that. I just wanna have a laugh down there, nothin' more."

"Ya a fuckin' puff then," Danny said.

"Leave it out, Danny," said Mickey.

Everyone laughed apart from Danny. He was broody now and was just waiting to explode.

"But I'm serious, lads – the match and a few pints for me, that's it." Darren didn't want to rock the boat with Danny. He might need him in the future, especially with the trouble in town he'd had. A man mountain backing you up was great. No, he'd have to appease him, and the best way was to keep his mouth shut.

Nobby, meanwhile, bored with all the talk of footy and violence, had moved himself over to two middle-aged birds, dolled up to the eyeballs in lipstick and mascara. They looked a right pair.

"All right, ladies, how are ya?"

"Great," one said.

"D'ya wanna drink?"

"Two half ciders, please?" the other said in her *really* common Brummie, making Jasper Carrot sound like Reginald Jeeves.

Nobby didn't have any money though.

"I'm sure I've sin ya in here before," Nobby said seriously. This was his banal pulling line which he always used.

"Yeah, it was in me fuckin' bed, I think," the first woman said. They burst out into laughter, obviously enjoying their joke more than Nobby did.

Nobby went to the 'toilets' for a slash. The bogs, rank with the smell of stale piss and wacky-backy, and looking like they hadn't been cleaned since the times of Gil Merrick, were where all the seedy business went on in the pub. Whether you wanted draw or speed, this was the place to come. The two cubicles were where you could get your gear. The landlord, Arthur, knew what was going on, but let it go. He was doing good business and that was all that mattered to him.

Nobby looked down at his limp dick. He started pissing into the urinal, already full of pubes, chewing gum and even a Tenant's lager beer mat lodged in between the plastic mesh guard, now soggy from the constant rain of acidic piddle.

"Ah," he sighed. It was the pleasure every man knew, the pressure within the bladder released itself. "Ah," he went on still, his flow now in full rhythm, smacking against the white, porcelain sides, splashing up and falling to the urinal cake. The smell rising up, a mixture of piss and deodorizer, was a peculiar fusion of the good and the bad, all at once, full on and in your face.

Suddenly beside him was Danny, towering over him, leaving a dark shadow in his corner.

"All right, mate," Danny said, now the worse from the lager himself. He hadn't been in for long, but he drank beer like others drank lemonade.

Danny unzipped his flies and took out his meaty fucker. Nobby, glancing down at it, caught a glimpse.

"Fuck me, Dan," Nobby began, slurring, "ya got a right one there like... have ya ever thought about starrin' in a fuckin' porno or summat?"

Danny looked around the bogs. He was paranoid: people could think he was bent.

"Fuck off, ya prick," he answered. If he hadn't been Darren's best mate, he would've lamped him.

Danny left the bogs, quickly and in shame, though luckily the toilet was empty.

Shaking his prick for any excess piss up his tubes with his right hand, Nobby had his left hand up against the wall for support, as he could hardly stand. His dick back in his pants now, he felt the warm trickle of piss running down his left leg, soaking through instantly, leaving a small, wet stain of urine on his stonewashed, lightly coloured Levis.

"Fuck it!" he shouted, leaving the bogs. Nobby went hysterical: he'd been right all along, Mickey had chosen The Jam. "Fuck me, Michael, I knew it. Are ya doin' this just to piss me off?"

"I dayn't want ya to call me 'Michael', all right?" Mickey hated the name 'Michael' - only his grandmother called him that. "And another thing, ya aiyn't even really me mate, so dayn't call me nothin'."

"Okay ladies, that's enough of that, I think," Darren said, trying to calm the situation.

Nobby mumbled something or other before he walked off to another part of the Lounge, disappearing into the smoky void.

The Lounge was a big place, full of small nooks and crannies, a fireplace, and a square bar, much like the one in the American sitcom *Cheers*. The Bantam Cock had been built in the early 1920s and still retained much of the décor from that era. The carpet was red and axminsterish in appearance but still looked reasonably well kept. The bar was made of oak, though its surface scratched from decades of hands, coins and the bottoms of pint glasses hitting it. On a busy night, usually on the weekends and on holidays, it was chocablock, and you could hardly move. Once you lost someone to the crowd, looking for them could take you a while.

The toilets separated the Lounge from the Bar and the Smoking Room. The Bar itself was a mess, and about as clean as a Balti house takeaway on the Stratford Road. It was in here you found your ex-cons playing pool like hustlers and your barley wine sipping alcoholic pensioners talking to themselves or to their emaciated whippets under the table, so all in all it wasn't the best place to be seen. The Smoking Room, in contrast, had a more relaxed atmosphere about it and was full of the true regulars, most of them over sixty five, bespectacled and flat-capped, who'd been using the place since time immemorial. Yet, the true soul of the pub was in the Lounge. That was where all the fun happened – if you could call it fun – and where Darren and his crowd drank.

Behind the bar in the Lounge, hanging proudly for all to see, a blue and white striped scarf, worn by the gaffer in the victorious 1963 League Cup final matches against their bitter rivals, Aston Villa; a picture of Trevor Francis in his prime wearing a Blue's strip; and finally, a team photograph, now old and faded, of Small Heath F.C. from the 1892-93 season, after winning the first Football League Second Division title. It was a Bluenose pub, and all the locals wanted you to know about it. Villa supporters were not welcome here. If they wanted to drink, then they'd have to drink round their own end: in Erdington or Handsworth, places that gave even your average Birmingham City supporter nightmares, because they didn't feel right there, like it was something in the water, the beer in the pubs. Maybe over yonder, to the north, where the Villa masses lived and reproduced, things were different.

At school, Darren had only known one Villa supporter, one James Kershaw, who'd actually moved with his family to Darren's area from leafy Sutton Coldfield. Darren had only known him as a swot who'd always got the best marks in school for every subject with the minimum of effort. He'd found out Kershaw was a Villa fan after he'd been mouthing off about the 1977 League Cup Final victory, which was only two years after Villa's first, in 1975. Kershaw had been blagging on about how it was revenge for their defeat in the 1960s. Well, Darren exploded, as could have been expected, along with three quarters of the boy pupils in the school. They first steamed into him with a few kicks, debagged him, before giving the poor lad a real good present of a pile on. Kershaw came out of it alive, but never opened his mouth again.

Down in the south of the Second City, word was rule. The Blues nation tolerated nothing from their claret and blue enemy. Birmingham fans laughed at your Liverpool-Manchester United, Arsenal-Spurs and Portsmouth-Southampton rivalries. Apart from the Old Firm derby up in Scotland, nothing came close in terms of hatred and bitterness as far as your locals in The Bantam Cock were concerned. Both sides were witness to that. Although the football on the pitch was usually nothing to get excited about, when the teams met you knew trouble would be on the agenda – the most recent occasion had been a few months before when the Zulus had won the day against the Villa lot on Lancaster Circus, chasing them away.

"So, Danny, serious like, what's ya prediction for tomorra?" Darren asked him.

"I told ya, mate, I dayn't give a fuck about the score... who does? It's just a rumble for me."

Darren turned his attention to Mickey:

"I saw Alan Irving?"

"Shit, where'd ya see him," Mickey said with a laugh. He took out his fags and crashed. "Yeah, carry on, where was he?"

"I saw him on the number 11."

"Is he goin' down tomorra?" he asked, lighting his fag.

"Yeah, with a couple of mates in a car..."

The bell rang for last orders and the lights flashed on and off like a poltergeist was in the house. Everybody knew what it meant, and a stampede ensued. The Lounge had cleared a bit, but not enough to make it entirely comfortable to get to the bar. Usually Darren got a couple for last orders. He couldn't tonight, though: London was calling and he needed the money.

They were pissing themselves: Nobby was sitting down in the corner, next to the fruit machines, which he'd been gazing at with fascination until he'd fallen asleep with half a pint left in his glass on his lap, and it was on the verge of tipping out all over him. This was an opportunity too good to miss:

"Go on, mate, do it," Mickey said to Danny.

Danny, however, didn't need any prompting. He walked over to the sleeping Nobby, first slaloming in and out of punters, his massive body knocking them on the way – not a complaint went out. He took out his packet of Benson and, with childish giggles all the way, proceeded to stick three fags in Nobby's mouth, one in each nostril and one in both ears. The pub cracked up when they saw what was going on; Nobby, still deep in sleep, didn't stir. Danny delicately took the pint glass from Nobby's hands, betraying the awkward brutishness he was known for, and poured it without a trace of mercy in Nobby's crotch area.

"Ah, come on now, that's goin' too far," Darren remonstrated.

"Shut up, Daz," Mickey said, "the fucker deserves it – he's bin a head-doer all night."

Still Nobby didn't move. It was like he was trapped in some place that he didn't want to return from. There was a smile on his face, even as Danny was doing his worst to him. The jukebox was playing Shakin' Steven's *Green Door,* and it would've been enough to wake up Sleeping Beauty, but not poor Nobby, now with saliva falling from the corners of his mouth.

Bagpuss was closing up:

"Can ya see ya drinks off now, ladies and gentlemen?! Please, it's late, we all wanna go home...See ya drinks off, come on! Hey, Daz, any chance ya can get that dope home?"

"Fuckin' leave him there," Danny said. He was now heavily drunk himself.

"Yeah, dayn't worry, mate," Darren said to Bagpuss.

Darren went over to his best mate and woke him up. It wasn't easy, mind you, but he managed it in the end.

Nobby opened his eyes slowly.

"Where am I?" he said.

"In hell, ya dick," Danny said, walking out.

"Daz, we'll see ya tomorra... half eight... dayn't forget... New Street... we'll have to buy the tickets first," Mickey said, following Danny out of the door.

"Daz, that Danny's a right tosspotter, ya know?" Nobby said, when the two had already left.

"Yeah, I know."

"Goodnight, lads," Bagpuss said.

"See ya later, Arth."

It was a cold night, quite unusually so for November, and only a degree or so below zero. Darren and Nobby were freezing their balls off, as they weren't really dressed for the weather.

"Fuck me, Nob, it's brass monkeys out here tonight."

"I dayn't feel the cold at all."

"Yeah, coz ya pissed up." Darren's teeth were chattering. "It's fuck off freezin'."

The pub was a ten-minute walk from Darren's, but tonight it was taking longer, no thanks to Nobby's stumbling and puking up all the way.

"Fuck, I'm gonna have it hard in the mornin'," Nobby said, wiping the vomit from his lips with the sleeve of his Smiths sweatshirt.

"Ya shouldn't have drunk so much."

They walked on a little more, Nobby further behind Darren, his steps slow, off tempo and awkward in their movement, until Darren finally reached home.

"I'll see ya tomorrow, okay?" Darren said as he opened the gate to his parents' semi-detached council house.

Nobby walked on silently, impervious to everything.

In bed, Darren had time to think about the next morning: There was the operation, the match, and the guilt he felt between the conflict of the two. Yet now there was a new problem – Danny: could he go to London with him? He'd been in two minds anyway, but now with this thrown into the mix, going looked more and more unlikely. Should he stay with Lynsey? Her magic seemed to be working again, only this time through the actions of a third party.

It had been another sleepless night. Darren had the train in two hours to London; in three, the operation.

When he got downstairs his mother was busy doing some cleaning in the kitchen. Saturday was her only chance because she liked to rest on the seventh day and there was also the Sunday dinner to prepare, a task that could take upwards of four hours if prepared in the proper way.

"Anythin' to eat, mom?" It was Darren's usual question.

"Nah, ya'll have to make ya own today, I'm too busy."

He'd expected a fryup or something which would've knocked the alcohol still in his system asunder with its cholesterol infusion. Beans on toast or corn flakes would have to do. He hated making his own grub, though. It was partly his old lady's fault, however – she'd spoiled him all his life in that way and he'd got used to the routine of first-class service.

"Put the kettle on?" he asked her.

"What time are ya goin' to the hospital?"

"About half ninish."

"What time's the operation?"

"Err, at ten, I think."

No, he couldn't go, he couldn't do it – he'd only regret it in the end if he did. It was the one opportunity to prove to himself how much of a man he was.

The enemy was strong – far stronger than them in many ways. His friends would agree with him on that. It was either a win or a loss, no half-measures. In the end, with all their effort, they hoped – him at least – to walk away from the place winners; and if they didn't, then at least he'd be able to say he'd been there, lending his support to the cause, which was important, not only to himself, but to all those connected to the struggle. In this fight there was an underdog, yet he'd be behind it forever.

And it was the right choice as far as he knew.

Nah, I won't go, I can't go, he thought, staring down at the plate of piping hot beans. *I'll have to do the other thing instead. I know they aiyn't gonna mind and that they'll understand why I didn't turn up... if they dayn't, then it's coz they're too sensitive to what's goin' on around 'em. I'm gonna miss out on a lot.*

"We can pick ya up later from the hospital if ya like," his old lady said. His eyes were fixed on the plate in front of him. "Darren, did ya hear me?"

"*What?*" said Darren, snapping out of his daydream.

"D'ya want us to pick ya up later from the QE?"

"Nah, dayn't bother yaself."

16: Morrissey Mark II

He was bollock naked, and his head was throbbing from the previous night's overindulgence. He always said it: the day after when he woke up, that he'd never drink again, the mouth spitting out the words from his dehydrated mouth with all the honesty of a person with a hangover. The promise always came to nothing - he expected the same today. As soon as he had a bit of dough in his pocket and he passed a pub - it was the same with his best mate, Darren.

Because Nobby lived alone, he didn't have his old lady at his beck-and-call like Darren did. Not that he minded – in fact, he had always said he had it better than Darren, anyway: independence was a gift. He'd grown up a lot since he'd moved into his one-bedroom flat. His parents had told him to get out, so he'd had no choice in the matter. Although they still talked and he went down there every Sunday for his dinner, relations between them weren't the best. They thought he was a waster, and should've followed his dad into the building trade instead of the career path he'd actually followed as a factory worker with no future.

Everything from the night before was a total blank. He hadn't drunk that much since the last time he'd drunk that much, and that hadn't been so long ago - maybe only even the day before, but he wasn't sure.

He got up from the bed, holding his right hand up to his forehead in an effort to relieve some of the pain there. Then, in an upright position, he pressed the palms of both hands firmly against his temples, trying to break the pain in the veins of his head. This, luckily, gave him some joy, though he knew at some point he'd have to let go. Eventually he did, and struggling to the kitchen - every step a feat in itself – he opened the bottom draw, only to find there were no painkillers. It was the kind of scenario everyone dreaded: you were dying and out of the only thing that could help you. The day before, you had plenty, they were everywhere, on the table, on the side, next to your bed, saying 'hello' to you.

But bad luck – he didn't have any; he'd have to go to the shop. Well, he was in no mood for that, so he went back to bed in a hope it would just go away.

It was no good. What seemed like an eternity lying was only a few minutes and he still had the headache. Again he climbed out of the bed and, with a ceaseless pain of pins being stabbed into the soft, moist tissue of his brain, he managed somehow to get to the shop, wearing his pyjamas, slippers, and his coat.

Nobby bought the tablets with a can of Irn-Bru and swigged four down for good measure. As always, he didn't forget his 45p copy of the *NME*, the edition's title: *The GREATEST ALBUMS EVER MADE, NME NAMES ITS 100LPS*. Like the way to the shop, the way back – even if it was only a hundred yards, was slow, yet by midway, he could feel the effects of the painkillers already.

Fifteen minutes later he was as good as gold. It was only then that the events of the previous night came back to him: He remembered Danny: how could he have forgotten that cunt? He remembered getting sick and the dirty middle-aged slags. No, he'd been out of order and he knew it.

He had a bath, got dressed in his usual gear: a Smith's t-shirt and a pair of Levi's 501s, brushed and styled his hair with Brylcreem, then put on his *Meat is Murder* album, like he always did. He'd listened to it countless times since it had been released in February, and if you'd have asked him how many times, he'd have been at a loss to tell you.

The stylus on his new record player cut through the multiple notches and craggy avenues of the black vinyl surface. The lyrics and the melodies Nobby knew more than he knew himself. He'd often created comments to the lyrics, ways of imposing his own understanding on them to his own time and place. They were good if you ignored the grammatical mistakes and logical inconsistencies of the paragraphing. He put everything in a scrapbook: pictures, newspaper cuttings and his own thoughts on their lyrics. He'd done the same with their first album too.

Nobby had a couple of slices of bread in the cupboard, so he made himself some cheese on toast and a cuppa.

His scrapbook was on the table, next to the copy of the *NME* he'd bought. The scrapbook, soiled from the constant touching and stroking of an artist's admiring hand, had been on the table since the previous Saturday, when he'd cut out an image of Morrissey from *Smash Hits*. He picked it up again, before having second thoughts. No, maybe he'd check, just to see – he was curious, how good were they in regards to music's other bands and artists?

His heart sank – *Meat Is Murder* came in at number 64, below such mediocre shite as The Beach Boy's *Pet Sounds* at 20 and Dexy's Midnight Runner's *Searching For The Young Soul Rebels* at 34, though he had to admit he liked their song *Geno*. *It was a massacre of common sense*, he thought. *How could the so-called music journalists and professionals be so callous to Manchester's finest?*

Angry, Nobby threw it back down on the table, vowing never to read the *NME* again. He then picked up the scrapbook - he had a few more pictures to add to it. On the front were images of Morrissey and the band glued on. Inside it were more of the same pastiche collages of his heroes. Over a couple of the faces and newspaper clippings of album reviews, interviews and chart positions, in thick indelible pen, both in black and red, Nobby expressed his own feelings in succinct perspicacity. Back nearly a year before, his words had been spontaneous.

He flicked through the pages one by one, looking at all his scrawlings. He went back to the notes he'd originally written in February on the release of *Meat Is Murder:*

1)HEADMASTER RITUAL: WHAT DOES 'BELLIGERENT' MEAN? IT HAS A GOOD TITLE AND I THINK IT SAYS A LOT ABOUT SCHOOL. GHOULS OR GHOSTS MENTIONED AT THE BEGINNING, WHICH IS ALWAYS A SCREAM. THE INTRO IS GREAT AND REALLY GETS YOU ON YOUR FEET. IT'S ABOUT MANCHESTER SCHOOLS, I THINK, AND HOW THE TEACHERS TREATED HIM THERE AS A BOY. GREAT CHORUS, TOO, WITH PLENTY OF GOOD REPITITION. REMINDS ME OF MY OWN DAYS AT SCHOOL AND THE TORTURE ME AND DAZ GOT FROM THE CANE OF MR BRENT.

2) RUSHOLME RUFFIANS: SEEMS TO BE ABOUT VIOLENCE AND STABBING AND STUFF, AND THEN PULLING BIRDS OR FANCYING THEM OR SOMETHING. GREAT UPBEAT TUNE, LIKE SOMETHING FROM ELVIS OR BUDDY HOLLY, WHICH YOU CAN DANCE TO IN A CLUB.

3) I WANT THE ONE I CAN'T HAVE: BIOLOGY AND MENTALITY AND SOMETHING, NOT REALLY SURE? IF YOU CAN'T HAVE IT, THEN LEAVE IT, STEPHEN. RICHES OF THE POOR? I THOUGHT THE POOR *WERE* POOR?

4) WHAT SHE SAID: MENTAL INTRO, LIKE THE TASMANIAN DEVIL ON SPEED OR SOMETHING. WHAT SHE SAID: SHE'S DEAD, THAT'S OBVIOUS, BUT WHO CARES APART FROM HERSELF AND THE BAND?

5) THAT JOKE ISN'T FUNNY ANYMORE: GUITAR INTRO AT THE BEGINNING IS GREAT. THE SOUND OF STEPHEN'S VOICE IN THE SONG IS MAGICAL. DEATH AND DYING. WHAT JOKE? DYING? WHAT BONE IS NEAR MY HOME? EVEN WHEN THEY FALL DOWN... WHAT IS THAT? DOMINOES? THE GUITAR FLOWS AND THEN GETS A SURPRISE WITH A REPRISE.

6) HOW SOON IS NOW: BLURRY INTRO AND THE GUITAR OF JOHNNY REPEATS THROUGHOUT THE SONG. SON AND HEIR... OF WHAT, STEPHEN, I DON'T UNDERSTAND? THIS RHYTHM IS A HOOK. SOMEBODY IS LONELY AMD WANTS TO DIE BECAUSE THEY ARE LONELY. THE BEAT IS DRIVING ME ON NOW BECAUSE I AM DRUNK WRITING THESE WORDS. GREAT, MAN, THE SWAYING BEAT IS FUCKING SORTED.

7) NOWHERE FAST: DROP MY TROUSERS TO THE WORLD, YES, SHOW YOUR ARSE TO THE QUEEN, THAT'S GREAT AND I AGREE WITH YOU.

8) WELL I WONDER: GOOD GUITAR WITH DRUM COMBINATION. AND HE IS HORSE. AND HE WONDERS. MAYBE HE SHOULD HAVE TAKEN HIS 'TUNES', 'BECAUSE TUNES MAKE YOU BREATHE MORE EASILY'.

9) BARBARISM BEGINS AT HOME: GREAT RIFF. IT'S SO FUNKY. SEXUAL PERVERSION FROM TEACHERS AT SCHOOL. CRACKING HEADS AND ALL THAT WHICH I ACTUALLY EXPERIENCED FIRST HAND.

10) MEAT IS MURDER: I LIKE THE COWS SCREAMING AT THE BEGINNING AND THE WHOLE SONG IN GENERAL. I LOVE MEAT MYSELF BUT I CAN SEE WHERE STEPHEN GETS THE IDEAS

FROM. COME ON, STEPHEN, START EATING MEAT. I HEARD IN SOME REVIEW THAT THIS IS THE BEST SONG ON THE ALBUM BUT I DON'T AGREE WITH THIS. MINE IS *THAT JOKE ISN'T FUNNY ANYMORE*.

17: The Letdown

She was hoping he'd come but also expecting it. Well, he was her boyfriend after all, and that was what boyfriends were supposed to do. Recently, her memory had waned and she couldn't remember a lot – even Darren's visits.

"Howaya, sweetheart?" her old man said, stroking his daughter's hand.

"Where's Darren?" she asked.

Christy rolled his eyes. Darren had taken his place as the number one man in her life and he didn't like it. This jealousy - illogical and all-consuming - was eating him up inside.

"He'll be here in a little while, chicken, don't be worryin' yerself about that like."

"Howaya, sweetheart?" her mom asked.

They were sitting on either side of the bed.

"Weak."

"I know," her mom said with a nod, smiling, as if she understood the pain her daughter was going through.

"Do yer wanna a cup o'tay, Teresa?"

"Yea', that'll be grand like."

Christy went to the hot drinks machine outside the hall next to the ward.

"I'm tired, mom."

"I know, chicken, I know."

"What are they doin' to me?"

"They have to, chicken... It's to make yer better again."

Lynsey looked at her mom sadly, like she had already been defeated by the disease.

"But, mom, I can hardly move and me back's killin' me."

"I know, but yer operation's today, Lynz," she said after a pause, her tone changing to a deeper gravity with every word she uttered.

Lynsey, wrecked with fear, looked at her mom.

"Operation? *What operation?*"

She knew this already, as the doctors had informed her.

"What... yer don't remember?"

"Of course I remember but I dayn't wanna operation."

"But it's for the best, love."

"I dayn't wanna hear 'it's for the best' or 'it's for ya own good'."

"Calm down, chicken," her mom said, putting her hand on Lynsey's face and gently stroking it.

"Mom, get off me," Lynsey said, moving the loving hand away quickly. She started sobbing.

"Don't cry there, chicken."

"How? Look at me, mom? I look disgustin'."

Two elderly Asian patients, who'd been reading in the two beds opposite, glanced up, surprised at the disturbance.

"Now, come on, yer bein' silly."

Her father came in holding two piping hot teas in plastic cups.

"What's all this in here then, ladies?"

"Nothin'," her mom replied. "Maybe yer can talk some sense into her, Christy? She's bein' all negative and all that like."

"Now, Lynsey, me little treasure, what's this I hear about yer actin' like a big eejit?"

He took his seat next to her again, passing a tea to his wife.

"Is there one or two sugars in that?"

"Two, just like yer always have it, love."

A silence ensued: it was awkward and uncomfortable for them all.

"I'm gonna die," Lynsey said, breaking the temporary hush. Tears started rolling down her face once more.

"There yer go – ya mother's right, yer bein' a right fecker," her dad said in a tone bordering on the humorous.

"I dayn't care, dad, ya aiyn't the one dyin' and in pain and all that – it's me, ya know?"

"Yer not dyin' there, love... Christy, tell her."

"Then what's this disgustin' thing inside me... this leukaemia... I hate it, it's just disgustin' and it aiyn't fair... *Why me, mom?*"

"Don't be gettin' all worried, love, I'm tellin' yer it's gonna be grand," her old man said.

"Where's Darren?"

"He should be here in a minute... what's the time, Teresa?"

"Twenty past nine."

"He aiyn't comin', is he?" Lynsey said.

"Of course he is," her mom said, caressing her hand again. This time Lynsey didn't notice and her mom continued.

"Nah, I dayn't think so."

"There yer go again, actin' the gobshite and feelin' sorry for yerself," her dad remarked coldly and authoritarian-like.

Lynsey tried to lift herself up from the bed - but it was no good – she didn't have the strength.

"Lynsey, love, don't do that, relax yerself – yer in no fit state to be humpin' around," her mother said, almost jumping on Lynsey in an attempt to hold her down.

"I can't stand this hospital no more... I can't stand this bed no more."

"Listen, Lynz, ya goin' into theatre in a bit so calm down," her old man said, this time his soft country accent even more bruising in its delivery.

"Where's Darren? I want Darren."

"He'll be here when he's here," her mom said nervously.

He couldn't let her down, she wouldn't allow it. She knew that at any minute he'd walk in, hold her tightly and assure her that everything would be okay, and that she would survive and they'd live together happily for the rest of their lives. This was because Darren would make it okay. She thought she could count on him, and especially now, at such a critical time. When she saw him everything would be better; when she saw him the illness would disappear; when she saw him she would get up from the bed and leave the hospital, never to return. But hold on, she was daydreaming again – it was the drugs. There'd be no happy ending, only strife, though at least with her loving boyfriend at her side she'd be ready as ever to battle on.

"Where's Daz?" she asked again, but this time calmly, like she was asking a stranger the time on the street.

"Lynsey, love," her dad began, "will yer ever give over and give it a rest, you'd give anybody's arse a headache. Don't be worryin' yerself, it'll be grand."

"Dad, stop it," she said with a giggle "Ah!" she then screamed out in pain, as her laughing brought a short, sharp pain down the length of her body.

"Are yer all right, love" her mother asked.

"Yeah, I'm fine, but where's Darren?"

Her mother smiled, before saying: "Yer brothers will be here soon."

"I dayn't care, mom, where's Darren?"

She turned to her husband: "Christy, will yer forever go and see where that youn' fella is?"

"Yer want me to go and get him?"

"Yea', go and pick the fecker up."

"Ah, don't be talkin' to me woman, I hardly know where he lives."

"All Saints Road, Kings Heath... Number 17," Lynsey said.

"Bloody fecker, I have to be goin' all the way there?"

"Christy, yer a pain in the face. Just go and pick the lad up, will yer."

Christy went in his green A reg. Austin Ital van to Darren's house. Fifteen minutes later he was there.

"I'm Christy Moriarty, Lynsey's father... Is Darren about?"

"All right, nice to meet ya," Vera, Darren's mom, said.

They shook hands.

"So, is yer son here like?"

"D'ya wanna cuppa?"

"No, I can't be stayin', I've got to get back to the hospital."

"Oh, yeah, Lynsey's operation's today, aiyn't it?"

"Tis, yeah... so, is he around like?"

"Nah, I'm afraid he aiyn't. He just left five minutes ago."

"Where'd he go?"

"To the hospital, I suppose."

"Okay, love I've gotta be headin' back... she'll be goin' into theatre in a minute."

"All right, nice to meet ya anyway... Maybe next time, with ya wife... a cuppa, yeah?"

"We'll see."

"Give me love to Lynsey, poor thing."

Christy got in his van and headed back as quickly as he could. When he got to the hospital, he discovered Lynsey's empty bed.

"Where are they?" Christy asked one of the Asian women in the bed opposite.

"I don't know. They left ten minutes ago with a nurse and two doctors," she replied in broken English.

"And where the hell have ya bin like, Christy?" Lynsey's mom asked at the top of her lungs. She was all ruffled and nervous.

"Where d'yer think I've been?"

"*Yer* tell me?"

"Feck off, woman, and leave me to God and peace."

"Where's Darren?" she asked.

"He wasn't there – his mother said he'd already left for the hospital."

"Well, I haven't seen him."

"Then he must be here somewhere."

"Where Christy?"

"How's me daughter doin'?"

"She's gettin' ready in surgery."

"Are yer gonna tell her Darren's not here yet?"

"No, Christy, that'd be silly now, wouldn't it?"

The train had just passed the city of Northampton. They were sitting in a second-class carriage, full of families eagerly looking forward to a day out in the capital, as well as a few Birmingham City supporters, though not the kind to cause trouble – the Scarf Brigade in other words. It was pretty quiet, really, and Mickey and Danny still looked a bit conspicuous in their designer gear, though they'd toned it down a bit, not wearing any stuff with logos. It would be better that way. Yet they still looked the part; you couldn't change a mullet hairstyle if it was part of the way you moved and talked – that kind of thing was innate, because Mickey was all about style. He was only wearing Farahs today, their little orange label on his right arse cheek the only giveaway of his 'casual' existence.

The ticket inspector had already been round checking tickets, so now they could relax a bit. The last time on an away trip to London to watch the boys play QPR in September, the ticket inspector had been a bit suspicious of them and called in the transport police in Watford. The police ended up throwing them off the train. Danny had been noisy then and promised this time to keep it hush. Luckily they had made that game at Loftus Road by hitching a ride from a builder on his way to London. They'd regretted it in the end, though, because they were hammered three-one. Their only consolation from the day had been why the Old Bill hadn't escorted them on the next train to Brum - as usually was the case - at which they'd had a great laugh about. The lads one, the Old Bill nil again.

"Where'd he go?" Danny asked Mickey.

"For a slash."

"Gis one?"

"What, one of these?" said Mickey.

Mickey took out a can of Carling from a plastic bag and gave it to Danny.

"It aiyn't even cold," Danny said, sighing.

"I know, I bought 'em last night and there wasn't no room in me old lady's fridge to put 'em in.

Danny opened the can, took a huge swig, burped and then handed it to Mickey.

"Oh, that hits the fuckin' spot – there's nothin' like a liquid breakfast."

"Stay off that shit," warned Mickey, "ya dayn't wanna be pissed up and outta ya fuckin' tree if we get in a scrap, d'ya?"

"Ah, fuck it, I'll be all right."

"Okay, but keep it down, we dayn't wanna get our arses thrown off again."

"All right, Mickey, leave it out."

"All right, but just take it easy, will ya? Ya got jumped and caned a bit by them Man. City wankers if ya remember. *No* drinkin'... not yet, anyway... later."

"Fuck, Mickey, gis the can."

He took the can from Mickey and polished it off in one.

"I told ya, Dan, I aiyn't gonna give ya another one, I swear."

"I'll buy me own then."

"Do it then."

They sat in silence for a while, all the time Danny's eyes fixed on the plastic bag at Mickey's feet.

"Gis one, Mick?" Danny asked.

"What d'ya think of the view – it's great, aiyn't it?" Mickey commented.

They were going through the Northamptonshire countryside, bleak in late November, but the epitome of a little England lost to industrialism.

"What?" Danny asked – he was still ogling the cans in the bag like it was the only alcohol left on the planet.

"The view, ya twat? It kinda reminds me of school – d'ya remember Mr Hornman, Danny, and Music?"

"*What?*"

"Mr Hornman and his music classes. I'll never forget when we did about that Edward Elgar bloke or summat and the teacher said that we had to close our eyes and think of the English countryside."

"What the fuck are ya on, cunt?" Danny said. He wasn't interested in anything except getting another can of lager.

"Mr Hornman?"

"Of course I know the cunt – tried to get me expelled, didn't he?"

"Yeah, but only coz ya stuck a pencil in Matt Gaston's fuckin' ear."

"The twat deserved it."

"Oh, yeah... I wasn't in that lesson, I wagged it with a few of the lads... we went to the Bristol City game at Ashton Gate... When was that?"

"Seventy-eight," Danny said, "Gis a can now?"

"How d'ya know that?"

"I aiyn't that fuckin' thick, mate."

Although a self-confessed thug, Danny wasn't an out and out dimwit: his sole hobby, apart from fighting, was the history of Birmingham City F.C, from which he had a considerable programme collection dating from the 1950s which his old man had given him on his deathbed.

The train entered the Home Counties.

"Where is the cunt?" Danny asked, now considerably irritated at his 'companion's' disappearance.

"Fuck knows," Mickey replied, only half listening and reading the week's edition of *Shoot* magazine.

"*Match*'s better, Mickey, ya should know that?"

"Whatever."

"So maybe ya should go and check where he is?" said Danny.

Mickey got up with a sigh, picking up the bag of lagers next to him.

"I'll check the bogs then.

"Yeah, maybe he fell down one of the fuckers."

"Ah, Mick, ya can leave the lagers with me if ya wanna like."

"Fuck that."

"Dayn't ya trust me or summat?"

"Like I trust a Villa supporter, son, like a Villa supporter."

Clatter, clatter, the interminable noise of the train wheels hitting the joints of the tracks, moving ever forward, ever on. The rural scene quickly changed to an urban landscape and the town of Luton.

Mickey was gone well over fifteen minutes before he returned.

"Well, where is he?" Danny asked.

"Fuck knows? I checked the bogs and I couldn't find him. He musta pissed off or summat and done one."

"Did ya check the other carriages?"

"Nah, just the first one."

"Ah, he probably jumped off somewhere then - couldn't handle it with the men, I say."

"Ya think?"

"What took ya so long?"

"I was lookin' outta the window."

"Soft cunt."

Another few minutes passed by and they'd just left Luton and were on the final leg of their journey to the Cockney badlands.

"For fuck's sake, Mickey, gis a can, I'm parched."

"*Patience*, Daniel, patience. After the match, not before."

"I'll buy me own then... Yeah, a couple of Breakers."

He walked in.

"Where the fuck have ya bin, *Tony?*" Mickey asked.

"I had the bleedin' shits, didn't I?" replied Tony, casually, as if he'd gone for a minute, not for over an hour.

"But I checked the bogs." Mickey said.

"Yeah, but I went to the far carriage toilets - all the other shitters were busy or had piss all over the seats – dirty bastards didn't even have the decency to clean up after they had a dirty fuckin' slash."

Tony was seventeen and skinnier than the handle of a brush. If there was going to be any fighting in London, he wasn't going to be much use to them.

"For a minute we thought ya'd fucked off like that letdown Darren," Danny said, pulling a can from the bag.

18: A Knight in Shining Armour in Search of Tony Butler

Lynsey had been in surgery for an hour when Darren came strolling into the hospital.

"Where have yer been, Darren?" Lynsey's mom asked, angry but not openly showing it.

"Ya wouldn't believe what happened to me?" he responded.

"What? Shock me? Lynsey was waitin' for yer, Darren, and yer let her down."

"I fell asleep on the bus and ended up in Stechford."

"Well, that's no excuse in me book... D'yer know Christy went to yer home like to pick yer up, and yer weren't there?"

"*Did he?*"

"Yea', he did, and he wasn't pleased – he was put outta his way when he should've been here with his sick daughter."

"Teresa, listen, I'm really sorry, honest."

"It's no good bein' sorry to me, it's to Lynsey that yer should be doin' that to, and now it's too late... And when Christy sees yer, he's gonna ring yer neck, yer little fecker."

"What for?"

"Yer know why," she answered, giving him a look, if not from hatred then at least from disdain.

They went to the waiting room just outside the operating theatre where Lynsey was having her transplant. Her two brothers were sitting next to their old man.

"Oh, oh, here he is... They seek him here, they seek him there, they seek him everywhere... The Scarlett Pimpernel... Hey, son, where the feck were *yer*?" Christy said, his eyes glaring with madness and his face as distorted as Jack

Nicholson's in *The Shining* when he was chopping down the door of the bathroom to get to his family.

"It's a long story," Darren replied as he sat down.

Now Darren was in a worse position with her family than he had been; it was beyond any reasonable doubt he was now *persona non grata,* not even on the periphery now, a total outcast with no chance of reprieve.

"Yeah, sit down, go on, relax, that's the only thing ya Brummies are used to," Owen said, Lynsey other brother, angrily. Although Birmingham born, he was a Fenian and a Villa supporter.

What's their problem, Darren thought to himself. He hadn't done anything personally to antagonize any one of them, yet here they were giving it loads to him and thinking they were better than he was. No, it wasn't true; they were Irish, and that was where everything had its roots.

They waited and they waited – in silence mostly. The ancient clock above their heads, tick-tock, tick-tock, tick-tock in its cadence, the only sound breaking the monotony and fear. Yes, there was that too: Fear in how everything would turn out. They all shared this. Reality cast them as enemies, but here, in this critical moment, they shared everything as one like supporters on the stands.

Occasionally, Lynsey's parents or her brothers exchanged a few words with each other, while ignoring Darren.

Sick of the treatment he was receiving, Darren went to the kiosk to buy himself a paper, a Mars bar and a can of Coke. When he returned, he sat down and began chomping and slurping, oblivious to the fact it was irritating them. He didn't care, though. With malicious intent, after he'd realised it was causing them distress, he began to ruffle the pages as he perused the newspaper. Sam Fox was there again, her double assets curvaceous and as sexy as ever. He turned to the back page and sighed. It reminded him of what he should have been doing.

He looked at the fixtures, his finger running down each one, most of them catching his eye: Liverpool v Chelsea, Luton Town v Manchester City, Southampton v Everton, Villa v Spurs, West Ham v WBA.

He made predictions in his mind. It didn't matter really, he only hoped Birmingham survived the season, but it wasn't looking good, with only five wins and a draw from seventeen games which had them third from bottom of the table. The Arsenal match would be important if only to give the lads a bit of confidence. His team was now above Ipswich and WBA who were really struggling, and a seven point gap had developed between those two and the rest. Leicester, Oxford and Man. City were only two points ahead of Birmingham on eighteen. Darren knew they could do it, but they'd let him down so many times before he didn't want to talk too soon.

A doctor walked out from surgery. He pulled down his surgeon's mask. Everybody threw themselves up.

"What is it, doctor?" Christy, Lynsey's dad, asked.

"No news yet," he said, almost running down the corridor. They all gasped, including Darren.

The tension was too much.

The long hand had gone round the clock several times and it was approaching kickoff at Arsenal. Darren had his fingers crossed for all eventualities as he put out the last fag from the box. He thought for a moment before he realised he'd already smoked fifteen just waiting there.

Seeing as there had been no action up to then with Lynscy, he decided to go for a walk around the hospital. The real method to his madness was to find a radio somewhere to listen to the match - or at least the updates - of his own team's fate.

He asked a cleaner mopping a nearby corridor where the best place was to listen to a radio. The cleaner, a diminutive Asian women in her fifties, didn't understand a word he said. He walked on, and a little further he spotted a male nurse.

"Excuse me, mate," Darren said politely, "d'ya know a place where I can get to a radio... I wanna listen to the footy?"

"Well," the black man began in his coarse West Indian accent, "ya can always go home... ya got one a dem at home, aiyn't ya?"

"Very funny," Darren said. "But I'm serious, where?"

"Ya'll be wantin' the ambulance drivers and the mechanics for stuff like dat... But I wouldn't if I waz yu, them be a funny lot, know what I mean? Nasty bhoys... yeah, they is a right nasty lot."

"Which way?"

The nurse, laughing his head off by now, gave the nervous football supporter directions and Darren quickly darted off.

Finding himself in the ambulance bay, he approached a paramedic.

"All right, mate, got a radio round here somewhere?"

"What d'ya wanna radio for, mate?"

The ambulance driver had a weasel face and looked more miserable than a Muslim at a pig farm.

"I wanna listen to the footy."

"Why would ya wanna listen to that?"

"Have ya got one or what?" Darren asked, his tone now discourteous, a mark of his impatience and desperation. It was already after three.

"Over there, in the garige – Dave's usually got it on... Ya know ya shouldn't be here?"

Darren ignored the admonition and walked over to the mechanics' garage. There were two ambulances: one had its bonnet open and the second had been lifted high above the pit. In the corner, around a small table, two mechanics were listening to the radio and the voice of Tom Ross. Darren knocked on the big door.

"It's open!" a voice cried out from inside.

Darren walked in.

"All right, I was just wonderin' if I could listen in for a bit?"

"Who are ya?" one of them said.

"I'm a relation of a patient and she's havin' an operation at the minute like... and well... I just wanna listen to the footy."

They looked at him strangely.

"Well, mate, this here's a restricted area and yow shouldn't really be here, but I dayn't give a toss – pull up a chair and sit yowself down," the older of the two said. He was over sixty with an oil-smeared face and sad looking, beady eyes. Both of them looked as filthy as Welsh miners down the pit.

Darren sat down quickly before they changed their minds. Above his head, to the right, was the small transistor radio. He hoped for a victory and he was praying inside himself – but not to God, it was the god of football, whoever or whatever it was. If they were going to score, who would it be, the hardman Kuhl, Dicks, maybe Bremner? Yes, that'd be ironic, an ex-Villa man.

He listened till halftime: it was still nil-nil. So far, so good. Luck was on his side.

He went back to see if anything was happening with Lynsey.

"And where did yer feck off to?" Christy asked, again with an acerbic tongue. He couldn't help it: he'd never liked him and never would. He was English, and Christy didn't like the English.

Christy's father, Padraig, a civilian at the time, had been injured by a Black and Tans' bullet in June 1920 and had lost a hand because of it. The bitterness he had given to his son had been passed on to Owen too.

"I went for a walk... Is it against the law?" Darren said sarcastically.

There was a silence.

"Nah, we aiyn't heard anythin' yet," Noel declared, playing the peacekeeper, trying to calm the situation. Owen was his antithesis in spirit, fiery and he liked an argument.

As four rolled by, sick of looking at their faces, Darren got up again and made his way back to the garage.

He came back forty-five minutes later with a smile on his face. The Blues had managed a nil-nil draw somehow against the Gunners, a team at the time packed with stars such as Viv Anderson, 'Champagne' Charlie Nicholas, Tony Woodcock, Kenny Sansom, and two promising young players in Martin Keown and David Rocastle. Although in seventh spot, they had been up to then disappointing in the league under the charge of Don Howe, and were not expected by the football pundits to do much in the season. However, it was a precious point for Birmingham, a point they had desperately needed, as Ipswich and WBA were hot up their arses at the bottom.

When he got back to the corridor Lynsey's family was nowhere in sight. He went to reception.

"Lynsey Moriarty... she's just had an operation... eer, where is she?"

"What's your relationship to the patient, sir?" the nurse at the desk said.

"Boyfriend."

"She's been taken to intensive care."

Darren rushed over there, his heart beating fast. How would she be?

When he walked into the intensive care unit all his fears became a reality. She was unrecognisable and covered like an Egyptian mummy in bandages with a pipe sticking out of her mouth. Only God knew the reason for her continual suffering, though He seemed to be powerless to stop it. This was Darren's assumption, anyway, because he wasn't religious in any sense of the word, it puzzled him. Yet her family believed in their Divine Almighty unconditionally – and what was *He* putting them through? Yes, something so wretched it was unforgivable.

Well, she was connected up – this time more than before and looking none the better. Darren believed the whole operation had been for nothing. Her family was around her broken and limp body, teary-eyed and angry. They looked back at the man who had broken their privacy once again: their eyes as irate as a lodge of Freemasons disturbed by a stranger in the middle of a secret initiation rite. They wanted this moment alone. They wanted to resume their vigil, but he was still behind them and disturbing in presence – he was a pollutant, simply.

"Where did yer feck off to again?" Christy said angrily.

"I just nipped away for a bit like."

"Just nipped away for a bit, did yer? That's feckin' convenient," Christy went on.

"Yeah, but I had to - I wasn't gonna sit round and wait for summat to happen."

Darren wasn't endearing himself to them at all with his glib responses.

"And sittin' round and waitin' for some feckin' news about yer girlfriend's very hard to do – I mean, it takes a lot outta a lad like?"

Darren was never going to win.

"Why dayn't ya just leave it out, Christy," Darren said.

"And why should I?"

"Dad, let it go," Noel imparted.

"Keep out of it, Noel," said Owen. He wanted to say something to Darren himself, but at the moment he was keeping quiet.

"Then tell him to leave, Noel," Christy went on.

"All of yer stop, d'yer hear," Teresa said, trying to calm the situation. "Lynsey's tryin' to rest and all yer can do is argue – all of yer leave if yer want."

They shut up.

"So, what did the doctors say?" Darren said. He was putting on a brave face but was embarrassed by everything – especially their boorish behaviour.

"She's very bad now, Darren, very poorly like, can't yer see?" Teresa said

"Yeah, I can, but what did the doctors say?"

"She has to remain here in intensive care."

"But is she in a coma or what?"

"It's all too complicated... We're just countin' on the doctors."

"But is she gonna be okay?" Darren asked, frustration and torture intermingled with every word. "What about the transplant?"

"They said-"

"And I dayn't want none of that medical bullshit," he interrupted her.

"...they said she..."

"So, nobody really knows nothin'?" Darren said after Teresa was explaining the situation to him for more than five minutes.

"It's all in the hands of God now, Darren, d'yer understand like?" she said calmly.

There they were again, giving it loads in their trust to God, and Darren couldn't understand it. He wanted to speak out to them about their God but thought it would only make things worse. He was an inch away from fisticuffs with Owen. He wanted a piece of him and Owen likewise.

"Yer know now, Darren, so yer can go. Leave us," Christy said, his face enough to convey what he felt. Words were superfluous.

"Yea', Darren, yer better be goin' now like," Teresa warned, *"we're* not even supposed to be here... somethin' to do with hygiene in the unit and the need for a sterile environment - we'll have to be leavin' ourselves in a minute."

Darren left and went straight to the pub. He was exhausted from the day behind him, so a couple of pints were well in order.

19: Memories Are Made of This

It was starting to fill up, but not too much, though it was still early. Charlie was sitting in his usual place at the bar talking to Tina, and quite a few locals were also in.

"Gis a pint, Tine?" Darren said.

"Good result today, wasn't it?" Charlie said to Darren, while rolling another cigarette with a Rizla.

"Great, let's just hope we get a win against Watford next Saturday."

"No problem there, mate."

"Ya think?" asked Darren.

"Yeah, dayn't worry, we'll stay up this season."

"Have ya sin Nob, Charlie?"

"Yeah, he was in at lunchtime... He was after Phil Simmons for some reason."

"*Phil*... what for?"

"Dunno... but he looked wrecked. He had a bit too much pop last night if ya remember."

"What time was it?"

"Lunchtime, like I said."

"Did he tell ya if he'd be in this evenin'?"

"Nah, nothin'."

"One-thirty please, Daz," Tina said, handing him his warmish pint of lager.

"Hey, Daz, I thought ya were goin' down there today with a few of the lads?" Charlie went on.

"I was supposed to, but I changed me mind at the last minute."

As Darren was making his way to the table where he always sat when he was alone, Bagpuss made an entrance to the cheers of the locals.

"All right, Arth, great result today," one said.

Bagpuss raised his hands in the air, before saying: "Yeah, what a fuckin' result."

Bagpuss had seen it all: the highs - particularly from the mid-1950s to the mid-1960s - and the lows: more of them, mind you, torturous in their reliability and never giving him solace. Darren, meanwhile – though never having been spoiled for the good times in the Arsenal or Liverpool sense – had at least seen them – except for the 1979-'80 season and the last one when they had been in the Second Division – mix it regularly with the big boys. And it wasn't so much heartache, anyway, to see them relegated, because they always seemed to pop back up the following season. Twice married Bagpuss, his two ex-wives hadn't been able to extinguish the football fire within him. He was by definition a 'Bluenose pedigree', and there was no imitation with that. His party piece, telling any poor soul who had the patience to listen to the 'best day of his life': 27th May 1963 at Villa Park.

The League Cup couldn't compete with its older brother, The FA Cup, in terms of prestige, but it offered teams another chance at winning some silverware. For Birmingham City in 1963 this meant a two-legged tie against their bitter, cross-city rivals Aston Villa. If it had been City's greatest day, a few would have argued for the 1960 and 1961 Intercities-Fairs Cup Finals, though they'd lost in both matches – not least because they followed on from 1956 when they had become the first British team to compete in a European competition. For Bagpuss, though, this was a no-brainer.

He'd been there, on that late May day in the 'Lion's den, as well as four days before, on their own turf, in the flesh, singing

– no, screaming vitriolic from the heart and for the good of the cause. In the first leg at home there had been over thirty thousand supporters – the great majority of them, naturally, backing the blue Brummies. He remembered everything. Rattler in hand, scarf round his neck, giving it everything he had.

"I was thirty-four back then, and all I can remember of St Andrew's is a blanket of blue and white – ya know, the scarves, the woolly hats and stuff. It wasn't like nowadays. Showin' ya colours was a necessity. They'd laugh at ya today, son, if ya went down the match wearin' a hat - it's sadly all about fashion today and punchin' somebody's fuckin' head in," Bagpuss began to an unsuspecting punter, a nephew of one of the locals, who was only there because he hadn't wanted to stay at home with his aunt to watch *3-2-1* with Ted Rogers and Dusty Bin. "... and I looked over, though I didn't wanna... Yeah, The Vile were there like – I can't remember how many, a couple of thousand probably... but they were the enemy... the tosspots."

"What did ya do?" the nephew asked in anticipation.

"Well, son, ya may not believe it if I told ya."

"*What?*"

The nephew was starry-eyed and looking at Bagpuss with all the reverence usually reserved for an ancient bard.

"I spat at 'em."

"Ya what?"

"I gobbed on 'em even though they were miles away in the away end and it blew back into another bloke's face."

"What did the bloke do?"

"He didn't even realise it was gob, silly prat. Me guess is he thought it was fuckin' drizzle."

"Was it rainin'?"

"I was so caught up in the moment and the emotion that I aiyn't gotta clue."

The inspiration on recounting his past memories was now in full flow and nothing would have been able to stop him.

"What was the lineup?" his new acolyte then asked.

"Scholfield, Lynn, Green, Hennessey, our captain, Smith, Beard, Hellawell, Bloomfield, Harris, Leek, Auld," the names just rolled off his tongue like they were second nature to him.

"Who scored?"

"Leek a brace and Broomfield."

Did the lad want more, because Bagpuss could go on forever.

"And at Villa Park... what about that?"

"Well," Bagpuss began, his face converting to a smile, "it was a bit of a foregone conclusion really. We knew we'd won even before kickoff."

"But how?"

"We all just sorta knew like."

"But what was it like winnin' the cup at St Andrews?"

"Of course it was great, but I think we coulda done it in better style – I mean we didn't even score a goal."

Unlike the 'young' and 'impressionable' visitor before his eyes, Darren had information overload in regards to Bagpuss's fables about the Blues. He'd heard everything all before – almost word for word. He remembered the first time he had become a victim at sixteen, and how enthusiastic he, too, had been. All that had passed now, however. It was only gibberish. He was sick and tired of hearing about the past, about 1893 and 1963 - there was no progress found there. 1986, '87, '88 – that was the future, and it was no good thinking about anything else. Moving forward. Evolution. Development. Advancement. These were all words Darren liked in respect to his club but he knew they were alien to Bagpuss's lexicon.

Smirking to himself, Darren sighed. Bagpuss now had tears in his eyes as the nostalgia had become too much for him. Was it sincere? Darren didn't believe it was. It was an act put on to impress his punters and get them to buy more beer. Business was business, after all.

"Just bein' there, though, at Vile Park, was enough. It was a gift, ya see. God had allowed us to humiliate 'em..." Bagpuss continued.

Darren could stand it no more, especially when Bagpuss had used the 'god' word. He walked out of the Lounge and went into the Smoking Room. A couple of locals were there sipping their halves whom he knew just to say 'hello' to.

He sat down alone, as he was in no mood to talk to any of them. They were boring and old and small talk annoyed him anyway when it wasn't about footy or music. He would talk to people, no problem, but it gave him no pleasure as it did Nobby, who would talk the hind legs off a monkey if given half a chance. People didn't dislike Darren, yet they weren't transfixed with him, either. Nobby, on the other hand, had no problem making friends and influencing people, and it was natural for him to give out the blag – nothing came easier. Conversation was his analysis of real expression, like his hero Morrissey did in his lyrics. Maybe Nobby was just copying his hero, maybe he was trying to be the world's greatest psychologist.

And what made it worse for Darren was Lynsey. His introspection was reaching new heights.

He could hear from the Smoking Room the Lounge was filling up quickly. It was nearly eight. In another hour the football crowd would come steaming in fresh from the capital, amongst them Mickey and Danny.

What would they say? Now he was thinking about it. What would be their reaction? Darren had sided with his conscience and just hoped they wouldn't take it the wrong way, especially Danny. He expected Nobby to be in the Lounge at any time but he wasn't in the mood for a chat with him. The other two, maybe a little later – at tennish if they were lucky, and if they hadn't decided already to make a night of it on the town in London. They'd be tanked up for sure on the train, and best be avoided. He didn't want an argument with them.

Darren slowly finished his pint and went home for an early night.

A couple of minutes after Darren left, Nobby walked into the Lounge.

"Hey, Charlie, have ya sin Daz?" he said.

"Yeah, he was here not twenty minutes ago – he must be in the Bar or summat."

Nobby scoured the Smoking Room and the Bar.

"Nah, Charlie, he musta fucked off."

"What, ya didn't find him?"

"Nah."

Nobby was still hungover from the previous night and just ordered a lemonade.

"Rough one last night, was it?" Charlie asked. He had a smile on his face. He'd been there the night before and knew what the story was.

"Fuckin' too right, mate."

Nobby went over to the fruit machines and put a coin in the slot.

"Here goes nothin'," he said to himself, his fingers crossed. He lost, so Nobby put a couple more quid in. Same result.

"Turn it in, Nob," an acquaintance commented, sitting around a table with his girlfriend next to him. "It'll never pay out, that thing."

Nobby just smiled, thinking what a twat he was. After losing a fiver he went back to talk to Charlie at the bar, who was in a deep, philosophical conversation over the day's matches with Bagpuss.

"Good draw... And it's good the Albion got hammered but Ipswich won, which aiyn't great," Charlie said.

Bagpuss pulled out a pink *Sports Argus* from under the bar.

"Mmm," he began, scanning the back page for the day's results and the league tables. "Leicester lost to Newcastle... good... but Ipswich won at home... like ya said to Wednesday... not good... Man. City lost to Luton... which is good too... Ah, Charlie, dayn't be worryin' yet."

"But it's Watford next week and they got a great result today away to Man U."

"It's gonna be a piece a piss, Charlie boy. We'll kick Barnes and the rest of their arses and give 'em a good hidin'."

"Well, whatever happens, at least the Villa lost. How many points are they above us now?"

Nobby was bored – for them the world started and finished with kicking a leather bag full of air into a small space where you scored something called a goal. It was all wrong, in truth – but who was he to tell them how to go about living their lives. He slowly – and without them noticing him do it – walked away from the bar and their uninspiring natter. He thought about putting another couple of quid in the fruit machine. Rummaging in his pockets, he realised he only had enough for another lemonade.

"Are ya gonna put anymore in there, Nob?" the same local asked him.

"Nah, I'll fuck it... Skint, ya see."

Nobby wanted to put a couple of tunes on then, but it was either that or the lemonade.

The doors opened and the bitter November wind penetrated the Lounge, creating a momentary rush of fresh air against the tobacco infused seclusion. In walked Mickey and Danny, both bleary-eyed from a concoction of alcohol and spliffs – maybe violence too. Mickey looked around, searching for someone. Danny, meanwhile, went straight to the bar to allay his monstrous thirst.

"All right, sexy," Danny said to Tina, his speech slurred and his intentions carnal.

"What d'ya want?" she replied, sighing. Tina barely knew Danny.

"Apart from a kiss... two pints and two double whiskys."

"I think ya've had quite enough today, son," Bagpuss said in a patriarchal tone as he was walking in from the backdoor that connected the Lounge to the Smoking Room. He looked like a sheriff from a town in the Wild West, all tense and looking though he was ready for a fight, though much, much uglier than Gary Cooper.

"I think it's up to me how much I wanna drink."

"Come on, mate, dayn't get silly now."

Danny was getting irritated. If it hadn't been the gaffer talking to him, the bloke would've already found himself on the deck. "Just gis the drinks."

Mickey, noticing the potential fracas from across the way where he was talking to a couple of locals, moved in.

"Hey, big man, come on... Sit yaself down over there, I'll get this round in," Mickey said, placating his goliath companion with a hand round his massive shoulders.

"All right, mate," Danny said calmly. He went over to a chair vacant next to the jukebox without further argument.

"Thanks, Mickey," Bagpuss said. "How was the match today?"

"Ah, ya know, not bad – at least we earned a point."

"Any trouble down there?" Charlie enquired.

"Nah, not really: the Old Bill had everythin' under control."

Mickey's eyes glanced around the Lounge once more. He noticed Nobby by the fireplace, hidden from view. After getting the pints in and giving one to Danny, he went over to him.

"Hey, Nob, have ya sin Daz around?" Mickey asked.

"Nah, mate," Nobby said, looking up, not realising whom he was talking to. He had a headache again, a sorry after-effect

of his previous night of fun, "I was lookin' for him meself...
He's probably fucked off or summat."

"Ya think so?"

"So, what happened, did he scarper in the middle of a
scrap?"

"Nah, nothin' like that," Mickey answered, smiling
sarcastically.

"Then what?"

"The cunt didn't even turn up at New Street."

"Well, that dayn't surprise me, coz I knew he didn't show
up, he was in here earlier. Charlie told me," Nobby said, his
smile like a Chesire Cat.

"He's a cunt, aiyn't he?"

"That's Daz's way, Mick – get used to it."

"Yeah, some way... Lettin' down a mate."

"Anyway, it was his bird Lynsey's op today or summat, so he
was probably down the QE"

Mickey's face turned serious, then he said:

"Fuck me, Nob, he didn't even tell me nothin' about an
operation."

"I thought ya knew like?"

"If ya askin' me whether I knew she was sick, then yeah...
but fuck me... This... I didn't know, I swear..."

A loud voice rose from the floor to the ceiling, filling the
Lounge with the sonority of Danny's out-of-tune voice:

Shit on the Villa
Shit on the Villa tonight
Oooh-ahaa...
Shit on the Villa
Shit on the Villa tonight...
Oooh-ahaa
Shit on the Villa
Shit on the Villa tonight...
Shit on the Villa

'Coz they're a load of shiiite.

"Eh, Mickey, take that dick head home, will ya?" Bagpuss said from behind the bar.

Mickey did what he was told, though not without protest from Danny, who was now so far gone he was weak on his legs. Eventually though, with a bit of force and the help of Charlie and another couple of locals, they managed to get him out of the door and into a waiting taxi. The taxi driver, an Asian who didn't seem to speak a word of English, was unwilling to let Danny into his car as he was afraid 'his customer' would do 'a runner'.

"Here, mate, here's a fiver. 75 Brandwood Road, King's Heath," Mickey said.

The taxi driver took Danny home.

Mickey stayed for another couple of minutes before he, too, went home.

20: Lord of the Telly and Suburbia

Sunday mornings were always the same in the Acheson home. Lazy, especially for the two men. Darren's mom on the other hand was scorned with the burden of endless housework – housework her male folk would barely help her do. Additionally, there was the Sunday dinner – that institution of British family life which she'd have to manage on her own as well. For Darren, who spent the day hovering between the *News of the World* and the telly, it was heaven on earth, his favourite day in the week, apart from the thought that he had work the next day. Inactivity ruled and slovenliness was king.

This day, however, it would be different, like most of the previous Sundays, there'd be none of that. He'd be off to the hospital again.

After a bath he went downstairs to eat breakfast. The hissing of the bacon and sausage cooking in the fat of the frying pan was a sound Darren had been brought up on – Les Ross too, whom his old lady, Cynthia, loved. Darren and his dad weren't overly struck on the bloke, as they found his voice annoying. But the law was the law, and on a Sunday, every Sunday, it was Les Ross and nobody else.

After scoffing his breakfast, he left.

Darren's house, a three-bedroom, semi-detached number owned by the council, was where he'd grown up. His dad had had the chance to buy it in the early '70s from them on the cheap, but never had. Now he was starting to regret it. Not that it was anything to write home about in terms of beauty or elegance: it was your usual working-class family home that had been built after the Second World War in Birmingham to allay the housing shortage due to the damage caused by the German bombings. The second great wave of council house construction had come in the 1960s and '70s in places like Chelmsley Wood, Castle Vale and New Oscott, and Darren's old man had even contemplated moving to the latter – seen then as an area of Birmingham on the up because of its close proximity to Sutton Coldfield - in 1979; that, like everything else his dad had ever tried to do, came to nothing. His mom often felt let down by Les, but what could she have done about it anyway? He was the family's breadwinner. Everything was in his power, even if it was the other way round in reality.

How would it go? The usual nerves he got when he thought of them were there again, because he knew it was a battle of wills. It was getting like a theatre. The three of them: Christy, Owen and himself. He'd have to watch Owen especially – he was a real fiery bastard. If anything worse than what had already happened between himself and the Moriarty clan was going to happen, then Darren knew it would come from Owen's divisive mouth. Had he been some knob off the street, Darren would have just decked him on the spot to end it all. But Owen wasn't just a nob off the street – he was his girlfriend's brother.

The morning was clear and warm for the first day of December. Christmas was under a month away. Presents, yes – he'd have to buy those too; and then there was New Year's Eve to think about. He couldn't be bothered, really, but he knew he'd have to make an effort.

When he got to the hospital Lynsey was as she'd been the day before, only now there were more pipes and machines than in a scene from the film *Blade Runner*. That signified only one thing for him: no news was good news. As expected, Owen was with his parents, but Noel was nowhere to be seen, sadly. Darren wondered why he was there – was he a sucker for punishment? Lynsey was out of bounds to everybody but her parents: any infection – even the smallest flu-like symptoms – could kill her. He wanted to say if there was any point to him being there, yet he was reluctant to stir anymore of the hatred they had for him. No, he'd remain silent, sit there a while, read his paper and smoke a few fags, then leave. The hospital was the best place he could've been anyway. Lynsey was close - at least in body. Her mind, however, he was clueless to its location. He reckoned people didn't dream in comas, and she was dead as any stiff.

A couple of hours went by uneventfully and it was already afternoon. His dinner would be ready soon. Ravished with the hunger, Darren made his way home without telling them.

Darren ate his tea greedily. That was the way he liked it. His mom was always very proud when he cleaned his plate. It was the signal her son had enjoyed it.

After dinner he sat down with his old man with a cup of tea and a slice of Mr Kipling's Bakewell tart. Usually they'd be watching the afternoon game on *Match of the Day*, but a blackout of all the televised matches had put an end to that. It was to do with the T.V. rights of League football going on between the BBC and ITV. The negotiations were progressing, and the paper talk was that an agreement was in the pipeline. This, however, wasn't helping Darren. It was a good job, though: Cynthia had the last word when it came to the telly, in particular on a Sunday, when she had *The Antiques Roadshow* on. Cynthia was the Commissioner for Television in the Acheson home

Whenever his mom mutinied the box on a Sunday, Darren would go upstairs and put some music on and read something. It was the usual fare, *Match, Shoot* and *The Sports Argus* for the footy; *The Face* and the *NME* for music and a lash of culture.

His eyes were closed.

"Hey, Daz, somebody's on the phone," his old man shouted up from the bottom of the stairs.

"Who is it?"

"Dunno?"

"Ask, will ya?"

"What did ya last servant die of?"

His dad came back a second later.

"It's Mickey."

"Mickey, what the fuck does he want...? He dayn't even have me number," Darren said to himself, climbing off the bed and walking down the stairs.

"All right, mate, what's goin' on?" Darren said, expecting a bollocking.

"All right, mate, how are ya?" Mickey replied in a friendly voice.

"Ah, ya know."

A silence, temporary and nerving, followed.

"Err... so how was the game? Sorry I didn't make it, but-"

"It's all right, mate, I know what's goin' on."

"Ya what?" Darren asked.

"I know about the op and the hospital and stuff."

They talked for a few minutes.

"... and are ya comin' with us on Saturday?" Mickey asked.

"Yeah, wouldn't miss it for nothin'."

"Ya out tonight for a tot?"

"Nah."

"What about in the week?"

"We'll see, but I'm skint at the minute..."

So Mickey had understood and, just when Darren had least expected it, forgiven him. It was a good job he hadn't gone – I mean, what had he missed, apart from a dull, goalless draw and the prat Danny making a show of himself and almost getting arrested in Euston Station?

Yes, he'd definitely be going to the Watford clash at home. That'd be a right one, more so for the fact Luther Blissett and John Barnes would be in the team for The Hornets, both

England internationals and black. The racist chants and banana throwing you could expect at places like Leeds or Cardiff with their white, working-class racial homogeneity; but at the St Andrews, it was something of an anomaly. At their home game against the Villa in September, Darren had witnessed constant abuse of the opponent's black player, Mark Walters, and had been shocked by it.

"Fuck off back to Africa, ya black Villa cunt!" The screams of hate went off from supporters all around him – in pockets on the Kop. The taunts, apoplectic and fused with a rabid hatred, were so blind of reason that Darren had had to leave halfway through the match. Some of the sickest name calling had come from Danny and Danny's cousin, the prick Dave Stirchley. After the game in a pub in Small Heath, Darren pulled Dave aside:

"Are ya fucked up, Dave, or what?"

Dave was nearly thirty and should've known better.

"*What?*" Dave replied.

"All that fuckin' name callin' to their black player?"

"Who? Ya mean Walters? Daley?" he said with a huff.

"Yeah."

"Ah, fuck off, Daz, they're just Villa coon cunts."

A year or two earlier Darren had been as bad as the any on the terraces when it came to racism, though it was for no other reason than he knew no better: everyone was doing it: ten thousand strong, so why not him – but not anymore. Noel Blake, a hard-nosed He-Man of a defender from Jamaica who'd just gone to Portsmouth, had been one of his heroes at St Andrews, but that hadn't stopped Darren shouting abuse at the other teams' opposing black players. He was ashamed of his past, even if he was the only one who cared about it. At the ground on Saturday he'd be keeping his trap shut, like he had ever since his Lynsey had told him to.

21: I'm Considerably More Intelligent Than Yow

Monday morning. Everybody knew what it meant, and Darren was no exception. He was hoping for a week's more casual, and according to Yam Yam that was exactly it – a week and no more.

It was as cold as an Eskimo's balls again and the weather forecast had predicted snow. If it came or not was another story altogether - yet it still held the city in childish anticipation. Well, it was December after all, and apart from New Street decorated in Christmas lights that were simply over the top, a festive mood had descended.

The day started ordinarily enough for Darren. Yam Yam got him on some multitasking: separating odds and ends again, cleaning the antiquated toilet that smelled worse than a pirate's armpit and, to really take the piss out of his unfortunate employee, made him shine all the number plates on the scrapped cars. That took till lunchtime, when over a pasty and a cuppa, Darren took out his day's copy of *The Sun* and started, like he always had since he'd been sixteen, to leaf through it, sports pages first, working his way backwards like a Muslim reading the Koran to the tits and page three, then going through the rest – or 'cack' - as he called it.

"Anythin' in it today?" John asked him.

Darren was sitting in the gaffer's chair, feet on the desk, smoking a fag.

"Err, not really – nice tits on her, though, what d'ya think?" Darren responded, showing him the paper.

"How was the match on Saturday?"

"I didn't go down."

"Why?" John asked, surprised.

"Ah, ya know how it is."

"What, skint?"

Darren didn't want to go into the nitty-gritty of his personal life; it was his own business and he wanted to keep it that way.

"Yeah, summat like that."

"Good result that - puts us in a better position now."

"Yeah, but it wasn't a win."

"Ah, we'll get three points soon enough."

"How's the daughter?" Darren asked after a pause.

"Great... Had another argument with that slag again," replied John.

"Who, ya ex?"

"Yeah. She wants more child support off me."

"How much are ya given her?"

"A tenner a week."

"Fuck me, John, it'll hardly break the bank, will it? Give her a bit more, ya tight cunt."

"Dayn't *you* fuckin' start."

John took a massive drag on his fag, infuriated: the tobacco burnt down to the end of the filter, and the red hot ash died. Angrier now, he stubbed it out, his twists and stabs of the nub in the astray expressing his fury at his life and all its unfortunate vicissitudes. Yet, if he'd known Darren's predicament, maybe John wouldn't have moaned and felt so sorry for himself.

Yam Yam walked in with his usual miserable face.

"And yow can get yow fuckin' feet off me desk and yow backside off me chair for starters," Yam Yam ordered Darren, who jumped up without complaint.

"Ya cunt," John said to Darren, laughing. He thought it was funny Darren had been caught red-handed.

"Yam Yam sat down and Darren put his arse on a small step ladder next to the door. Once there, the door opened and in walked Sid, carrying his lunchbox and a small flask of tea.

"All right, mate," Darren said, addressing Sid. "Ya can sit here if ya wanna, I've finished me pasty anyway."

Darren picked up the rest of his pasty from the plate and pushed it into his gob, the pastry flakes falling onto the floor and his overalls like a Siberian blizzard.

"I hope yow gonna clean that tip up later, son?" Yam Yam asked, referring to the crumbs that had settled all around him.

Darren looked down at his feet: they had also covered his red Samba Adidas trainers, now the worse for wear after working a week in a scrapyard.

"Ah, this?" Darren said.

"Yeah, *that*."

"All right, it aiyn't a problem."

They were one, big and happy family, sitting around eating and reading newspapers.

"Anythin' interestin', Daz?" John asked.

"Ya already asked me that."

"But there's gotta be summat?"

"Just some shite about Scargill."

"Poor bastard. Maggie really wants to hang him by the fuckin' balls," lamented Sid.

"Fuckin' Tory cunts," Darren said.

"Yeah, I hate 'em," added John.

"Yeah, they're the fuckin' ruin of this country," Sid said.

"Why can't they just leave the workin' man alone?" said Darren.

"Coz it'll never happen," Sid commented.

"The only thing I know is that things'll only improve when that bitch's shot or summat," John declared.

"That's a bit harsh, son," Sid said.

"Why's it?" John asked.

"I mean, I dayn't like the woman much meself either, but I wouldn't go that bleedin' far..."

While they were all arguing about politics, Yam Yam was smirking to himself smugly, like he knew something they didn't. The verbal disagreement continued for a few minutes between the three of them, though Sid was the least vocal; their gaffer, meanwhile listened on passively, observing, thinking.

"Yeah, Sid, ya right - I dunno that much about politics but I do know the Tories have ruined this gaff... I mean, come on, The Specials even sing about it," Darren said.

"Who are 'The Specials' when they're at home?" Sid replied, puzzled. He looked at his youthful interlocutor - there was too much of a gap in the generations.

"It dayn't matter, Sid, it was just an example... What I wanted to say was everythin' and everyone's against her. Yeah, I'm sure of it... All The Smiths songs criticise her – even if it's only in a small way."

This was all getting a bit out of hand; Yam Yam would have to say something: Darren and John would have to be put right once and for all.

"Hey, dickhead," Yam Yam said, interrupting Darren in mid-sentence," "d'yow really know what yow are talkin' about?"

"Yeah," Darren replied, "and I know no workin' man who likes the bitch."

"Ahr, that may be fair game, but listen ta this..." Yam Yam lit a fag; something serious was coming. Taking a drag, he closed his eyes, exhaled, creating a smoke ring, before opening them again. A smile, subtle in expression, gave away the contempt he had for Darren's opinion. "Yow know that piece a shit yow read every day for 18p, that piece a shit that over half the country reads – d'yow know what lies behind it and who it supports?" their gaffer declared severely and with an air of arrogance.

Darren hunched his shoulders and gazed at Yam Yam – he had no idea; John too.

"Well, I'm gonna tell yow," he went on, taking another puff, "I'll tell yow all: Yow are all arfsoaked and yow mek me sick... I can safely claim that ta be true. And d'yow know why?" he then asked, turning to them all one by one. Only Darren and John were paying him any attention; Sid was eating his sandwiches and had his head in *The Mirror* doing a crossword, engaged and uninterested in the teenage-like squabble erupting before his eyes. "It's coz *The Sun* fights against everythin' yow blastid believe in and fight for."

"I dayn't understand," Darren said.

"The paper's a piece of shite, me muka – yow dunno nothin' yow talkin' about."

"And *ya* do?" Darren said.

"Ahr, all the fuckin' miners and the war in the Falklands and the unemployment – especially them on the dole – *The Sun* fabricates the fuckin' statistics... How many are on the dole? One, two, three million – we dunno."

Sid looked up with a wry smile. The two young dimwits didn't have a clue to the answer and looked at their gaffer like a second head had just sprouted from his neck.

"Well," Darren said after a pause, "I only read it for the footy anyway."

"Ahr, and there's a fuckin' excuse – 'yow read it only for the footy'... What, yow dayn't read nothin' else loik?"

"I have to agree with ya there, Dave," Sid put in. "That's what they all say." He put a fag in his mouth and lit it up. "Yeah, I've heard that excuse loadsa times." Sid turned his paper around so everybody could see it. He pointed to the red masthead with the white *Mirror* logo and with his finger said: "That's what ya all should be readin'... this, yeah... this is the proper workin' man's paper," his pronouncement muffled by the fag in his mouth.

"Nah, Sid, it's the God's honest truth," said Darren, clearly embarrassed now.

"Ahr, a Christian, ay yow? Can yow swear to God?" Yam Yam asked.

"Yeah, I knew... err, really."

"Ya knew what, Daz?" Sid asked.

"I knew it was a Conservative paper."

"Garroway – over me dead body yow did!" his gaffer replied.

"Nah, I swear."

"Listen, I know yow probably think me doolally, and I know I dayn't look much, but did yow all know I passed me eleven-plus exam?" Yam Yam stated proudly.

"What, when ya were twenty-five?" John said, pissing himself laughing.

"Shut yow cakehole or yow'll find yowself out of a fuckin' job... Ahr, I passed it and went to a grammar school in Wolverhamptun – first and last person in me family ever to do so."

"And what's that gotta do with anythin'?" Darren asked.

Yam Yam stubbed out his fag, opened the bottom draw to his desk, pulled out a small bottle of Bells Scotch whiskey, picked up the flask of black coffee he always brought to work next to his feet, poured some coffee into his favourite 'Who Shot JR?' mug, added a decent-sized shot of the water of life, before taking a healthy gulp from it.

"And what's that gotta do with it... what's that gotta do with it? I'll tell yow: It clearly states the fact I'm smarter than any of yow arfsoaked Brummie wasters and that I know more about the world and what's goin' on in it."

"Is that right, boss?" John asked bluntly.

"Ahr, I knaw I look a thick twat but everythin' can be deceptive in life... I mean, come on... at least I gotta bitta education."

"Have ya got A-Levels?" Darren asked.

"Unfortunately, I aiyn't."

"CSES or whatever they were called back in the Stone Age when ya were a boy?"

"Cheeky cunt... but I aiyn't got none of them, either."

"So ya dayn't have nothin' then, d'ya?" Darren went on – pushing it now to the limit.

"In a word, yow are correct."

"Like us?"

"I suppose."

John laughed, before adding:

"Yeah, I suppose ya one of us like."

"That's highly unlikely."

"Why?" Darren asked.

"Coz I got me business for starters... while yow miserable wasters dayn't – yow are only forced to work for a cunt like me coz yow are thick twats."

"Hold on a minute, mate" John said, angry now a little and feeling insulted in his own estimation, "It aiyn't our fault millions are on the rock-and-roll and we have to take such jobs."

"That's only an excuse, mate. If yow wanted a better job, youw'd find one, now problem. Dayn't go blamin' everythin' on poor Maggie."

The two young men looked at their gaffer with a stare drifting on disbelief. If it had been some dumbo in the pub defending their 'beloved' Prime Minister, they'd have decked him there and then – or at least threatened to. They smiled, mistaking it for a little lunchtime banter between work colleagues to liven up the atmosphere.

"That's unbelievable, Dave?" John said.

"And lads, I'll tell yow again and for the last time – dayn't be readin' that excuse for a paper. It's one thing while tryin' to be the other - a duality of contrastin' views. I aiyn't read it since '74."

"What d'ya read now?" Darren asked.

"Tellin' yow the truth, I dayn't read nothin'... George Orwell."

"Who's he?" John said.

"A writer. Maybe yow did him at school?"

Now the lads were in unfamiliar territory – they lifted their arses up and quickly went back to work.

The day dragged on. At the end of it, Darren asked the gaffer to pay him everything at the end of the week, rather than at the end of every working day, so he wouldn't piss it all up the wall, leaving him penniless before Saturday and the match. He'd be leaving the hospital too – at least for one night. He'd go on Tuesday, maybe.

"How's Lynsey, love?" his mom asked him, as he was walking in the door.

"I dunno."

"Why's that?"

"Ah, it's a long story."

After tea he watched telly for a while, then had an early night again.

22: A Chat with Nobby

Tuesday, second day of the working week and four away from Saturday. Work was the same, apart from Yam Yam acting all high-and-mighty with himself over the day before. He thought he'd got one over on them, and he felt good about it – keep your underlings, underlings – and let them know about it, was one of his sayings.

The day went by quickly, and after work Darren went home for a wash and then to the hospital.

"All right, I'm here to see Lynsey Moriarty."

"Are you an immediate member of the family?" the receptionist asked.

"Nah. I'm her boyfriend."

"It won't be possible for you to see her - only immediate family members are allowed."

"What... I dayn't count?"

"I'm afraid not, sir."

"Why?" he replied, angry.

"It's hospital policy."

He wanted to see her but he couldn't. He left, his heart heavy and his mood low.

At home, later than usual, Darren ate his tea of faggots, peas and mash that his old lady had put over the gas for him. After it, he spent the evening in front of the telly.

"What's on tonight, mom?" he asked.

"Leslie, give Darren the paper, love."

His dad gave him the paper. Darren turned to the TV listings:

"Okay, what have we got," Darren said, scanning it, "*EastEnders... Juliet Bravo* at eight... Mmm, *Points of View*... ah, there aiyn't nothin' on?"

"I'm watchin' *EastEnders* and *Juliet Bravo* anyway, so ya and ya father can do what ya like."

There was nothing to do as usual – except for the self-torture of *EastEnders*. Darren didn't like watching Cockneys – they disturbed him. His old man too. He couldn't get used to Wendy Richards as the matriarchal figure of Pauline Fowler, when for years he'd enjoyed watching her as the sexy Miss Brahms in *Are You Being Served?*

That meant he'd be upstairs again on his tod listening to music.

After five minutes of *EastEnders* he picked up the phone and carried it out to the hall where he could talk in private.

"All right, Nob, it's Daz... What ya up to?"

"Watchin' telly."

"Are ya goin' out for a jar tonight?"

"Yeah, probably."

"Lucky cunt."

"So ya aiyn't?"

"Nah, I'm skint."

"And tomorra?"

"Yeah, if I can get a couple of quid off the old lady."

"Fuck me, ya always skint, what's wrong with ya? I thought ya got some casual."

"Well, it aiyn't permanent, is it."

"How long ya got there?"

"A couple of weeks max... it'll probably see me all right till Chrimbo?"

"How's Lynsey?"

"She's bad."

"Why, what happened?"

"I dunno exactly – it's some kind of infection from the op or summat like that. To tell ya the truth I'm in the dark over everythin' meself."

"It's too bad, mate."

"Yeah, and her mom and dad aiyn't actin' like they should."

"What d'ya mean?"

"Nah, it's just we aiyn't gettin' on and that like."

"That's a bummer."

"Where were ya on Saturday?" Darren asked after a moment.

"What d'ya mean?"

"I was waitin' for ya half the night... what, ya just didn't turn up?"

"Yeah, I did... I was a bit hungover from Friday and didn't stay long."

"Nob, ya were wrecked on Friday, I swear." Darren said, laughing.

"What happened, Daz?"

"Nah, nothin' really, ya just made a bit of a show of yaself, that's all."

"How?"

"Nothin', honest."

"Come on, dayn't play with me?" Nobby asked. He was impatient now.

"Ah, Danny was pissin' round a bit."

"Fuck, I knew it was summat to do with that cunt... What was he doin'?"

"Nah, nothin'."

"Come on, ya supposed to be me mate. Tell me?"

"All right," Darren said after a moment, sniggering a little, "he was stickin' fags up ya nose and stuff... it was all a bitta fun, that's all."

"Oh, yeah, I bet ya all had a great laugh with that?"

"Come on, Nob, it was only a joke."

"Ha, ha," Nobby replied sarcastically."

"A joke, that's all it was – there aiyn't no need to get upset about it."

"Jesus, Daz, I *dayn't* remember fuck all."

"Ya should keep off the pop then."

"I didn't drink that much, *did I*?"

"Ya did... But anyway, what about the The Smiths gig, are ya still plannin' to go?"

"Yeah, too right I am."

"It'd be great if I could make it."

"So come then."

"It depends how me financial situation is."

"Well, it's in February, so ya still have a bitta time left."

Ireland – did he really want to go there? If all the people were like Lynsey's family, he'd rather not. But it was *The Smiths*. Yes, they were a good reason to go – and anyway, he'd have to see them at some time, so why not then?

23: The Generation Gap

Darren had overslept – not long, but long enough to be fifteen minutes late. Luckily, the gaffer wasn't around and he got away with it.

Sid got him working with him in the morning and they had a good old natter. Sid was a quiet man on the whole, though with a touch of sarcasm when he said something.

"So, Daz, tried to get one over on him, didn't ya, son?" Sid said.

"Ah, ya have to try these things from time to time, dayn't ya?" Sid smiled. "Ah, Sid, d'ya think they'll be work till Christmas... or, ya know, summat a bit more permanent like?"

"Nah, I dayn't think so, mate – ya only here now coz we had a loada cars in from Smethwick and it was a bit much for us to cope with... I'd say before Christmas, but no later than that."

"At least that's summat."

"And it gives ya a bitta time to find summat else."

"Yeah, but that aiyn't gonna be easy just before Chrimbo, ya know what I mean like."

"Yeah, it's a pity, really," Sid said, "ya a good little worker."

Darren didn't really know anything about his older colleague and wanted to find out something:

"So, Sid, d'ya like footy?"

"Well, ya know, not as much as I used to."

"Who d'ya support?"

"The Blues," Sid said, but in a tone that hid any pride or emotion.

"D'ya still go down much?"

"Ya must be jokin', mate... not with all them bleedin' yobs down there at the minute... I aiyn't bin down since... err... since '81."

"It aiyn't that bad."

"Ah, son, I can remember fifty thousand at St Andrews without a spot of bother... and today we can hardly get a fifth of that in and the place is like the Battle of Waterloo on some days... It's all broken bottles and knives... A bloke dayn't feel safe. I remember as a teenager if there was a bitta aggro it was all fists and nothin' else – ya know, ya'd end up with a black eye which ya old lady would put a cold pack on for twenty minutes and that'd be it... But today," his face went serious now, "ya end up down the A & E in some hospital with a stanley knife in ya face."

"Not everybody's like that down there, Sid."

"And how d'ya explain all the palaver back in May then?" Sid asked emotionally.

"Well, I can't... Maybe it was a one off... I mean, I wasn't there so it'd be hard to tell ya."

Sid laughed; he didn't trust the younger generation when it came to interpreting their view of what supporting your team was all about.

"Listen, Daz," he then began, "I dunno how ya feel about it, but I reckon football's lost its soul – ya know what I mean? It's a generation thing, probably, and summat that most of us old-timers can grasp quite easily... Just wait, in ten or fifteen years' time ya'll be sayin' the same things to ya nipper and his mates, I suppose... And another thing, when it happens ya'll be sayin' it with all the frustration and cynicism that I have now. I never thought it would end this way, but that's progress." Darren just nodded, neither agreeing nor disagreeing. "Like I said, when I was a lad all the supporters' attention was on the pitch, what the game was like, the passin', crosses – ya know? Today, though, ya all seem to have another agenda... beatin' the shit outta each other for one thing... Tell me, Daz, is it true?"

"Nah, it aiyn't... And ya aiyn't bein' fair to say it."

"From where I'm standin' I *am* bein' fair."

"I know, but from a packed house of say... I dunno how many thousand, how many people actually cause trouble?"

"Beats me, Daz?"

"Not many... a handful, that's all."

"Well I dayn't believe ya."

"Ya dayn't have to, but it's true."

"And are ya one yaself?"

"One 'what'?"

"A hooligan?"

Darren smiled, before saying:

"Ya think so much of me, Sid?"

"Nah, I dayn't wanna offend ya, I was just askin' a question."

"Nah, I aiyn't."

"But have ya ever bin?"

"Nah."

"Well that's good to hear."

"Ya know what, Sid... it's strange ya aiyn't bin down in ages?"

"Why, have I bin missin' summat?"

"In a footballin' sense, nah, but it's still a laugh."

"Yeah, for ya young ones but it aiyn't for someone like meself."

"Too old, are ya?"

"Yeah, that could be the very problem," Sid answered with a laugh.

"Listen, why dayn't ya come down with me on Saturday against Watford?" Darren asked after a moment, his voice containing a touch of embarrassment – maybe Sid would be offended? It came out anyway and now it was too late to take back what he'd said.

"Thanks for the offer, mate, but I think I'll give it a miss."

"Why?"

"Ya know, wrong crowd for me and I wouldn't fit in."

It was Sid's choice. At least he'd asked him. Darren left it at that.

24: A Word of Warning

"Hey, mom, lend us a fiver, will ya?"

"And what about the rest ya owe me plus this week's housekeep?"

"Ya'll get everythin'. I'll be workin' till Christmas so dayn't worry about that."

"What d'ya want the money for... Ya off down the pub again?"

"Can ya give it me or not?"

She gave him the money reluctantly.

"And dayn't forget: I want it back Friday."

That evening in the pub Nobby got in early like he always did. Wednesdays were usually quiet in the Lounge with only a few locals in. Charlie, the seven day a week man was there, sitting on his usual stool.

Darren got in after nine.

A couple, that was all it would be – well, with a fiver he had no choice, anyway.

"How's Lynsey, Daz?" Nobby asked him.

Darren was sick of the same old questions.

"I wasn't up the hospital today – no change, I suppose."

"What's the situation with the fuckin' in-laws?"

"No comment there," said Darren, rollin' his eyes.

"Is it *so* fuckin' bad?"

"Couldn't be better, mate, couldn't be better."

He was feeling guilty again: he'd skipped the hospital for a few pints.

Although present in body, Darren's mind was someplace else all throughout the long hour he was there.

"Are ya goin' down on Saturday?... Are ya goin' down on Saturday?" No reply... His eyes - fixed on the flashing lights of the fruit machines which Nobby was beside, throwing his hard-earned coins down with a passion - were glazed and painted an other-worldliness. "Are ya goin' down on Saturday or not?" the voice called out, this time impatiently.

"What?" Darren asked, returning to reality.

"Are ya goin' on Saturday?" It was Charlie. "Are ya deaf or summat?"

"Sorry, mate, didn't hear ya there?"

"Are ya goin' to the Watford match?"

A wave of putrid, stale breath flew in Darren's general direction.

"Eer, yeah," he replied, holding his breath, "... course I am."

He was in no mood for small talk again, so he slid over to Nobby.

"Nob, listen, I'm gonna make a move – I aiyn't really up for it tonight... And anyway, *Sportnight's* on at ten - it's a good excuse to save me dough for the match. I'm already down a skydiver from the old lady plus all the other shit I owe her..."

"Hey, Dave, are ya gonna keep me on till after Christmas or what?" Darren said. After their little performance with him, he was doubting his gaffer's willingness to it, but it was worth asking anyway.

Yam Yam smiled – he knew he was in control, and his employee was the hunted against the stronger predator.

"Nah, Christmas and that's it."

"Has this summat to do with the other day?"

"Nah, not at all – why ay yow askin'?"

"I just thought it was, that's all."

"Nah, nothin' of the sort, mate... And it's okay, anyway – I didn't tek offence."

He still wasn't allowed to see Lynsey. The trips to the hospital were starting to become a waste of time.

"Hey, Noel, maybe ya could help me?" he said to Lynsey's brother, who he'd invited for a coffee in the hospital canteen, and the only one that Darren thought was reasonable enough. Darren's fuse was about to explode. He needed positive feedback.

Whether it was true or not he couldn't say for sure, but Noel – though aware of his Irish heritage as much as Owen – felt more attached to the city of his birth, and was less inclined to show hatred for Brummie and English culture than his brother did.

"Listen, Darren, I aiyn't gonna stop ya, but I think me brother and dad will."

"What's their fuckin' problem, mate? I've done fuck all to 'em and *you* and ya mother... I treat Lynsey well... I dayn't understand none of this."

"They dayn't like ya... they've never liked ya."

"But why?"

"I suppose they have their own reason for that."

"What does ya old man want from me?"

"He wants ya outta Lynsey's life."

Darren looked and Noel, his eyes full of the odium he had for his brother and dad.

"But it's up to Lynsey to decide about that, dayn't ya think?"

"I agree – but I doubt he does."

"What about ya brother?"

"Oh, he's just bin listenin' to the Wolfe Tones for too long."

"But I think I have the right to see her."

"I agree."

"Then why can't I?"

"Listen," Noel began after a momentary pause, "a little bitta free advice for ya: don't push it... make them believe ya really care about me sister – and that means not soddin' off down the pub or to the match or summat... Act as if ya with her, waitin' with us in the hospital night after night, sufferin' with us... But just bein' there, ya know what I mean? It's about ya presence more than anythin'... Ya silent but as a person ya around... And then, after all that, maybe they'll look at ya in a different way... D'ya know, Darren, how stressed we all are over what's happened... I mean, come on... probably ya aiyn't got no idea-"

Noel had crossed the line now.

"Hold on a minute - I dayn't need ya to tell me about worry and hurt and pain," Darren said, "coz I know about all of them things like all of ya. Ya have to remember that I love ya sister too."

"Yeah, but how long have ya known her for?"

"What's that gotta do with it?"

"It's got everythin' to do with it."

Noel had spelt everything out in clear terms – there was ambiguity. The facts – the immutable state of affairs – gave Darren food for thought. He couldn't use excuses from now on. If he took heed, then maybe he could win them over.

But did he really want to acquiesce to them? The gulf in mentalities was apparent and maybe beyond repair.

After the hospital Darren went home to think over what Noel had told him.

25: The Gaffer's Revenge

He woke up high in spirits: it was Friday and Darren was looking forward to getting a bundle - it'd been quite a while since he'd got his last weekly wage packet. Over a hundred quid. One hundred big ones. His old lady would try and steal most of it, but he planned to blag her yet again. Yes, it would be easy – she was a soft touch.

"All right, mate," Darren said to John, walking in the office. John didn't appreciate his work mate's pre-weekend chirpiness and just tutted. "What's rocked *your* fuckin' boat?" Darren asked, tutting himself to counter it.

"Nah, sorry, just had a bad night."

"What happened?"

"Ya know, the usual."

"What, problems again with ya ex?"

"Yeah."

At lunchtime a conversation sprang up somehow over the AIDS virus. Since doctors had first reported on the disease in Britain at a London hospital in the early 1980s, many people had begun to panic at its threat, and by the mid-decade gays were generally despised.

"They should all be shot," Yam Yam said to Sid, Darren and John.

"That's goin' a bit over the top now, Dave," Sid commented, "but to put 'em all on a desert island to fend for themselves – that'd be all right."

It was obvious, to a greater or lesser degree, the scrapyard was full of homophobics. Or was it?

John stood up, but in an assured way; his face, looking like he'd just lost the winning pools coupon, eyeballed them all with a veiled fury.

"What's wrong?" Darren asked.

He didn't reply.

This time Yam Yam asked, thinking authority and age would get the answer. Still nothing.

Darren and Yam Yam looked at Sid.

"What's wrong, John?" Sid asked, taking the stares from his gaffer and work mate as a cue to ask himself.

"Ya bastards," John then said in a quiet and determined tone, "ya fuckers... me uncle died of AIDS last year..." Well, that was it. All three felt like huge pricks at a Jewish wedding, and they didn't know what to say or where to look – in fact, they couldn't have really, anyway, as John continued on with his tirade: "... Only forty-four, he was... Took him so fuckin' quick too... I mean, me mom was cut up about it as well, coz she loved her brother... And yeah, before ya ask... yeah, he was gay, but I dunno why that's got anythin' to do with it – it aiyn't important-"

"Nah, nah, I dayn't," Yam Yam interrupted, his face green - not white - from shock, and looking more like Master Yoda from Star Wars with all his mid-life wrinkles and wispy grey hair, "mean nothin' by it, yow know? It was just a laugh, mate, yow know what I mean lioke?" His voice was ruptured with humility, something which John and Sid - both long time workers in the scrapyard - had never heard before.

"Yeah, it's the truth," Sid added. He was looking away from John, ashamed at what he'd said.

"Ya cunts," Darren remarked under his breath. Up to that point he'd been quiet on this one, and now he was beginning to be grateful he had.

"It wasn't me fault," the gaffer continued, "it was a slip of the tongue... Yow know sometimes we all play the goat and act like arseholes... Honestly, John, I didn't mean nothin' by it, it was just summat... well... how can I explain it?"

"There aiyn't no need to explain nothin', coz I already know how ya all feel about it... All I can say is for me uncle Nigel's death was a struggle to the very end... I believe wherever he is now he's a happy bloke – even if he was gay, I dayn't believe it matters much in the eyes of God, do *you?*"

"Nah, nah," a chorus went out.

"That's good to hear... So, *Dave*, ya really sorry for what ya said?"

"Yam Yam took John's hands in his own and held them tightly, before saying:

"Ahr, mate, truly. I didn't mean nothin' by it, I swear... And another thing, I'll never say such things again... It... it... was stupid of me... Ahr, what a cunt I was."

"Yeah, I'm sorry as well, mate," Sid said, head bowed.

Darren looked on at the two of them. Yes, they'd been put in their place, even if personally his attitude to benders was the same.

"So next time ya'll know... AIDS is summat that affects everybody, not just the people it kills... It's like any disease – cancer, one of them tropical fuckin' killers... I dunno, malaria or summat..."

Cancer. Cancer – well, leukaemia to be exact. When John said that all the seriousness of Darren's own situation came to mind. John's uncle, whoever the poor fucker had been, didn't care now because his battle was over. Lynsey's, however, was still ongoing, and Darren hoped she'd be fighting to the end.

"We're all sorry, mate," Darren then said. He'd only laughed at Yam Yam and Sid's comments, but felt guilty nonetheless.

Then, unexpectedly, John's thespian-like stone face changed, and a smile, slowly though, brought on a joviality that only a minute before would've seemed impossible.

"I was jokin', ya cunts," John said.

"*What*?" Yam Yam asked, not hearing quite properly.

John repeated himself.

Yam Yam pulled his hands violently from John's clutch.

"Yow what?" Yam Yam asked.

"I was havin' a fuckin' laugh, that's all."

Darren and Sid stood there gobsmacked; Yam Yam, meanwhile, had his fists clenched and was ready to land one on his worker's chin.

"It was a bit of a laugh," said John, coolly, like nothing had happened.

There was no way Yam Yam was going to let John get away with humiliating him. He knew he couldn't hit him without it ending up in a fight, and he was too old for that shit.

"Yow sacked, yow hear me?"

"What?"

"I said yow sacked."

"Ya jokin', *yeah*?"

"Nah, I aiyn't."

"But why?"

"Just pack yowself and get the fuck outta me office and yard."

Yam Yam didn't look like he was joking, but John thought it was a counter to his own game:

"Come on, Dave, ya jokin', aiyn't ya?"

"I've never bin more sure about summat in me life."

He doubted his gaffer was being serious, so he asked him again:

"Come on, Dave, it was just a bit of a laugh."

"Nah it wasn't."

"Sorry, Dave," John said, his tone now full of gravity.

"I dayn't care. Pack yow things and go... What d'yow think this is... someplace where yow can just tek the piss?"

"Dave, I swear, I didn't mean it."

"Listen, get yow stuff and go... I have to admit, yow had me for a minute, but it wasn't funny... I mean, people are dyin' every day, and dyin' in the most horrible ways – like me old lady, for instance: breast cancer at thirty-two... Ahr, have yow ever had someone close ta yow really die and suffer?"

John hadn't.

Yam Yam sat down:

"The doctor just gave me the latest test results and yow can imagine that back then they meant nothin' to me and me old man. I sat down next to her on the bed in the hospital. She was skinny and white and the cancer had eaten her from the inside out lioke – she was a ruin in a word... I held her hand but she was too weak to feel it... Seein' her die was a terrible thing... I was only a nipper meself, and hardly ready for such a thing... After some time the doctors said to me old man and me that it was hopeless... Yow have to remember the way things were medically back then – not much, I tell yow. She lost the strength to speak or move and she even had problems lookin' at us... There woulda bin no point her dyin' in that there hospital, so we took her home to die... Even though it was difficult for her to communicate with us we knew it was what she wanted – so we granted her wish... And then she started to go. It wasn't pleasant seein' the woman – who was still only young then, remember – fadin'... And I knew it, yow know, that she'd mek it, that she'd be in the arms of the Lord – coz me mother was a religious one – she'd be at the service every Sunday with Reverend Byfield at our local church in Wolverhamptun... Ahr... and then the funeral... well, what was that like..."

A tear came to his eye.

"Are ya all right, Dave?" Sid said in a compassionate voice.

"Ahr, fine." Yam Yam got up from the chair. "Yow still here?" he then said to John.

"Well, I thought-"

"Think nothin'," Yam Yam said, cutting him short, "just go... As I said, yow dayn't work here no more."

26: Spaghetti Catenaccio

The Friday night before the match was raucous for the lads. Nobby completely ignored Danny, though, for obvious reasons. Darren, meanwhile, was moody. He'd been given the opportunity to try and put his relationship with Lynsey's family on a good footing, yet here he was doing what he'd been told was what irritated them the most about him.

Darren realised nothing would change – not until Sunday or Monday anyway – so he quickly got back into the groove with Nobby.

"Scores, lads?" Bagpuss said to Darren and Mickey at the bar.

"Two-nil to us," Mickey replied.

"A draw." Darren was being negative; John Barnes was in the team.

"Is that it – where's the confidence in ya team, Daz?" Bagpuss said. He handed them their pints.

"Well, I tell ya what, lads," Mickey began, "that Luther Blissett won't do shit... I mean... Ya go to Italy... everybody expects ya to do summat... and what happens? He goes and makes a whole dog's bollocks of it."

Bagpuss's face grimaced, then he said:

"Difficult over there, though. They've got that *Catenaccio* system, know what I mean? Defence is everythin'... Hard to break 'em down like, ya know? Even someone like Blissett... well, ya aiyn't really gonna be as effective. The English league's more of a goal scorin' league... I mean, if Rossi were here, me God, wouldn't he score a few..."

They knew Rossi – 1982 and all that – but the 'Cat-a-what'?

"Ya bin watchin' too much of that Italian cinema from the '60s," Mickey said in a knowledgeable tone, though really he didn't have the foggiest what Bagpuss was on about.

"They play the game the way it should be played: with the brain, ya know, son... nah, maybe ya dunno – *am I right?*"

Mickey, ever the wide boy, wiped all the sarcasm off with a simple shrug of his shoulders.

"So, Arth, how d'ya know all about this Italian football then?" Darren asked, interested but also wanting to take the piss at the same time.

"Well, ever since John Charles, really... Ya know, as a younger man he was a bit of a hero for me. D'ya know he played both as a forward and as a central defender?" They both looked at Bagpuss clearly showing their ignorance to the question. Although they'd both heard of John Charles and knew he had been a player, they were oblivious to any of the finer details, something which Bagpuss, as a self-confessed football aficionado, was proud of and used to boast about no end. "All right, lads, it dayn't matter, anyway... But let me tell ya – he was the first of all the British players to go there and the only one in me honest opinion to have made a success of it."

"What about Wilkins? Souness? Brady?" Darren asked.

"Brady's a Paddy and dayn't count," said Bagpuss.

"Okay, but the other two do – dayn't they, Mickey?"

"Yeah," Mickey answered with indifference.

"Yeah, but ya have to remember after Charles all the players who've ever gone aiyn't bin as successful – and I'm talkin' about the ones there today and all... Charles' goalscorin' rate for Juventus was summat like a goal a game if me memory serves me right and that's summat to be proud of... Take today, though - take any of ya goalscorers in the First Division who can hit twenty-five to thirty a season and watch that drop to

under half – maybe even to ten – in the Italian First
Division…"

Bagpuss went on like that for twenty minutes without a
break. You had to expect it, though – it was all part of his
service and hospitality.

"How' the job, mate?" Mickey asked Darren.

"It's all right – one of us got the fuckin' sack today… John
from school."

"Why, what did the cunt do?"

"Ah, it's a long story and I dayn't wanna get into it."

"Pissin' off the gaffer, I bet?"

"Yeah, that's it."

Danny, who'd been in the Bar, approached Bagpuss and
Tina who were pulling some pints.

"Hey, Arth, who's that new Scotch bloke next door?"
Danny asked, annoyed.

"Keith."

"And where's Pat?"

"Patricia had to leave – summat about her mother bein'
sick."

"Fuck me, he can't even pull a bastard pint properly, and he
looks a right dim twat – are ya tryin' to lose ya customers in
there or what?"

The rest of the night flowed by like it always did on a
Friday: before anybody knew it, the bell for last orders rang out
signifying the end of the alcoholic intoxication. All the hard
drinkers hated that sound – for it ended what they were on the
earth to do. They'd have to wait another twelve hours until
lunchtime and the two precious hours of afternoon drinking,
and then until six and another five more. It was only in the
City Centre that some of the pubs opened all day, but most of
the locals tried to avoid those places like the plague, as they
lacked the atmosphere of The Bantam. The U.K had some of
the strictest publican laws in the world, and if you liked a tot –

like most in The Bantam did – it was sometimes a hell on earth.

Nobby, for obvious reasons, kept his drinking to a minimum. He had The Smiths gig coming up in Ireland and wanted to save for that. Danny, drunk as always, ignored Nobby all night.

Everybody started to leak out of the doors. A couple of locals, not yet drunk enough, asked Bagpuss for a 'lock-in'.

"Sorry, not tonight, maybe tomorra."

"Come on, Arth," one implored.

"An hour tops," said another.

"Nah, nah, not tonight... See ya drinks off ladies and gentlemen, please!" Bagpuss then screamed out, adamant he'd get his way.

Darren had a lot on his mind as he walked home, and the alcohol could only dim a little of it: Lynsey, as usual, her dad and brother, the money he owed his mom and the retribution he was dreaming about getting on the Villa scumbag. He'd hardly thought about the last one since Lynsey took ill, but now, remembering it, he wanted to do whatever it took to kick the ten living shits out of the prick. He knew he wouldn't be able to handle it on his own – he'd have to ask Mickey and Danny for help, maybe Nobby too.

There was the question on how to do it. Darren wondered as he strolled through the cold King's Heath streets on the way home a plan that would see him all right in regards to the reprisal. Just then the idea came to him: In a week, on the 14th, Manchester United would be in Birmingham for their league match against the Villa. Because the Red Devils had one of the biggest teams in terms of success and the toughness of their firm in town, it would be a great decoy to get his own back on the Villa casual without stirring it up too much. The plan was a good one but there was only one problem with it: on that very day the lads would be down in East London playing the

Hammers. It was like a dream come true: the ICF on their own territory. Yet Darren wasn't really that much of a hooligan anyway and thought it a bit dangerous too. He knew Mickey and Danny would be going, but this time, instead of going alone, they'd probably try and hook up with what remained of the Zulus or some other City firm. The East End of London was a dangerous place if you didn't know where you were going. Darren had been to Upton Park only once before in a League match in September '82 – one of his first away matches to the capital – when the Hammers had slaughtered Birmingham five-nil. And it wasn't just on the pitch that they'd got a good hiding, but all along Eversleigh, Lawrence and Heigham Roads to the East Ham tube station and safety. After that Darren had had enough of London until the 1984-85 season, when he'd built up enough courage to go back down there for a clash at Craven Cottage with Fulham. Now, the Fulham Suicide Squad was no ICF, and along with a nice one-nil victory Darren had tagged along with a few Zulu hardcore who had done their city proud by breaking the jaw of some emaciated Westender.

All that was in the past, nevertheless, and he wasn't sure if Mickey and Danny would agree to stay behind in Brum to beat the shit out of some Vile casual while their team was playing West Ham United on the enemy's turf – it could be too much for them to miss.

It was Watford the next day, anyway. Darren would go – there'd be no forsaking that again for the hospital – watch the match, have a few jars before and after, and propose it to them.

27: John Barnes and Grace Jones We Hate You

It was Saturday morning and the match was a little over five hours away. Darren was well up for it, but he'd decided to take Noel's advice seriously and he headed off down the hospital to try and see Lynsey, and if that failed, at least show his gormless face to them and show to Noel he was trying his best.

Well, when he did get there, it was the usual story: Lynsey was still in a coma and he was still not allowed to see her. It was unfair, really. Nobody – even his parents – knew how he was feeling. He knew he could have a drink down the pub, a laugh with his mates, and anything else too, but that didn't stop any of the things that were happening to Lynsey. Yes, he was suffering as much as anybody. Yet here were her old man and older brother thinking they were the only ones in pain – no, there were other people too, and Darren was one of them.

He stayed at home till noon before heading off slowly towards the ground, hoping to meet a few of his mates and Mickey and Danny later on the terraces. Before that, though, he'd have a few drinks alone in a pub close to the ground on the Coventry Road.

The match itself, which ended in a two-one defeat for Birmingham, was a good game with John Barnes showing his usual flamboyant skill in front of goal and embarrassing the City defenders all day. The match – as matches had gone so far that season – was a quiet affair in regards to trouble. The sole dark spot – almost in a literal sense – were the racist chants directed at Watford's black players, though everybody had expected it.

"Fuckin' black cunts!" Danny shouted at the final whistle.

"Come on, mate, leave it out," Darren scolded. "There's no need for that."

Danny walked off.

"Mickey, I've got a proposal for ya tonight – are ya goin' for a tot?" Darren said to him as they were walking out of the crowd between a swarm of other supporters. Some of them, casuals by the way they were dressed and in a rush, were trying to get to the Watford supporters before the Old Bill could offer them any protection.

"Look at 'em," Mickey said, smiling.

"What, ya wanna join 'em?"

"Nah, not today... I'm savin' meself for next Saturday."

"So, ya'll be in The Bantam tonight?"

"Yeah. Me and Danny and a couple of the lads are goin' into town now – see what's goin' on there."

"Okay, I'll see ya later... Remember, I got summat to talk to ya about."

After the match Darren went straight home to avoid any aggro. When he got there his parents were sitting in front of the telly doing what they always did best in the opinion of their son. He intended to relax until eight by having his tea and a short kip. Saturdays were usually like that, especially during the footy season and when there was a home game. Playing away totally changed all that.

"Darren, where's me money?" It was his old lady again.

"I don't have it all."

"Ya a pissin' liar – talk to him, Leslie, will ya?"

Darren's dad was about as assertive as a shopkeeper to a mob boss in Brooklyn; his old lady ruled the roost and she laid down all the rules and held infinite power – his dad's only job was to verbalise the orders she'd established.

"Do as ya told, Daz," he said phlegmatically.

"Ya hear ya dad – ya owe me thirty quid, and I wanna go to the Co-op on Monday and buy some shoppin'."

Darren pulled out a wrinkled tenner from his pocket and handed it to her.

"There, I'll give ya the rest when I've got it."

"And when will that be?"

"I'll probably be gettin' a full-time job outta this casual at the scrapyard – John, one of the lads there has bin sacked like."

His old man let out a laugh.

"What for?" his mom asked.

"Ah summat to do with the gaffer."

"Daz, be quiet, *Blind Date's* on in a bit, so me and ya mom want some peace, okay?" his dad said, irritated.

"*Blind Date*, what's that?" Darren asked.

"A new show hosted by Cilla Black," his mother replied.

Leslie loved Wendy Richard, but for Cynthia, after Les Ross, there was only Cilla. She'd loved her since the 1960s and was always singing *Anyone Who Had A Heart* to her husband and son's irritation every time she took a bath.

That night a solemn mood gripped the pub because of the day's defeat, though it wasn't as bad as it could've been – Liverpool had beaten the Villa three-nil at Anfield, and that gave at least a little satisfaction. Bagpuss, *Sports Argus* in hand like a western gunslinger's Colt 45, analysed – like he had ever since he'd been a young lad – the day's results with meticulous intention:

"Okay... Ah, yeah, Leicester and Man. City drew... good result for us... Ah, Spurs hammered Oxford five-one... Ipswich lost to Man. Utd... Mmm, the Albion lost, which keeps 'em at the bottom."

They were still third from bottom after the defeat against Watford, but because Leicester and Manchester City had only earned themselves a point in their clashes, and Spurs comfortably beat Oxford, Birmingham was still in touch with them.

"Charlie, Charlie, we couldn't win with an OAP in a wheelchair," Bagpuss went on.

"Arth, come on, what d'ya expect, mate?" Charlie replied.

"Mickey, I need a word with ya," Darren said, five minutes after Mickey and Danny had walked into the Lounge. They were both clearly drunk, though as usual Danny more so than Mickey.

"What about, mate?"

"I told ya today, remember? Come into the Bar for a minute."

They both walked through into the Bar. It was busy too, but at least there Darren was able to sit down with him and get a bit of hush. They planted their pints on the table.

"So, what's this ya want from me – and dayn't be askin' again about no pirate videos coz I told ya a month ago I can't get ya none," Mickey said with a sardonic air.

"Nah, nah, nothin' like that... It's just, well, ya know I had a bitta trouble with that Villa tosser a few months back in town?"

"Yeah?"

"Well, I need ya help with summat."

"What, ya want us to help ya pan the cunt?"

"In a word, yeah – I wanna get me own back."

"Sorted, mate, no bother. *Is that it?*" Mickey said, gettin' up.

"Yeah, but I wanna do it sorta soon like."

"When were ya thinkin'?"

Darren knew what was coming next could change everything:

"Next Saturday." Mickey started laughing. "I know it's West Ham away next week," Darren continued, "but it'll be the perfect chance."

"Ya havin' a fuckin' laugh or summat, aiyn't ya, mate? Ya want me to stay in Brum next week to deck some Villa cunt while the lads are down in deepest, darkest London doin' their best to defend the pride of our city?"

"Well, yeah."

"Fuck that, Daz, we can do him in any time."

"I know that but they've got Man. Utd next week and I'm sure the Villa will be up for it."

"Okay, so they'll be up for it, but what's that gotta do with ya fuckin' bloke?"

"It'll be a diversion."

"I'm fuckin' lost, mate, honestly" Mickey said, lighting a fag. "Nah, Daz, not next Saturday – no-fuckin'-way-Jose... And I hope to fuck ya aiyn't gonna miss this one – ya are comin' down with us?"

He'd have to exact revenge sometime and he scanned his mind for a quick solution.

"What about against Chelsea in two weeks' time? We could do it then?"

"Why the fuck does it have to be a match day, Daz?"

"Coz the cunt's always in the same pub for Villa's home games."

"I thought ya had this trouble with him in the summer?"

"I did."

"So how d'ya know he's a regular there on match days?"

"I asked around."

"Ya fulla shite... Listen, don't be worryin', we'll get him... But Daz... not when there's a game, all right?" Mickey tapped Darren on the shoulder patronisingly. "Dayn't worry, mate, ya'll get ya comeback."

They went back into the Lounge where it was a bit more exciting, though by The Bantam's usual standards there wasn't much of that around. Everybody always took a loss badly, especially when it was against the Villa. Watford paled in comparison to them, but three points were always three points. Everyone's hopes and dreams had their roots in football, and when your life was as mundane as theirs was – with all the shift-work and monotony of the factory floor if they were lucky enough to have a job; and if they weren't so lucky the tedium of interminable queues at the Jobcentre and rejection after rejection at interviews for jobs that offered the minimum wage anyway – you could see why Birmingham City and the beautiful game were so important to them. Nevertheless, being a supporter was painful, like the night was showing, a massive contrast to the Saturday before when they'd drawn to Arsenal - when joy, okay, maybe not that, but relief – was on everyone's face in the pub, not least of all on Bagpuss'.

"But Charlie, it was a win for sure, or shoulda bin, and the lads go and mess it up," Bagpuss said.

On his stool as usual, Charlie Grozier sat there, nodding away, agreeing with everything Bagpuss was saying, but indifferent as well, tapping his long, spiny and manky-nailed fingers, yellow and stained with nicotine on the lager-spilt surface of the bar to the surging rhythm of Bagpuss's low, unmelodic Brummie accent.

"And so what now," Charlie commented after Bagpuss had seemingly finished, "I suppose it's back to square one?"

Maybe he'd just go after him on his own. Although not 'hard' in the classical sense of out-and-out brutality – that was Danny's area – Darren could look after himself if he had to. However, this guy *was* a hardman by all accounts, and he'd need real balls to try something on his own. If he did plan it without help, then at least he could do it his way. He was pretty sure the bloke wouldn't recognise him. The night it happened they had both been pissed and he supposed the bloke had forgotten everything by the next morning – Darren was just another Bluenose to him, like all the others he'd probably twatted over the years, a misty face now, gone from his lager-fuelled memory. But this 'ghost', of Kings Heath and proud, would get his fist full in recompense. The bigger they were, the harder they fell. Yes, he was Darren Timothy Acheson's for the taking.

"Get ya fuckin' hand off me arse, ya dirty cunt!" It was a violent scream. It belonged to a woman in her mid-twenties with the highest, most annoying high-pitched gob known to man. Danny, drunker by a mile than anyone in the Lounge, had put his huge manhands on her backside in the hope of pulling her.

Pissed off anyway at the day's result, Bagpuss acted without hesitation:

"Hey, Danny, finish ya pint off and get out – ya barred."

As he was saying it, Tina – next to him behind the bar - started pissing herself.

Danny looked up at Bagpuss: the stare, like the one he used on passing enemy supporters protected by the Old Bill, was menacing – no, more than that, it was murderous in intent. The gaffer, never afraid to stick up for himself when the need arose, looked on, at that instant frozen with fear; a second later, Tina, herself caught by the moment of her gaffer's heroics, stopped laughing too, along with a few others close by. Darren and Mickey were over the other side of the large Lounge, and only realised after another few seconds had passed.

"I'm sick of ya, Arth. Ya a fat cunt and ya won't bar me – this is *my* pub... I pay me money like everyone else. Just coz ya ate all the pies dayn't give ya the right to fuckin' think ya summat special!"

You could hear a pin drop.

"Just get outta me pub," Bagpuss said bravely.

Mickey then arrived on the scene and grabbed Danny by the arms, ready to take him outside, quickly followed by Darren. They proceeded – after Mickey had said something in Danny's ear – to drag him by force outside until, resigned to the situation that at least for now he wouldn't be allowed back in, he walked off into the night, fuming.

"Ya can't bar him, Arth?" Mickey said when everything had died down and returned to normal.

"Listen, Mickey, I can't have twats actin' like demented perverts in me pub, ya hear?"

"I know, but he was only havin' a laugh."

"If that's a laugh, son, I aiyn't fuckin' interested."

Darren thought about Nobby's nemesis – all eighteen stone of the hulk – had been sorted right true and proper. He'd have to tell him the good news when they next met.

"I tell ya what, Daz, I'd love to give her one," Mickey said after he'd finished his conversation with Bagpuss and had briefly talked to Tina, looking as tasty as ever in a tight-fitting red dress.

The Word Girl, a song by Scritti Politti, came on the jukebox.

"Lynsey loves this one," Darren said with open pride, even though he wasn't keen on the band himself. And she did: it'd been part of the background to their first summer together, and its melody brought only happy memories flooding back.

"How is she anyway, Daz, I forgot to ask, mate?"

"It aiyn't good."

An awkward silence came next; Mickey was obviously lost for words.

"And what are the chances of a full recovery?" Mickey then said, knowing he had to say something, and it *was* something.

"Dunno, mate, I really dunno."

He hoped everything would be okay, but Darren wasn't a doctor. As the song played, he wished he and Lynsey would be able to dance to it like they had in the past, smooching to the hit on all the dance floors of Birmingham's nightclubs. The song stopped and Grace Jones' *Slave To The Rhythm* came on.

"Turn that shit off," a voice yelled, followed by: "Who put that on?"

"It was me," a young woman said – no more than thirty with peroxide blonde hair – putting her hand up. She was sitting in the corner with another couple of middle-aged men and women. All of them weren't regulars. She immediately started jumping up and down like some hyperactive jack-in-the-box. Her musical taste was far apart from everybody else's in the place – even her own company. She started to move, and it quickly erupted into an erotic kind of dance, hips swaying and arms spread out over her head in a mesmeric concoction well suited to Grace's deep voice and unflinching rhetoric. Once there, caught in the moment of ecstasy, the woman took an empty Mann's bottle from the table next to her, got on her knees, and began singing, eyes closed, into the bottle. Her voice, raspy at best, gave no credence to the song already condemned by everybody in the pub. It was a depressing finale to a depressing day and to top it all off the bell for last orders exploded into life and the lights flashed on and off as the very last note of the song faded away.

But somebody was going to do something about it.

Bagpuss, a little worse from the alcohol after a few snidy shots of whisky from behind the bar, started clapping, before entering into his own imperfect rendition of Jeff Lynne's *Mister Blue Sky:*

Sun is shinin' in the sky...

By the end of it – though his voice was inferior to the woman's – a universal round of applause went up, indicating he'd won in the popularity stakes: Arthur *un point,* lady-with-Grace Jones-complex and disgusting yellow hair *nuls points.*

28: Signing Off

They were all there, tired and moody, like always, their eyes, casting doubt and prejudice. Noel, his newly found ally within the enemy camp, gave him a wink – nothing too sure, mind you, but just enough to put Darren at ease.

"She's still in a coma, Darren, and the doctors don't know if she'll come out of it," Teresa said

"And what about the infection?"

"*Antibiotics*," Christy said, singly and with meaning.

"What? They're workin'?"

"Nah, they're givin' 'em to her through a pipe," said Noel.

And still there was nothing; he knew as much as two – no, three weeks before. Was there any point to any of this? He pulled Noel aside.

"Listen mate," Darren began, "I dayn't wanna cause no offence like, but the situation's startin' to piss me off... What's goin' on? Come on, be straight with me?"

"We dunno nothin' too."

Owen looked at them in conversation; he was angry, suspicious.

"Well, ya should."

Her parents looked tired. A month had almost passed since the nightmare began, and it had started to show on their faces, particularly on Lynseys mom's. Teresa had had enough of torture, and her spirit for a fight was slowly draining away; Christy, ever the patriarch, had the heaviest load to deal with – the suffering of his daughter had started to affect his eating and sleeping habits. He was drinking more too, and he'd lost weight. Noel as well. Owen, however, expressed none of the suffering his parents were going through. His only emotion was hate, which manifested itself in its purity to Darren. This was not to say Owen's love for his sister was frosty in nature, it was just the hate for her boyfriend was stronger – at least now; intensely so, growing, in fact more than he knew how to control. Darren felt the intense revulsion directed at him, but said nothing – what would've been the point? Intensify the odium further and end up in a fight with him?

"Listen, I aiyn't stayin' round here for nothin'," Darren said after a moment.

"Okay, go then, but dayn't expect no sympathy from none of 'em," replied Noel.

Darren walked out undeterred, Owen tracking him with his mad, glowing eyes the whole time like a radar until he disappeared around a corner.

When Darren got home, he spent the whole afternoon and evening in his room, listening to The Smiths, sinking deeper in harmony with their moribund lyrics and into his own haven of depression - which had regrettably been made worse by the knowledge he would have to work the next day. But then he stopped to think about it: he had a job; many didn't. Maybe he'd get something full-time from the gaffer now thanks to John's sacking. Darren closed his eyes as *Meat is Murder* finished and the crackling eruption of the stylus played out the end of the record, leaving only the echoed murmur of static from the speakers, where knowing this, he fell asleep.

On the Monday, as expected, Yam Yam offered him John's job:

"Sow, d'yow wanit?" the gaffer said over an early morning cuppa.

"Well, yeah," Darren answered rather indecisively, as if, in fact, he didn't want it, "I suppose."

"Millions on the dole and only a 'I suppose', ahr?"

"Nah, nah, I wanit."

Did he feel bad about taking his mate's job? A little, but what could he do? John had child support to pay, though in Thatcher's Britain it was dog eat dog.

Sid and Darren were still embarrassed by John's sacking. Sid had known Yam Yam a long time and had never seen him act as he had.

"I just wanna apologise for Friday, Dave," Sid said. Darren looked on too shame-faced. The gaffer smiled.

"What ay yow apologisin' for, mate, nothin' happened?"

"Nah, we were all outta order."

"What, yow think that story about me old lady was true? She's alive and well, livin' it up in an old people's home in Wombourne."

Talk about taking the piss.

They both stared at their gaffer. Clearly at the forefront of their emotions now, the anger seething within them both expressed itself in their faces. What could Darren say, though, without getting the same treatment as his former workmate? Nothing. He'd have to leave his contempt inside.

Darren and Sid agreed when they returned to work and had a talk that their gaffer had done it all out of spite, and it had been some kind of one-upmanship on Yam Yam's part to get his own back on John for the disrespect he'd shown him. Now, however, it wouldn't be just John suffering but his toddler too.

Because they were a man down from John's unfortunate sacking, Darren now had to work twice as hard as he had been. Adding to this the particular cold weather, it was rather an unpleasant time for Darren. Pissed off, Darren had to grin and bear it, but not before complaining to Sid about it first.

"Hey, Sid, I hope Dave's got plans to get another bloke in like I was here for John?"

"Stop ya complainin'."

"But I'm knackered."

"John managed all right."

"Well I aiyn't John."

Strong words. He should have been grateful, though he wasn't – did he want to be interviewed again by some four-eyed twat in the Jobcentre? Sid guessed he did.

"Oh, and by the way," Yam Yam said to him as he was leaving, "I hope yow gonna sign off – can't be riskin' none of that shit around here, get it lioke?"

"I'll need the mornin' off to do that."

"Ahr, but now tekin' the piss – I want yow here by eleven. Got a few mowtas comin' in from Shard End that I'll need yow to start strippin'."

Darren wanted to make quick work of it: in and out, like a thief in the night – any longer than an hour in there gave him a headache, so he wanted to avoid that.

"Yeah, dayn't worry, I'll make it back on time."

29: Sylvester Stallone or Chevy Chase?

Tuesday and Wednesday were crazy – like the weather: from rain, to sleet, to snow and back again. Darren's mood too: he hadn't listened to Noel's advice and had skipped his visits to the hospital the previous two days. He was tired, you see, due to all the extra work Yam Yam had given him – but who cared about that other than himself? The Moriarty clan surely didn't.

"How's Lynsey, love?" his mom asked, the third time in as many days. He was starting to hate it now.

"I dunno... it aiyn't good."

"Maybe me and ya father should visit her at the weekend?"

And out of everything, this was the one he wanted least of all. They hated him so they would naturally hate his parents too.

"Ya met Christy, dayn't ya?" Darren asked her.

"Well, he was here – but I'd hardly say we met."

"What d'ya think of him?"

"Hard to say after only a minute... Why ya askin'?"

"Nah, I'm just curious, that's all."

"D'ya get on well with 'em?"

"Yeah, it's all right," he answered, lying of course.

"So, will it be all right to pop over there to the hospital on either Saturday or Sunday?"

"Nah, I dayn't think so."

"Maybe next week then?"

"I dunno, we'll see."

He'd signed off, in what had been a surprisingly painless process, though he had thought about delaying it for another couple of weeks on the sly. In the end, though, he'd decided against it, as the paltry sum wasn't worth the risk. Maggie could stick her poxy dough where the sun didn't shine – well, that was at least what he was thinking as he was walking out of the Jobcentre for what he hoped would be the last time in his life.

"Sow, yow signed off, didn't yow?" the gaffer asked him on the Thursday morning.

"Yeah, Dave."

"Did them mowtas come in?"

"Yeah."

"Did yow strip everythin' inside 'em?"

Yam Yam had been off for a few days.

"Yeah."

At lunchtime, the three sat eating their sandwiches and reading their papers.

"Everythin' sound at home, Dave?" Sid asked in a concerned tone.

The gaffer looked worn out. Something was up, and judging by his face it was something serious.

"Nah, it aiyn't really, but what can yow do."

Whatever it was, Darren had his own troubles.

"Now that ya got a full-time job ya can give me the rest of the money ya owe me, Darren. I aiyn't takin' no more excuses – I want it next payday," Darren's mom said to him over dinner.

"Yeah, whatever," Darren replied indifferently, like he always did with his mom.

Darren walked up to the solitude of his bedroom, can of Lowenbrau in hand, switched on his record player, took off the record *19* by Paul Hardcastle, and replaced it on the turntable with *The Word Girl*. He wanted a bit of Lynsey with him. He played the song over and over again.

It was pub time. Usually he'd be out on a Wednesday night, but because Nobby was doing something else he'd decided to stay in and wait until Thursday night, when Nobby would be there.

Darren knew his best mate was in before he'd opened the door to the Lounge – *This Charming Man* was playing, and there was no doubt in Darren's mind who'd put it on.

"All right, son," Nobby said, welcoming him with in a joyous tone, then slapping him on the left shoulder playfully. Yet again, it was obvious Nobby had started drinking as soon as the doors had opened at six, and he was hammered already.

"What did I tell ya, Nob?" Darren said, frustration evident.

"I dunno, what did ya tell me?"

"Just stay off the pop."

"What's this?" he said, lifting up his pint. "Ya havin' a laugh, aiyn't ya?" Nobby then burst out into a childish giggle, before downing the rest in one.

Darren got himself a pint in.

"Where's mine, ya tight cunt?" Nobby said, furious with his mate's selfishness.

"I aiyn't stickin' in rounds tonight, so ya can buy ya own."

"Get me a pint in, twat. I aiyn't after an excuse."

Darren got Nobby another pint.

"How many's that tonight already, Nob?" Darren asked, handing him the pint of lager. Nobby grabbed it. The pint spilt, half the contents falling onto the floor, hands and sleeves of them both.

"Sorry, mate," Nobby said, still laughing.

"For fuck's sake, ya soaked me."

"Ah, stop actin' like a pussy, ya cunt."

Bagpuss made an appearance at eight, clad in his Sunday best, though it wasn't Sunday.

"Hey, Daz, come here, mate."

Darren walked over.

"Where the fuck are ya off to tonight wearin' that clobber?" Darren asked.

"Keep it down, will ya, but I'm takin' a bird out."

A few of the female locals were looking at him with smiles. They'd never seen the landlord look so dashing. Tina, too, was impressed.

"Ah," Darren smirked and gave Bagpuss a wink, "ya jokin', aiyn't ya?"

"Nah, us old cunts can still pull as well from time to time, ya know."

"What's she like?"

"Her name's Sheila. I met her at the bingo a couple of weeks back."

"Kept that secret, didn't ya?"

"Yeah."

"What's she like?"

"West Ham Saturday, mate," Bagpuss then said, changing the subject.

"Yeah, I can't bloody wait for it."

"Are ya makin the trip down there?"

"I aiyn't sure yet – if I do, it'll be with Mickey and Danny."

"Daz, a free bitta useful advice," Bagpuss said after a pause gravely, "ya wanna keep away from that loony-"

"Ah, come on, Arth, he aiyn't that bad," Darren said, interrupting.

"I'm tellin' ya, summat's gonna explode in that cunt soon."

"Dayn't exaggerate... I've known the bloke ages and he aiyn't that bad."

"I just hope ya aiyn't goin' down with him."

"Best bloke to have at ya side in a ruck."

"I tell ya, he'll land ya in deep shit one of these days."

"Ya aiyn't gonna bar him for life, are ya?"

"Well, I dayn't want him in this place again, if that's what ya askin' me."

"Arth, dayn't do it: he'll only start and get all funny, ya know what I mean?"

"So there ya are, the proof's in the puddin', aiyn't it: he's trouble or he will be – it's either one of 'em."

"He's a local, Arth."

The topic of conversation changed back again to what they both really loved: football:

"A win on Saturday, I hope," Bagpuss said, clapping his hands and grinning like a boy on Christmas Day.

"*Ya think so?*" Darren replied in disbelief.

"Why not?"

"They're flyin' high at the minute, Arth, and I can't see that we'll beat 'em."

"We've got to turn the corner sometime."

"Yeah, but not against the Hammers – maybe we'll get summat after Christmas against Man. City."

"Ya younger generation make me sick, ya know?" Bagpuss said, half in anger, half in jest. "Support ya team, be proud of 'em – I hate all this fuckin' negativity, it drives me mad."

"Nah, I aiyn't bein' negative, Arth, I'm bein' realistic."

"All right, but as long as The Albion dayn't catch up with us and we aiyn't relegated and the Vile come below us it'll have bin a successful season in me book."

"The Albion are already down, Arth, that's a cert."

"Anyway, must rush," Bagpuss said, taking himself a shot of whisky from the bar, "I've gotta meet this bird at half eight."

"So where are ya off to?"

"We're goin' to the pictures in town."

"What to see?"

"I dunno yet – it's between *Rocky IV* and *Spies Like Us.*"

"I'm fuckin' sure she aiyn't gonna wanna watch a comedy."

"Well, whatever we see I hope I get the shag at the end of the night." Bagpuss laughed.

"How old is she?"

"In her late forties, I suppose."

When Bagpuss had gone, Darren rejoined Nobby at a small table near the door. There was a draft.

"Jesus, Nob, coulda picked a warmer spot."

"Stop complainin', ya cunt."

"Got a full-time job now at the yard."

"Well done, son."

"Yeah, John was given the boot – that's how I got it."

"That's sound, that is."

Nobby wasn't really engaged in the conversation; he'd had too much to drink and his eyelids were sporadically opening and closing.

"Ya should get some kip, mate," Darren said, noticing Nobby's drowsiness.

Nobby suddenly came to life.

"Hey, Daz, what about the cunt Danny – I swear it, mate, I'll get him... yeah, I will."

As quickly as he said it, Nobby fell asleep, his back leaning against the wall.

30: Irish Tragedy Play

If Lynsey had been conscious at the time, what would she have thought of her boyfriend's behaviour? Only months before she had been healthy and full of life and joy in their future together. Now, however, things were different, and in the protection of her family's vigil she was a sleeping child. Death – if it was to come – had still time to wait. Darren, impervious to the fact – just as the doctors were – gave himself pleasure in the guise of beer and football, while her parents were driving themselves into a deeper psychological hell.

"Teresa, turn over – there's a good documentary on Channel 4," Christy said, as they sat in the living room of their small semi-detached in Moseley.

"I won't, I'm watchin' this," she replied.

They had just returned from the hospital. It was uniform now, day after day after day – a second home from their own. They had no idea how it would finish, but were praying to their God, the only thing on earth that could save their daughter.

Christy wanted a drink but felt ashamed. A pint would be just the therapy for his continual climb into the depths of depression. Yet his wife wouldn't allow it – *how could you*, she'd said two days after they'd found out about Lynsey's illness. Christy had just walked out and went down to his local. Half an hour and two pints later he was back at home. He had found Teresa, his wife of over thirty years, in tears on their bed.

"What are yer cryin' for, love?"

"I'm here alone and yer just don't care."

"I needed a jar – is it such a sin?"

"And what about me... I have to deal with all this too?"

The temptation, especially due to the stress, had now reached a critical point. The last week Christy had thought of nothing else but a pint and he'd drunk his share.

"I'm goin' out for a bit, love."

"Can't wait any longer, I see – off down the pub, are yer, yer fecker?" his wife said, rebuking him.

"Just for a while, love."

It was late anyway – almost ten.

"Why can't yer just sit here with me?"

"It's only for a couple." Christy looked at his watch. "It'll be last orders in a while, so I won't be long."

He made no more excuses and just walked out the hundred-odd-yards to his local on the Moseley Road.

In the pub Christy met Owen.

"Howaya there, son?"

Owen hadn't been to the hospital that day as he had been doing a foreigner. A brickie by profession, and from all accounts a good one within Birmingham circles in the trade.

"Ya know, dad, could be better."

Christy ordered two pints of Guinness. They sat together and drank.

"Ah, it'll be all right, son."

"How's Lynsey – *no change?*"

"Come on now, son, ya should know that."

"I suppose that boyfriend of hers wasn't there again?"

"He wasn't, the fecker."

"Fucker."

"Watch yer language, son… There's no point gettin' upset like. It's his loss if he wants to stay away."

"The cunt-"

"Watch the language," his old man interjected. He could just about tolerate the 'f' word, but the 'c' word was going too far. It's reference to female genitalia sickened him – Christy's wife and daughter were women.

"Dayn't worry, dad, everythin's gonna be sorted."

Christy didn't see it like that as he gazed forlornly into space, sipping the pint in front of him.

"Christy, son, what's the story?" It was Michael Brady, a friend from the pub.

"Ah, Michael, me old fella. Everythin' grand there?"

"I'm sorry to hear about yer trouble, Christy... How is the young one?

"Ah, yer know, Mick, it's not good, not good at all."

Owen left them to chat and went home.

As Christy walked home, neither in unity with happiness nor hope, the descent into grief had control over him. He was dreading the thought of seeing his wife again. Their marriage had always been a good one until recently, but now cracks were beginning to appear.

Luckily Teresa had already gone to bed when he did get home, and he could rest well in the thought that he wouldn't have to talk to her. It was getting too much, though his wife had no idea how he felt. She knew he was depressed and tired – but so was everybody else. Lynsey's illness, for obvious reasons, lay at the core, though there were other reasons as well. Whatever was going to happen to their daughter - good or bad – he knew the feelings for his wife would never be the same again.

Their daughter, meanwhile, unconscious and immune to everything going on around her, was at peace in one sense. Although not dead, in many ways it was like she was. There could be no argument that Darren's actions – if she had known about them – would've caused her great sadness and disappointment. Yet she had also been unaware of how her dad and brother felt about him. They'd hidden most of their true feelings from her. They loved Lynsey and wanted her to be happy but with some other bloke. They wanted her to marry one of her own – that was to say someone from the Irish community, or at least a Catholic. They'd never wanted to get to know Darren. Prejudices remained that wouldn't go away, in the past, present or future.

Darren had probably sensed Noel's advice wouldn't have made any difference anyway. He was doing what he was doing now because it was what he wanted to do; he needed some time to enjoy himself because he was tired, and the football was that one great escape. No matter if he was on the terraces with his mates, in the pub, in the hospital rooted to a chair or at home with his mom and dad watching rubbish on television - his thoughts, both directly and indirectly, would always be first and foremost with Lynsey and *of* Lynsey. What good was it waiting in the hospital and not being able to talk to her? It made no sense at all, that. No, he'd be doing his own thing until the time came when she'd open her big brown eyes once more and look him in the eye and tell him she loved him.

31: An American Bird and Down in the East End

It was the day of the West Ham game and Darren was waiting for the lads at New Street Station. Mickey and Danny were late, but they still had plenty of time before the InterCity train left. Darren had got a phone call from Mickey on the Friday, ordering him to go:

"Ya can't bottle it this time, Daz – not against West-fuckin'-Ham."

And well, after that, Darren couldn't have refused really. With about fifty quid in his back pocket – enough for a whole day of fun – he was well up for it but nervous too: walking into the jungle of the East End had its risks.

He was dressing down. Mickey had told him to. In bandit country dressed in designer labels was like wearing a sign across your chest saying: I'M A CASUAL FROM OUTSIDE OF TOWN, PLEASE JUMP ME AT WILL.

They wanted none of that shit, so it was just an old sweater and winter jacket his old lady had bought him from Debenhams a few years before. Shoes, black – like the ones he'd worn at school. He'd win no fashion contest, but at least he'd be inconspicuous – no easy target for the hordes of ICF casuals who would be prowling the streets like Jack the Ripper, looking for the Zulus and any other Brummie scum who thought they were hard enough to challenge them in a ruck.

His two brothers-in-arms arrived, ten minutes before the train's departure.

"Well done, son," Mickey said, dressed himself like Rodney from *Only Fools and Horses,* impressed by his mate's effort of dressing like one from the Scarf Brigade.

"Ya forgot ya scarf, though?" Danny said, pulling a blue and white stripped number from his pocket and looking equally embarrassing in his donkey jacket and woolly green hat like Benny from *Crossroads*.

Mickey, a veteran of many away days, was a bit dubious about wearing the colours. He thought it was a bit dodgy and no guarantee of safety: the ICF usually didn't pay any attention to the real fans because they were weak and unwilling to defend themselves. That majority, like most of the other firms spread far and wide across the country, stuck to a code of conduct: *We fight only our own kind or those up for it.* But a small minority, a very small, would be happy to lash out at any rival supporter just for the fun of it.

"Put ya scarf away, Danny – nah, better still, throw it away," Mickey said. Danny was twice his size and could have put him in intensive care with a punch.

Danny threw it away without argument. It was clear who was in charge.

They got on the train heading for St Pancras station, the very InterCity Mickey and Danny had taken a couple of weeks before against Arsenal. They looked like the Three Stooges in their Adrian Moleish attire, slipping into the temporary anonymity they craved for the trip. Around them, families and other supporters of the normal persuasion ate sandwiches and read the daily newspapers, happy at the possibilities of the day ahead.

"When was ya last time down here then, mate?" Mickey asked Darren.

"Eighty-two."

"*1982?*" Danny growled.

"Nah, I didn't mean to London itself, I meant to West Ham. Last season I was down here."

The plastic bag opened and the cans went around. Mickey, against drinking before a match, took a few sips and no more.

Darren and Danny, however, polished off four each between them.

The trip to London was filled with boisterous laughter and infinite expletives.

"Hey, Mick, why didn't ya brother come with us?" Darren asked.

"He bottled it – nah, only takin' the piss... Me old man would string me up by the balls if he found out I'd taken him to West Ham away."

"But he was at the Arsenal game with ya, wasn't he?"

"The ICF are a way different breed to them Gooners, mate. I aiyn't never worried for me safety in North London – it's where we're goin' that frightens me."

And he was serious.

"Hey, Daz, how's Nobby?" Danny asked, crushing a can and reaching for another in the plastic bag.

"Sound."

"He's a fuckin' cunt."

Darren ignored him.

They arrived in London at half past eleven. After getting fish and chips they went to a pub in Trafalgar Square to wash it down with a few beers. The pub itself was an upmarket place frequented by too many fat Americans with false smiles on their faces and Japanese with cameras the size of video recorders dangling round their necks. The lads looked out of place, like Eskimos on Miami Beach or blacks at a Klu Klux Klan convention.

"She's all right over there," Danny said, pointing rudely to a girl – a Yank judging by the way she was dressed in green and yellow baseball cap and matching sweatshirt – sitting with a middle-aged couple who looked like her parents.

"I dare ya to try and pull her, Mickey," Darren dared.

"*How?* Her mom and dad are right over there with her."

The couple was reading a menu. After a moment they got up and went to the bar to order some food. Their table was around the corner and hidden from the bar.

"There's ya chance, mate," Darren said, egging him on.

Mickey, ever the cool cat, walked over and plonked himself down beside her.

"All right, love," Mickey said.

"What?"

"I said all right, how are ya?"

"What did you say?"

His Midland's lilt was too much for her.

"I said how are ya?"

"Excuse me, but are *you* English?"

"Yeah, love, *I am* – and ya American, I suppose?" he said with some irritation.

"Yeah, American."

"Why are ya here so close to Chrimbo?" Mickey asked.

She looked at him again for a second in amazement, before saying:

"I'm sorry, sir, but I don't understand a word at all you're saying."

This was unbelievable, in fact it was beyond belief. He glanced over at his two mates; they were waving at him and pissing themselves.

"Where – are – *you* – from – in – A-mer-ic-a - love?"

"Oh, you mean which state?"

"Yeah, that'll do?"

"Texas, Waco, Texas."

"What? Wack what?"

"Waco, it's the name of the city."

"So, ya from Texas then?"

It took another milli-second for the young bird's brain to compute the dialect of Shakespeare once more:

"Yeah, Texas."

"Jesus, ya must know Larry Hagman then?"

"*Sorry?*" He repeated himself, this time reducing the pace even more and pronouncing every syllable, not eating them like typical Brummagen. "No, *Dallas* is a soap opera... err, hello?"

"I know, I was just takin' the piss, love."

"You were what?" she asked.

Mickey thought it was unbelievable.

"So, where's ya old man's cowboy hat? I thought them cowboys all wear hats and jeans and carry guns and stuff?"

"What's your name?" she asked, not understanding his question, her slow, mesmerizing Texas drool feeling good to his south Birmingham ears.

"Mickey."

She reached out her hand and they shook hands.

"I'm Mary-Lou."

Nah, Mickey thought, *a double-barreled first name as well in the mix,* which only added to her sexiness and appeal.

"What are ya doin' back home and what are ya doin' in England so close to Chrimbo?"

"Slowly, please?" He had to repeat himself again, this time replacing 'Chrimbo' with Christmas. "I'm a student at Baylor University."

"Ah, uni – ya must be ya clever sort then?"

"Sorry?" Problems, problems. He repeated himself for the millionth time. "Oh, no, not really." She added modestly.

"What are ya studyin'?"

"Business and Finance with a minor in Philosophy."

He'd run out of conversation. The gap in culture and upbringing was too great. Mickey, panicking, changed the topic immediately, so as not to look like a tool and feel out of his depth:

"So, Mary-Lou, why are ya here for Christmas?" he asked, this time slowly, like Prince Charles without the ears.

"I came with my folks... a pre-holiday tour of culture, they call it. We're only here for a few days... You know, to see the main sights, maybe catch a few shows."

"They're the old bucket and spade, aiyn't they?" Mickey was in London, so he thought he'd use a bit of Cockney rhyme-slang.

"You talk funny, Mickey – I don't think I've ever met anybody like you in my life," she said, laughing.

"I hope that's a good thing?"

"I thought the New Yorkers or Bostonians were hard to understand, but you are almost impossible... Where are you from... Scotland?"

"Nah, Birminghum."

"Oh, did you know that Birmingham Alabama was named after your town?"

He didn't.

"It aiyn't a town, love, it's a city," he responded sarcastically.

Mickey then looked over to Darren and Danny: they were waving at her.

"Are they your buddies?"

"Who? *Them?*" he replied.

"Yes?"

"Nah, sorry, I dunno them twats."

So much for loyalty to your mates.

"Can you say that once more?" He repeated himself yet again; this was becoming boring. "Well, whoever they are, they're looking over in our direction," she went on.

"Oh, just ignore 'em – Cockney wasters, probably... local like."

Her parents suddenly appeared.

"Oh, mom, dad-"

"Who's this, darling?" her old man, a big beast of a creature, said in a tone like a U.S Marine Corps drill sergeant. He reminded Mickey of the American footballers his younger brother would watch on Channel 4 every Sunday.

"Mickey, his name's Mickey."

"Please to meet ya both," Mickey said, not moving from his seat, eschewing the courtesy and niceties that the fine Texan couple were probably used to back home in the Lone Star State.

"Would you mind moving from my wife's seat," the dad then said, insulted by the Englishman's lack of manners.

"Oh, Willard, leave the boy alone," his wife put in, a portly woman with flaming red hair. "Don't mind him, dear, my poor husband's just grouchy over the poor service in this place."

Mickey felt it was time to trap. He said his goodbyes and rejoined his mates over at their table.

"Ya cunt," Danny said, pissing himself. "Was she up for it or what?"

"Come on, lads, we're leavin'," was Mickey's quick reply.

They downed their pints and left, got on the tube and headed for the Upton Park station.

The Old Bill was everywhere, and the ground a ten-minute walk away.

"Right, lads, keep ya voices down a bit and follow me," Mickey said.

They walked behind a small group of Birmingham City supporters – middle-aged men mostly, mixed in with some kids wearing claret and blue colours. This would be the perfect foil. No police and no casuals on their backs.

As they approached the Boleyn Ground, Darren became more ill at ease. His last adventure down these parts almost ended with him getting the worst kicking of his life. Only his quick feet, and quicker thinking, had got him out of what could've been something very nasty. Thirty crazy ICF hooligans on his tail hadn't been fun for him, no matter what Mickey and the maniac Danny thought about it. Yes, if he wanted fun, he could smoke a spliff or get totally wasted down the local or play Subutteo.

"Hey, Mick, where are we goin'?" Darren asked nervously.

"Keep it down, will ya" he answered in a whisper. "To the pub for a tot."

Darren had been to a pub the last time, in '82, called the King Arthur, and it had been from there that they'd been run out of the place by the West Ham casuals – he was sure they had been the ICF. Now, three years later, he'd wised up to everything.

"Nah, I dayn't wanna go to no pub, Mickey." Darren said, evidently showing his displeasure.

"Dayn't be a fanny, Daz," Danny said, sniggering. He was well up for it like always. The big man was excited: any chance of the row sent his adrenalin sky high; the same couldn't be said of Darren; Mickey, however, was somewhere inbetween the two.

"Nah, let's just go straight to the ground.

"Dayn't worry, mate," Mickey replied in a calming voice, before tapping him on the back reassuringly. "I've bin to this spot before – it's sound."

He'd have to take Mickey's word for it. A veteran of over a hundred away games - including cup matches - there was no better person to listen to really.

They arrived at the pub, and luckily for Darren it was packed with the scarf brigades of both sets of supporters and was a friendly enough place. They'd be safe here. Darren sighed in relief.

It was difficult to drink a pint without spilling half of it onto the bloke next to you, and that was why it took Danny – they'd asked him because he was the most physically imposing, and a natural 'parting of the Red Sea' formed by all those cacking it around him from fear of a quick smack in the gob – about ten minutes to get the beer in.

"Well, lads, this is nothin' here... It's Disneyland, in fact. Get lost here and ya'll find ya way out somehow... But Maine Road – it's a fuckin' labyrinth that place, and if ya get caught in there ya fuckin' finished," Mickey said.

"Yeah, is that right?" Darren asked. He didn't agree. His close-shave three years before had seen to that, when in the mazy streets of the East End he'd barely escaped with his bollocks intact.

A bit of trouble started at the far end of the pub from where they were, but it was quickly put down by the protestations of a few older West Ham supporters, shouting in the sharp East End Cockney: "Keep it shut, Adam, yer fuckin' muppet!" And that was the end of that.

After another pint they headed for the ground, whizzy-headed from the lager and tobacco smoke of the enclosed space of the pub. Any dreams Danny had had of causing trouble were quickly put down by the Old Bill. Birmingham and West Ham's casuals had earned themselves a right reputation around the country and the police were ready for anything. Swarms of them, on foot mostly, but some with Alsatian dogs, lined the streets approaching the ground. On the corners, groups of mounted officers looked on as the crowds passed them by. Lessons learned from the Luton-Millwall and Birmingham-Leeds matches had seen to that. No, there'd be little trouble today, other than from a few 'think-it' anoraked hooligans giving it loads to OAPs with poodles and zimmerframes. The real firms - that of the ICF and the Zulus respectively - were probably mixing it with each other good and proper in some derelict warehouse on the Isle of Dogs, miles away from where the game would be taking place and from the prying eyes of Big Brother, the Old Bill; or at least those Zulus would be that hadn't already been locked up or under house arrest for the Leeds tear up. There were always a few who escaped through the net, and so some trouble, no matter how small, would be on West Ham's manor.

And as for the match – the real casuals didn't care; it was little entertainment and dull anyway. No, they'd make their own fun.

They got into the away end fifteen minutes to three. Packed in like rice crispies into a cereal box, a crush ensued, but once the coppers closed the gates that eased and the supporters could at least breathe and follow the action on the pitch.

The game itself was entertaining enough, though yet again Birmingham came away without a point in a two-nil defeat.

"Fuckin' cunts, man!" Danny shouted out as the ref blew the final whistle to end the match. "Fuck off, Cottee, fuck off McAvennie!"

The away supporters trundled out of the ground, heads low and disappointed. The police were expecting a riot: outside, masses of them lined the route to the tube station. The lads moved on in the sea of movement. Up ahead, they heard the sound of screams and the smashing of glass. Something was going on.

"Move along now, please, move along," a copper said, no more than twenty. He looked afraid; it was probably his first ever matchday.

"Fuckin' cunt," Danny said to the young officer of the law, only when he was far enough away from hearing distance.

And the crowd was still moody. It could go off at any moment. They passed a few cars that had unfortunately had their windscreens smashed and side mirrors ripped off only a minute before.

"Idiots," Mickey commented, lighting a cigarette and crashing his box to the other two, "imagine leavin' ya fuckin' mowta round here on a matchday.

The escort took them to the underground station in record time.

"So, what are we gonna do now?" Danny asked as they were moving down the escalator stairs. He was disappointed – not so much at the loss, but rather because he hadn't had the chance to pound anyone.

"We can head down into central London to see what's goin' on there," Mickey suggested.

Even though they were all dressed like homeless urchins from the mean streets, Mickey wanted to explore a bit.

"Why dayn't we just head straight home – we can catch a couple in The Bantam? We all look like fuckin' mongs, so we aiyn't gonna have a chance of pullin' no birds anyway," Darren suggested.

"Fuck off, Daz," Danny replied aggressively.

They got on the tube and made their way to the centre of London again.

"I aiyn't goin' to no pubs or nothin' if that's what ya wanna do?" Darren protested.

"Then piss off there, Daz... be a bore," Danny said.

Darren wasn't going home alone, so he just kept his mouth shut and followed them.

They walked from place to place, had a few pints in one dive, before finding a nice little wine bar off Oxford Street. Bad weather was drawing in and sleet had started falling. They wanted to get in, get away from the wind and cold, but the bouncer on the door, a big black fucker, refused them entrance:

"Brummies, aiyn't yer?" he began with a broad south London twang.

"And what of it," Danny said, spoiling for a fight. He moved threateningly closer to the bouncer, but next to him Danny was a dwarf. "Have ya got a problem lettin' us in? Just look at the weather... it's pissin' down and we're fuckin' freezin' our arses off."

Danny hadn't come one hundred and twenty miles for nothing.

"Listen, geeza, just fuck off, yeah," the bouncer warned. He and Danny were face to face. A confrontation was unavoidable.

"So, what, ya want some?" Danny threatened.

"Let it go, Danny," Darren said, cacking himself.

"Yeah, let's go, Danny," voiced Mickey.

And that was it. Mickey had sorted it again.

"And don't come back 'ere, yer get me, yer fuckin' dimlos," were the bouncer's parting words to them.

"That was a close one," Darren said as they were moving away, the two more enthusiastically than their big mate, who was still looking back at the black goliath eyeballing him. Danny wanted a fight, but wasn't going to get one.

"Ya a cunt, Daz, and ya fuckin' bottled it," Danny said.

"Nah, I didn't at all - I just have some common sense: did ya see the size of the cunt?"

"It dayn't matter, he was outta fuckin' order, Mick."

"Daz's right, though, Danny, what chance did ya stand against him?"

"Ya stickin' up for him, yeah?" Danny asked

"I aiyn't," Mickey answered.

"Fuck me, ya gettin' as bad as him... Ya both bottled it big time," said Danny.

"Ya were like this two weeks ago, remember?" Mickey said. "Yeah, ya spoiled everythin' then too... I've had enough. Every time we go away summat happens, and it usually aiyn't good... Okay, I understand we wanna have a bitta fun but ya ruin everythin'... I mean, what the fuck were ya doin' back there with that coon? He woulda flattened ya with his fuckin' lips if he'd felt up to it like."

"Ah, I can't be dealin' with this shit," Danny said. Yes, he was pissed off – too much criticism for one day.

Danny steamed off in a huff without saying another word.

"Come on, Daz, let's go home," Mickey said

"What, ya just gonna leave him?"

"Dayn't worry, he'll be back."

They caught the train to New Street. The trip back was silent for them both, as neither Darren nor Mickey had any compulsion to speak – it'd been a difficult day, after all.

With the loss, Birmingham City found themselves in a precarious situation near the bottom of the First Division table, which hadn't changed much since the beginning of November. The team hadn't won in the League for nearly three months, and things were becoming desperate. If it hadn't been for Villa's poor performances too, most of the St Andrews faithful would've seen suicide as the only obvious way out to what was becoming a farce on the pitch.

At half ten – before which time Darren had nipped home to change into his Farah's and Slazenger sweatshirt – he walked into the Lounge of The Bantam. Mickey had promised to join him. Nobby was there, and as usual he'd had too much pop already. Bagpuss, at the bar, *Sports Argus* next to him, surveyed his kingdom. After exchanging niceties to Nobby, Darren strolled over to Bagpuss to get the pints in. Next to Bagpuss, like the day turned into night, was Charlie.

"They were takin' the piss today, Daz, weren't they?" Bagpuss said. His face expressed all the agony and passion for his club.

"We're fucked now, Arth – and we've got Chelsea next week, and I can't see us gettin' nothin' from that one."

Bagpuss turned to the back page of the *Sports Argus*:

"Ya right, kid... Mmm... Yeah, it's gonna be tough... We've got Man. Utd, too, on New Year's day – and we aiyn't gonna win that one."

"Can I see the table, Arth?" Darren said. He took the paper and looked: "Both the Albion and the Villa lost, Man. City hammered Coventry... But Leicester won away to Everton."

It didn't matter how many times they analyzed it, or in which way they looked on the other results - a fact was a fact: their team was struggling.

"It's a fuckin' conspiracy if ya ask me," Charlie put in. "Yeah, it's that cunt, Saunders – I dayn't trust the bloke and I never have. Ya'll see how things work with him; he won't be here long, I'm tellin' ya... That ex-Villa snide's the reason we're strugglin'... Get rid of him, I say... Yeah, get rid of him and all our hopes of winnin' some proper silverware might happen like... I reckon down in the fuckin' Villa boardroom that fuckin' Doug Ellis is pissin' himself... I told ya, it's all Villa conspiracy and Saunders is in on it."

"Anyway, Daz," Bagpuss began, ignoring Charlie completely, "how was it down there today – any trouble?"

"Nah, the Old Bill had everythin' sorted. Loadsa them, there were. Not a chance of the rumble."

"D'ya go down with Mickey and that dickhead, Danny?"

"Yeah."

As he said that, Mickey came walking in, dressed to impress as usual with labels on all and everything. He nodded to a few locals – in what was a bit of a Don Corleone entrance – on his way to the bar.

"Daz, Arth, Charlie," Mickey said, welcoming them.

"Where's ya mate, Mickey?" the gaffer asked.

"Somewhere... I dunno."

"Well, I hope he dayn't expect to drink in here tonight – he can piss off somewhere else and leave his trouble there."

"A pint, please," Mickey said.

Tina made an appearance after being in the Smoking Room.

"Did ya collect all them glasses in there and in the Bar, love," Bagpuss asked her.

"Yeah, I've washed 'em already."

She looked at Mickey; this was the best she'd ever seen him dressed, and he was always dressed impeccably.

"Nice sweater, Mickey," she said.

"Yeah, ya shoulda sin us today – we looked like three fuckin' dipsticks," Mickey replied, laughing and looking at Darren.

"Any scuffles down there, lads?" Charlie asked, as usual a fag hanging out from one corner of his crooked mouth.

"Nah, but it was a fuckin' buzz no less," Darren said. "I sorta sussed it there'd be no trouble, and we didn't wanna get nicked anyway."

"Fuck off, Daz, ya were shittin' it. Down in their manor, with a chance to really do some damage, and ya bottled it."

Tina laughed.

"Come on, mate, dayn't be like that, if we'd bin given the runabout I'd have bin well up for it."

"Yeah, like the last time ya were down in east London, I suppose?"

"Anyway, we lost again and it looks more and more likely we'll be playin' the likes of Grimsby and Barnsley again next season," Bagpuss said, resigned to the very fact of it. For someone who always advocated positivity when supporting your team, he was being negative *yet* again.

There was no celebratory mood, so after polishing off a few pints, Darren went home. On the way Lynsey's face jumped out at him in the cold darkness like a firecracker on Chinese New Year. No, there'd be no happy Christmas, he could feel it. An inconvenience, no doubt, yet what was he supposed to do? His bird and his team were suffering and there was nothing he could do about it. She'd been far from his thoughts the whole matchday, though now he couldn't blank her out. She was haunting him.

When he got home his mom was snoozing in front of the telly and his dad had already gone to bed.

"Get up, mom, go to bed." He switched off the telly. "Come on, go to bed," he said again.

She woke up.

"All right, Darren, how are ya – how was the match?"

Sensitive, that one.

"Okay."

"Did ya win?"

"Nah, we lost again."

"Ya tea's in the oven."

"What is it?"

"A Saturday fry. Just do yaself an egg in the pan and heat the bacon and tomato up in the oven,"

His mom went to bed and he ate his reheated food on the kitchen table, still moody and thinking about all the things he was thinking about: the match, Lynsey – and he wondered how it was all going to end. There was still a scalp to get from the Villa scum, and he was adamant one way or another - on his own or with his boys - to do him in.

There was Owen too. Yes, he had too many enemies.

Darren went to bed. And there were dreams again – of Lynsey and the guilt, because they *were* there, and there was no way he could deny it.

32: The War Just Got Dirtier

The next morning Darren woke to the predictable smell of an English fried breakfast, a breakfast his stomach was in no way willing to go through again. He opted for the healthier option of beans on toast.

He'd made his mind up to go to the hospital. A few days had gone by since Darren had been there last and he expected fireworks between him and her family.

On the way, he smoked a load of cigarettes – his nerves were playing with him.

At the hospital Darren found out there was no change in Lynsey's condition, though now she'd been moved to her own room. She was still lying there like she had been for what now seemed like an eternity in time. Lynsey reminded him of a beautiful statue all stiff and lifeless, but with the splendour of a queen. Her looks had completely faded, and she looked nothing like the woman he'd met all those months before.

Luckily, both Christy and Owen were at work, and Lynsey's mom was alone. When they saw each other they were both unable to speak: her anger - which he'd seen from her eyes – struck Darren instantly.

"It's a bit stupid yer bein' here now, Darren."

"Ya think so?"

"Owen wants to ring yer neck, yer bloody fecker."

"And what, I should be scared or summat?"

She looked at him – his arrogance wasn't doing him any good at all.

"I mean, how long's it been since the last time yer were here to see her?"

"I've bin busy."

"Yea', galavantin' off to yer stupid matches."

"I've bin workin' a lot recently."

While they were arguing, going back and forth with their opinions as a ball on a tennis court, Lynsey lay in the bed, an unconscious spectator. If she had had the strength or will of mind, she would've surely intervened.

Darren was even beginning to forget how her voice sounded now.

"So, yer got nothin' to say for yerself, have yer?"

"About football, then, aiyn't it?"

He leaned over Lynsey bed, trying to kiss her.

"Don't bother – yer don't deserve it."

He moved back.

"That's *your* opinion," he said.

"There's too much bad blood between us all now, and I'm sure Christy won't want to look at yer again... And Noel, bless him – he even told me he offered yer a bit of advice... Yea', he offered it and what did yer go and do – exactly what he told yer not to."

"I aiyn't gonna shout in here, Teresa, coz I can't really be bothered-"

"That's the very word," she interrupted, "'bothered' – yer English are always about that... Yer can't be bothered, it's all too much trouble, I've got me life to live and that's it... Well, Darren, yer got it all to come, I'm tellin' yer. Lynsey's a great girl and yer treated her like shite."

"Hold ya fuckin' horses, Teresa, hold on. I've always treated ya daughter with respect, and it'll continue for as long as we're together."

"Yer think me husband, Owen and meself will allow that like?"

"Allow what?"

"Yer won't be with *her*," she said with anger.

"Ya think so?" Darren said in a raised voice, but lower than actually screaming. Darren asked Teresa to move outside the room. He wanted to give her a piece of his mind without disturbing Lynsey. He knew he'd messed everything up – especially with Teresa and Noel, whom he'd considered at least his part-time allies in the feud with the Moriartys.

"I know ya dayn't want me to part of the family," he continued.

"Yer got it in one, Darren."

"But who said I ever wanted to be?"

"The only reason any of us tolerated yer was because Lynsey told us to – there's no other reason."

The truth was all coming out, but he wanted to dig deeper.

"I knew all along it was gonna be like this – d'ya think I'm a fuckin' idiot or summat." He moved to a hair's breadth of her face. "The thing is," he continued, "I didn't wanna rock the boat – it was all for Lynsey's sake."

Nothing would have given him greater pleasure than to smack the diminutive Irish bitch in the gob, but it was only his wish. Lynsey would have disagreed, naturally.

"Go on, hit me like," Teresa said, seeing the brutality expressed in Darren's eyes.

"Ya aiyn't worth it."

"Yea', because yer wouldn't last two minutes... me Owen would see to that."

"Ah, *you* and whose army? Ya son's a fuckin' tool."

"He'll sort yer out all right."

"We'll see about that, ya old fuckin' bitch."

Darren walked off, leaving Teresa open-mouthed from shock.

33: Intoxication with some Danish Gold

After buying eight cans of Special Brew from the offy, Darren went home – he intended to drink himself into oblivion.

He rang Nobby:

"Come over tonight, mate?"

"Nah, it's Sunday. I aiyn't drinkin'," Nobby said.

"Fuck off and get ya arse down here tonight," Darren replied, sighing.

After his Sunday dinner, Darren sat in front of the telly, watching, like always, what his mom wanted to watch. After a while, along with his dad, he fell asleep, only for the annoying baroque jingle of trumpets and *The Antiques Roadshow* end credits to wake him up some time later.

"Are them ya cans in here, Darren?" his mom asked, looking in the fridge.

"Yeah."

She went back into the living room to a snoring husband.

"Leslie, leslie, wake up." She shook him and he opened his eyes. "Leslie, have ya sin what ya son's drinkin' now?"

"Nah, what?" he replied, dazed and groggy from his kip.

"Special Brew – that poison."

"And what d'ya want me to do about it, love? He's a grown man, aiyn't he, he can drink what he likes."

She looked at her hopeless spouse, sighed in resignation, then walked out of the room, only to walk in again a second later.

"I'm puttin' up the Christmas tree tonight... can ya take it down for me from the attic?" she asked.

"Okay, love," her husband said.

Darren sat down again in the living room with his dad while his mom put the kettle on.

"Mom's makin' a cuppa."

"Smashin'... How was the match yesterday, Daz?" This was Leslie's great icebreaker with his son – football.

"It was great," Darren answered, sarcasm blanketing the words.

"Bloody rubbish."

"Nah, crap – we shoulda won."

"The Hammers are flyin' at the minute."

"Yeah, but I can't see it lastin' till Chrimbo."

Darren's dad had been an avid Birmingham City supporter as a younger man, but now he was happier listening to them on a Saturday afternoon on the radio and watching the highlights on *Match of the Day* on the night. He put it down to the changing game, like Stan from the scrapyard. He thought football had lost its charm and skill. The great players: Best, Moore and Gray were no longer around, and 'mediocres' had replaced them, in his words. Leslie hadn't been down to St Andrews since they had sold Trevor Francis in 1979, and had no intention of ever going back there. *What for*, he'd say, *when they can't even hold onto their best players*? He was quite the opposite to Bagpuss – cynical beyond belief and proud of it as he got older.

Cynthia brought the tea out on a tray with two succulent apple pies. This was Darren's utopia.

"Ya aiyn't havin' one, mom?" Darren asked.

"Nah, she's on one of them bloody diets again," his dad said, sniggering.

"Oh, leave it out, Leslie. I told ya not to tell him."

At seven, Nobby came round.

"All right, Nob," Leslie said. He was always pleased to see Darren's best mate.

"Where is he, Les?"

"Upstairs."

Nobby went inside.

"Ready for Christmas, Les?"

"Yeah, we're puttin' the tree up tonight."

"*No*, I'm puttin' the tree up," a voice cried out from the livingroom. It was Cynthia. "Don't tell lies, Leslie."

Nobby laughed and went up to Darren's room.

Darren was lying on his bed.

"Did ya bring some cans with ya, Nob?"

"Nah... I told ya: I'm takin' it easy tonight... I've bin drinkin' too much recently and I'm savin' me dough for Christmas and The Smiths now."

For a moment Darren disappeared, before returning with two cold cans of Special Brew.

"There ya go, mate, get one of them down ya neck."

"I aiyn't drinkin' this shit, if that's what ya think."

"Come on, Nob, dayn't be such a cunt."

Nobby took the can reluctantly, but didn't open it."

"So how's life... how's Lynsey?"

"Ya wouldn't believe it if I told ya," Darren said as he was putting on the *Meat Is Murder* album

"What, she aiyn't died, has she?" Nobby asked, the question embracing sincere anxiety.

"Nah, ya cunt."

"Then what?"

"It's that fucked up family of hers."

"What have they done now?"

"It's a long story."

"Well tell me."

Ttsss, the ring pull went on Darren's can of diesel fuel and white foam from the toxic mixture burst forth. He lapped it up, then took a manly gulp.

"Ah," he exclaimed, "that's summat else." Darren was ready for business.

"So what have they done now?" Nobby asked impatiently.

"Ah, it dayn't matter."

"What, ya had a scrap with her old man or summat?"

Darren laughed, before saying: "Not yet, but it's comin'."

"Well, rather *you* than me, mate."

"What is it about the Irish, Nob?" Darren asked after a moment.

"What d'ya mean?"

"Well, ya Irish so ya should know?"

"I dayn't understand what ya mean?"

"Listen, ya me best mate and have bin since we were kids, and I aiyn't never had no problems with none of ya family... Ya all Irish, so what is it... Why do I have a problem with 'em?"

"Listen, it aiyn't the Irish, it's them like – I dunno, maybe they've a fuckin' chip on their shoulder or summat... Why, what did they say to ya?"

Darren drank three cans opening his heart out, while Nobby, uncharacteristically, listened on, still holding the same unopened Special Brew.

"... and there it is," Darren finished.

"Fuckin' wankers, man."

"Are ya gonna drink that can or just look at it all night?"

"Nah, I aiyn't touchin' it – rocket fuel, that... Let's go down The Bantam for a bit?"

"Nah, I'm deafin' it tonight."

"Ya know ya aiyn't gonna get up for work in the mornin' drinkin' that and at the pace ya are?"

"Dayn't worry about me, mate."

Pissed already, Darren opened yet another can. Feeling thirsty just looking at him, Nobby asked Darren to get him a cold one, as the can in his hand had gone warmish.

"Well, here goes." Nobby took a sip, but it was the kind birds took with their half a lager in a City Centre wine bar on a Thursday night.

"Come on, Nob, dayn't drink like a faggot."

The topic of conversation changed:

"Can't wait for the fuckin' gig in Feb."

"How much is it gonna set ya back again?"

"With the coach and ferry I think I aiyn't gonna have change from a hundred."

"I reckon ya'll spend more."

"I told ya to come."

"Can't afford it."

"It's gonna be the dog's bollocks."

"Bit expensive for me."

"Dayn't give me that shit, Daz – ya probably spend that much at the weekend watchin' that shite."

The Smiths live: Morrissey's voice, Marr's guitar – in your face and LIVE. It sounded tempting, but no; he never wanted to hear another Irish accent in his life if he could help it. And anyway, there was Chelsea on Saturday, then Forest, then Manchester City away. He wanted to go to as many games as his budget would allow – he had to support the lads - that was the most important thing.

By ten, Darren had seen off five cans, and he was now in a world of his own.

"Daz, I'm goin' down The Bantam for the last half hour – are ya comin'?"

No response. Nobby asked him again, but Darren's eyes had closed and he'd fallen back onto his bed. He started snoring. With that, Nobby put the can he'd hardly touched and left, saying goodbye to Darren's parents on the way out.

34: A Lucky Escape

Nobody needed to place a bet on Darren making it to work on time the next day. He strolled in with a massive hangover after lunchtime. Miraculously, he hadn't puked during the night, so he thought he'd be all right at work.

Yam Yam was in the yard when he arrived through the gates talking to Sid, who was in the cab of the crane. As expected, the gaffer did his fruit:

"Where the fuck have yow bin, sleepin' bastard beauty?"

"I overslept."

"Well, blow me, some honesty for a change instead of the usual bullshit."

"Sorry, I had a few drinks, that's all."

"I know, and just for the fuckin' record yow smell like Oliver Reed's aftershave lotion... Big fuckin' bender, was it, mate? *With the lads?*"

"All right, son," Sid said, climbing out of the cab.

"All right, Sid."

Darren was in no mood to work and all he wanted to do was go home to bed.

"Listen, Dave, I can't work today, but I had the decency to come here and tell ya to ya face."

"Give the boy a fuckin' prize." Yam Yam looked at Sid, disbelief in his eyes at what his inebriated worker had just said. The *cheek of it*, he thought "Well, if yow feel like guwin home, go – but dayn't expect yow'll have a job here in the mornin'."

It was like Darren's brain had been scraped by a cheese grater, brutal and uncompromising.

"But I really dayn't feel up for graft today, Dave."

"Yow gow and yow finished, yow hear?"

"I'll take it as holiday."

"Ahr, yow won't."

"Ah, go on, Dave, give him a day off. Ya were never young and overslept coz of a tot?" Sid said, trying to work on the gaffer's compassionate side.

"It's fuckin' lunchtime, Sid, hardly oversleepin'."

And then, surprising even himself, Darren spewed his guts up all over the yard, just missing his feet and trousers. It was a deep amber colour – like the Special Brew he'd drunk so greedily the night before – laced with the usual concoction of chopped carrots and an assortment of other vegetables, the vestige of his Sunday dinner. The smell made the odour from a rubbish tip on the slum streets of Calcutta seem like a fragrance created by Coco Chanel.

"Pissin' 'ell, Daz," Yam Yam exclaimed.

Darren retched and wanted to puke again, which he then did in three short - but quick - bursts, followed by two more smaller ones of watery bile. It was only after this that the headache really kicked in, a throbbing nightmare of unimaginable proportions, made worse from the acidic aftertaste in his mouth left from the puke.

"Look at yow," the gaffer went on, "have yow no shame?"

"Let him go home," said Sid.

"Piss off, gow on," Yam Yam uttered.

"I'm sorry," Darren muttered, spitting out the excess pieces of finely chopped meat and greens from his old lady's kitchen.

"Ahr, and it gets docked from this week's wages, all rioght?"

Darren looked up, his face whiter than the giant marshmellow man's from the film *Ghostbusters*.

"Ah, dayn't worry, Dave, I aiyn't drinkin' again, that was the last time, I swear."

The way home on the bus was awful – worse than the way there, when the onset of a bad stomach was only just kicking in.

The indescribable smell of the West Midland Travel bus didn't help him either, and he only got relief when he stepped off at his bus stop, the cold but refreshing December air replacing the enclosed mugginess of stale fags, spliffs, alcohol and diesel fuel.

At home, after taking a couple of painkillers, he went straight to bed, not waking until the late afternoon, when he felt hungry.

"Where have ya bin?" his mom asked as he was coming down the stairs in his Birmingham City Patrick replica home shirt from the season before, emblazoned with the sponsor ANSELLS, a Midland's brewery, on the front, yellow y-fronts, and his left hand conspicuously inside them scratching his balls.

"I had half a day off – hangover."

"I told ya about drinkin' them Special Brews, didn't I? I remember ya uncle was the same, Special Brew or Breakers seven days a week."

"Leave it out, mom... Anyway, what's for tea?"

"Faggots."

"Ah, wicked."

Darren went into the kitchen and poured himself a pint glass full of orange squash, as dehydration had set in and his mouth was drier than a desert in a drought, before going back into the living room where he switched on the telly.

"And get yaself dressed, Darren, walkin' round half-naked in front of ya mother – ya should be ashamed of yaself coz it's disgustin'."

Moaning, Darren went upstairs and slipped into a pair of shorts, then straight back down again. *Blockbusters* was on – not his favourite thing on telly but it'd have to do. He still had a slight tingling in his head, though nothing that Mr Brains and his delicious faggots couldn't deal with.

Not being the smartest bloke when it came to intellectual pursuits, Darren had had enough of Bob Holness after five minutes when he failed to get: *What V is a river in European Russia?; and, What G is a city in Virginia where President Abraham Lincoln gave his famous address? Yeah, they could answer 'em*, he thought – but they were your middle and upper class twits, the cream of the crop and moneyed, getting something from university that they couldn't supposedly get anywhere else. Well, he could've given them a lesson or two, so he thought.

On Central *Crossroads* was on, but again after a few minutes of cheap sets and diabolical acting by plastic Brummies he switched off the telly completely.

His old man walked in the door from work punctually, and his tea was ready for him on the table. How his mom managed to do it Darren didn't know – he'd once put it down to telepathy, but it'd been that way ever since he could remember.

"He wasn't at work today, Leslie," Darren's mom said.

"Is that right, son?"

"What did ya go in for if ya had a hangover?" his mom asked him.

"Dunno."

"Bollocks," his dad said.

"Watch ya language, *Leslie* – not at the table."

"All right, love, sorry," he responded.

"And how's Lynsey, love?"

"Wrong question."

"Why, has summat terrible happened?" She gasped and her tone was grave, in line with her son's attitude towards the topic.

"Yeah, summat like that."

"Tell me then... Is she worse? Did she get a donor?"

Darren wanted to open up, yet he didn't want the third degree from them.

"Nah, it's nothin'."

"What d'ya mean, *it's nothin'*?"

His old man was munching away, oblivious to everything but the food on his plate. Darren was silent. He didn't want to give up the ghost. She asked again.

"Nothin'."

"Darren Acheson, ya'll tell me what's goin' on with that sweet little creature right this minute."

No, he wouldn't, so he blanked her out – it'd be too much trouble otherwise.

In no time at all Darren had cleaned his plate, and feeling much better after a decent meal, he went inside again to put his feet up and relax in front of the telly.

"Hey, Daz, ya mother wants ya to wash up?"

Darren was in his own world, looking at the newly decorated tree. The lights, different colours and flashing on and off, attracted him, and he couldn't stop staring at them.

His old man repeated himself, this time his son heard him.

"Nah, I aiyn't doin' it... I'm sick and knackered."

Five minutes later his mom walked in with a cup of tea.

"Ya can make ya own – ya didn't wash up for me," Cynthia said.

"But *mommy* dearest, I'm sick."

She was there to commandeer the box for the night. Darren had to leave, otherwise it'd be a night of *Coronation Street* and *Brookside,* and that was a big NO for him.

He went upstairs to his bedroom and lay down. From time to time he'd gaze out of the window, admiring the Christmas decorations and lights in the neighbours' windows.

It started snowing, the heaviest shower that Birmingham had had that winter. For a while, Darren just watched it fall, more and more, until there was a thick layer on the ground. In the mood for some music, he switched on his clock radio instead of his record player. At once Shakin' Stevens' voice flew out from the tiny speaker with *Merry Christmas Everybody.* Christmas was here, at least for the Welsh Elvis.

When that song finished, Grace Jones' *Slave to the Rhythm* came on, bringing a wry smile to Darren's face from the memories of the woman's bumping and grinding in the pub. He thought about The Bantam with all its crazy characters: Bagpuss, Charlie, Jack Delcourt, the seventy-five- year-old ladies' man; Pete, RIP, killed walking into an open manhole on the way home after an all-dayer there. These were only some of the many people.

"Darren, Nobby's on the phone!" his dad called out from the bottom of the stairs, like he always did, a classic case of lazyitus.

Darren went downstairs, and took the phone outside to the hall through force of habit:

"All right, mate, what d'ya want?"

"Ya smarmy bastard, ya know what I want."

"I dunno what ya goin' on about."

"How's ya head?"

"Top notch, son," Darren answered sardonically.

"Ya dayn't make it, then?"

"Make what?"

"Work?"

"I did, actually, but I was well hungover and told the gaffer I wanted the day off."

"Ya winged it?"

"Yeah."

"I told ya not to drink that stuff."

"I know, but anyway, what d'ya want?"

"I was wonderin' if ya wanted to come down The Bantam?"

"Nah."

"All right, dayn't bother then."

"Are ya goin' down on ya tod?"

"Dunno."

"Ah, it's a Monday - it'll be shit in there anywhere."

"Have ya sin the snow outside?" Nobby then said after a pause, his tone naive and full of the nostalgia of his childhood.

"Yeah, it's settlin' too."

"I think we're gonna have a white Christmas."

"Dayn't count on it," Darren replied, deflating his best mate's dreams.

35: Christmas Presents and the Nightmare of '82

When his alarm clock went off the following morning, Darren was up like a shot, and within half an hour was at the gates of the yard. Because it was early, nobody was in, so he had to wait for nearly an hour until Sid arrived to open up. Meanwhile, in the snow, which was deep to the ankle, Darren had time to do some thinking. He wanted to see Lynsey again but knew it would cause more trouble than it was worth. Her family had pushed him to the edge and they'd achieved what they'd set out to do: alienate him from Lynsey. He didn't know how she was and it worried him. Nobby and his mom had feared the worst the day before, but their assumption hadn't been as stupid as he'd thought. It was cancer, and cancer killed people. *What if she was already dead, a corpse, cold and alone in the hospital morgue?* He didn't want to think about it. Darren turned his thoughts to other things.

It was Chelsea on Saturday, a game they would have to win if they wanted to see themselves climb out of the relegation zone. Aston Villa was two points ahead of them on nineteen points, and Villa was playing QPR in the evening away. The London team was mid-table and the pundits favoured them for the win. Darren hoped and prayed for it: a Villa defeat was almost as good as his own team winning.

Yes, the Headhunters would be in Birmingham. The Zulus who weren't already in hiding from the Old Bill would be waiting for them, and if there weren't any Zulus, the Junior Business Bovver Boys would be up for the scuffle. These young lads would have to be on the top of their game. The Headhunters were brutal and had taken the end of many home grounds in the past. Darren hoped that Mickey and Danny didn't have any ideas for a tear up, because he had his own plans for one of them, *or maybe two.*

First of all there was Owen – that thorn in his side – who he wanted to bash up more than anyone. Darren knew sooner or later he'd come face to face with him and that they'd end up at it - the English lion versus the Irish Wolfhound.

The other bloke, the Villa scum, was a trickier proposition. If he wanted to take him out, he'd have to go to him – take it all to his manor or go back into town and find him there. He wasn't sure if Mickey would back him up, so he'd do everything on his own. And anyway, Darren could look after himself, or so he thought.

He worked his socks off the whole day; Yam Yam was ever watchful and Darren was paranoid he'd lose his job if he put another foot wrong. Luckily, the gaffer didn't say a word to him and the day went by quickly enough. At the end of it, Darren decided to go into town to buy his Christmas presents: one for Lynsey, one each for his mom, dad, his aunt Vera and uncle Des, as they'd probably be down for Christmas dinner. All his grandparents had died years before sadly, but it cut down on the cost of presents, so that was okay.

Darren didn't know what to buy Lynsey. It'd been the same for her birthday in August. Because he had been short of dough then, he'd just taken her to the pictures to see *Fright Night*, a film Darren had enjoyed but Lynsey had hated, and then afterwards for a 'romantic' meal at McDonald's

Fright Night was Darren's all-time favourite film. Its tacky formula of vampires that hated crosses and garlic was a throwback to the era of Bela Lugosi, one of Darren's heroes. The special effects weren't its strength, either. The vampires' fangs looked like they were made of rubber, and the facial appliances looked as real as a Denis Thatcher smile.

Lynsey had complained all the way through the film; she'd wanted to see *The Bride* with Sting, a drama about Frankenstein. In McDonald's after the film she gave her opinion on Darren's choice in no uncertain terms:

"It was me birthday, Daz, and we saw what ya wanted to see – why are ya so selfish?"

He looked at her before taking a bite of his burger.

"But wasn't Jerry Dandridge great?" he said, munching away.

"Well, he is handsome – what's the actor's name?"

"Chris Sarandon."

"Yeah, he's gorgeous."

"Well, I really enjoyed it. I aiyn't sin summat like that in ages. Some of them birds he was killin' were sexy like... Did ya see the disco scene, pure class, that."

"It was cheesy."

"Why?"

"There was no sense to it."

"It's only a film, Lynz, dayn't get all serious about it."

"Well, I didn't like it."

"What about Evil Ed... 'Oh, you're so cool, Brewster... The master will kill you for this, but not quickly, no, slowly, so slowly," Darren said, laughing his bollocks off and mimicking the voice of the character.

His self-centred behaviour back then had disappointed her, and now Darren wanted to make up for it by buying her a nice present.

It was still a week before Christmas and the shops weren't too busy – just how Darren liked it. He bought his parents' presents first: some perfume for his mom and a Perry Como album for his dad. Then it was his aunt and uncle's turn, before he only had Lynsey's to buy. He'd thought about perfume too, but didn't have the money for the one he wanted to get her, so in the end – after much humming and ahing - he went for a nine-carat gold necklace and matching earrings, which cost him just over a tenner.

As he was in town, Darren decided to stop by for a tot in the Yard of Ale. Although still nervous about what had happened to him in the summer, he thought he'd be all right in there because it was generally a pub full of locals and not your football headbangers after a fight. It was only two pints, in the end, but they'd put him in a good mood. He knew how it was: one, and he wanted a second; two, and he felt warm, sort of one with himself; three, mind you, and he was slowly losing his fight with intoxication, but not quite – anymore than that and he was well on his way to getting pissed up and whatever else would follow.

When he got home after ten, his old man had some bad news for him:

"The Villa won," his dad said.

"Ya jokin'?"

"Nah – one-nil."

"Who scored?"

"Dunno... I just heard on the radio."

"For fuck's sake."

"Ya tea's in the oven, Daz."

Darren went up to his room to put his presents away. The result made him feel sick and gave the Villa a five point lead on them, making the Chelsea game on Saturday all the more important.

"Did ya buy some wrappin' paper yet, mom?" Darren asked.

"Yeah, it's in a bag under the stairs."

"What did ya buy Lynsey, love?"

Darren showed her Lynsey's present.

"What d'ya think, mom?" he asked, valuing a woman's opinion.

"It's lovely, son."

"I got dad an album."

"Which one?"

"Perry Como."

"Oh, he'll like that."

He went to bed – all he could think about was the claret and blue climbing up a ladder, leaving the Blues below them in their wake. If they were going to be relegated, he wanted them down there with him and his team. He was sick to death of all the taunting that had been going on for years. One of the worst days of his life had been the 26th May 1982, the day the enemy won the European Cup. It was even worse than the year before when they'd won the League title. Yes, that was the pinnacle of football – only the World Cup could compete with it. He'd watched it at home with his old man, and for those ninety minutes they had been Krauts – a strange fact indeed for the Achesons, as Leslie father had been in a German POW camp during the Second World War. That was how much Darren hated Aston Villa. Peter Withe's sixty-seventh minute winner and the final whistle were moments that he'd live with for the rest of his life. At the time nothing compared to it in terms of heartache, but three short years later that belief was crushed.

Darren fell asleep and dreamt the Rampant Lion was pissing all over St Andrews.

36: The Knockout

Wednesday went by quickly, and when he got home Darren ate his tea and had a bath. Twenty minutes later he was ready to go out to The Bantam.

All the crowd was in there, that was no surprise, and Nobby was already drunk *again*.

"Hey, Arth, how was it with that bird?" Darren asked.

"Yeah, it went great like."

"What did ya go and see in the end?"

"*Rocky*."

"Was it good?"

"Yeah, it was okay."

"I'll probably go and see it after Christmas... Are ya goin' out with her again?"

"Yeah, probably... Aiyn't shagged it yet, though, so I'll have to, won't I?" Bagpuss said with a laugh.

"So *Rocky IV's* good?"

"It aiyn't like the first two but better than the last one – that was crap."

Nobby came over to the bar.

"Pint, Nob?" Darren asked.

"Yeah, go on then."

"D'ya wanna pint, Charlie?"

"Nah, I'm all right there, Daz... but thanks anyway, mate."

"How's the girlfriend anyway?" Bagpuss asked awkwardly. "Sorry I aiyn't really mentioned it much but it's a bit difficult for me to talk about, ya know what I mean?"

"Yeah, it's all right, I understand." Darren sighed. "It aiyn't lookin' good, ya know? She's in a coma still and the doctors know fuck all."

"But surely they know what's goin' on?"

"Her parents dayn't even have the foggiest."

"But did she have the operation?"

"Listen," Darren then began, somewhat abruptly, irritated, "to tell ya the truth I dunno what the fuck's goin' on or what they're doin' to her or nothin'. Her parents have bin keepin' everythin' from me."

"What for?"

"Fuck knows, mate... I was just talkin' to Nobby on Sunday night about it."

Bagpuss ranted on for a bit, until he got a phone call out the back and left. Five minutes later he returned and there was another topic of conversation on his tongue:

"Fuckin' Villa won, then, didn't they?"

"They're pullin' away a bit now, ya know what I mean like," Darren replied.

"And that puts the pressure on us for Saturday's game."

"Difficult one, that," Charlie commented, only his second sentence of the whole night.

"Ah, we'll win it."

"Come on, Arth, but where are the goals gonna come from?" Charlie said.

For Nobby it was like watching paint dry listening to Charlie, so he went over to chat to Dennis, which was like watching paint dry.

"How are ya, Dennis?" Nobby asked.

"I aiyn't too bad."

"Any winners today?"

"Nah."

"Yesterday?"

"Nah."

"So nothin' then?"

"Won on a horse at Chepstow a few days ago... a fiver I put on at 12/1."

"That was all right then..."

Mickey and Danny walked in.

"Are ya gonna cause fuckin' trouble tonight, mate?" Bagpuss warned Danny.

Danny, untypical of him, had his head low in shame as he walked up to the bar.

"I'm sorry, Arth, it won't happen again, I swear," he said.

"What d'ya say to him?" Bagpuss asked Mickey

"Nah, it's all sorted, Arth – *aiyn't it*, Danny?" Mickey said, smiling.

"Yeah, there aiyn't gonna be no more trouble, I swear."

"Well, all right, but if there's gonna be, ya out on ya arse... Okay, gentlemen, what can I get for ya?"

Nobby saw that Danny was in the pub and looked over to Darren, nodding his head, pissed off his enemy was within breathing distance.

"Long time *no* see, Danny – where the hell d'ya fuck off to down in London?" Darren asked.

"I caught the last train home."

"And what were ya doin' in London in the meantime?"

"Ah, ya know how it is... Lookin' round, stuff like that."

The lads got the pints in and they talked about the match on Saturday:

"So, are we all up for it then?" Mickey began, clasping his hands in anticipation.

"Yeah, it'll be an important game for us."

"More than that, Daz, it's fuckin' crucial, mate... But the match's summat else, what about the Headhunters?"

Darren was hoping that the topic wouldn't be brought up, but now it had.

"Listen, Mickey, what d'ya want? I dayn't understand all this shit with violence... I mean what, we go to the games every week and nothin' ever happens – which I'm happy about, but it's all this talk about it, ya know?"

Mickey and Danny were surprised by their mate's attitude. They knew already he was a bit of a pussy, though now they were sure he was nothing else.

"Daz, if ya dayn't wanna come with us, then fuck it... Go on ya own and mix it with the anoraks if ya wanna," Mickey said.

"Hey, ya bein' unfair now, I never said nothin' about not goin', it's just all this talk of doin' things and smackin' some bloke in the face – it's all bullshit really, aiyn't it? We dayn't have no intention – when was the last time I saw ya give it to someone – and *you* for that matter, Danny?"

Darren was treading on dangerous ground; they were embarrassed and it was a good job they were alone in the corner, away from ears.

"Fuck off," Danny said, insulted.

"Yeah, if ya wanna criticize someone, criticize ya fuckin' self... I mean, what's the story with ya girlfriend... I've heard from people ya can't even be bothered to see her?" Mickey said.

"And who'd ya hear that from?"

"It dayn't matter, but if ya wanna get all personal then I'm okay with it," Mickey went on.

"Okay, okay, fair enough, if ya wanna be like that, be like that... Some kind of hooligan, are ya, a *casual*? Then why the fuck aiyn't ya in with 'em then?"

"Dayn't be like that," Mickey said, looking at Danny, "it's outta order... Ya know I was part of the Zulus ages ago-"

"Bullshit, ya aiyn't never bin," Darren interrupted.

"Yeah I was, wasn't I, Danny?"

"Yeah."

Whatever he'd done or hadn't done, it didn't matter really; what mattered was Darren had crossed the line, a line he couldn't crawl back across from.

"And what, ya were in with all of 'em in Sara Moon's and on the Ramp – coz I think it's all bollocks."

"Are ya fucked up or what, Daz?" Mickey asked. His was now sat up in his chair in a more defensive position, like he was on a terrace on a Saturday afternoon.

"But it's a fact. I know a few lads in Dale End and on the Ramp and they know nothin' of ya – ya a fuckin' liar."

"Ya better fuck off now, before it bangs off in here... ya know what I mean?"

Darren smiled. He wasn't afraid, in fact, he was loving it. Did he have any ground to say what he'd said? Did he know such blokes or was it just for his own enjoyment and to crank up Mickey, the coolest customer he'd ever known?

Nobby walked over, hearing that things were a little heated; Bagpuss too, though he hadn't opened his mouth yet.

"All right, lads," Nobby said, "Everythin' okay here?"

"Just fuck off, Nobby," Danny said in a threatening tone.

It was two versus two now.

Something had gone inside Darren but he didn't know what it was. One minute he was okay, and the next, well, he'd cracked. There were too many things going on in his life and he seemed to be all confused.

"And ya can leave him alone, Danny, know what I mean..." Darren said, defending his best friend.

Darren didn't even see it coming – it was like he'd been struck by the hammer of Thor. He was down on the floor and dazed. Although still conscious, he was blurry-eyed and his head was throbbing. The taste of blood was in his mouth, and it felt like he'd lost a tooth or two. He could hear screams and shouts.

And then the voices died down and all was quiet.

A chubby-faced bloke was in front of him, but he was still somewhere between consciousness and unconsciousness, and had difficulty making out whose face it was.

"Daz, Daz, wake up, mate."

The bloke called out another few times.

Darren was tired and wanted to fall asleep.

"Hey, Daz, nah, dayn't go, dayn't go," the voice said. "Daz, mate, are ya all right?"

And then it clicked: it was Bagpuss.

The paramedics came and sorted him out. Darren had a concussion from banging his head on the floor – a floor that was luckily carpeted. He'd also broken one of his front teeth and another at the back was loose. The ambulance, with Nobby in tow, sent him to A&E to get himself sorted out and a copper came to question him.

"I've got a few questions for you, sir?"

Darren's headache was equal in fury to Monday morning's, and he was in no mood to talk, especially to the Old Bill.

"I feel sick." He vomited into a bucket beside him.

"Okay, but I'll be back later, sir... Have you informed someone of your whereabouts, sir? Parents, a spouse?"

"Nah."

"Your friend's here – can I get him to call someone?"

"Which mate?"

"Patrick Clark."

"Ah, *Nobby* - can ya send him in?"

A few hours later Darren was back at home in his comfortable bed. The doctor had ordered him to spend a few days at home. Rest was important for him now.

The policeman had questioned him before he left the hospital about what had happened. Danny had lamped him one and the police wanted Darren to press charges. Darren didn't want to. He wasn't a grass, so he put it down to boyish immaturity. And that was that – or was it?

"Ya gotta stay at home for a few days, love," his mom said, bringing him a cuppa.

"I can't, mom. I've gotta go to work - the gaffer will do his nut if I dayn't go in."

"Dayn't worry about him - ya got a doctor's note, so he can't do nothin'."

37: Pat Nevin I Hate You

Darren spent all Thursday and Friday in bed, from time to time getting up to go to the toilet or eat something, though he really didn't have an appetite. Looking in the mirror, he saw the gap where his tooth had been. He looked a right prat, or so he thought. Whatever would Lynsey think of him now?

On the Thursday night Nobby came to visit him.

"How are ya, mate?"

"Me head's spinnin' still."

"Fuck me, he planted a right punch on ya."

"And what happened next?" Darren was still unsure what transpired after he'd been smacked.

"I went for Danny but before he could land one on me Mickey got stuck in."

"And Bagpuss?"

"Bagpuss steamed in. Danny's bin fucked off, of course... He's gone – at least for as long as Arth has the pub. He won't be allowed back in there again."

"Jesus, I didn't even know why he did it."

He was lying through his teeth. It was all a wind up and Darren was as much to blame as Danny.

"Well it dayn't matter anyway – it's all sorted now."

"What about Mickey?"

"Ah, Mickey's as bad as that fuckin' cunt."

Darren wanted to go to the Chelsea game, but he didn't feel up to it. He'd give it a miss, and listen to the match on the radio.

At three on Saturday afternoon he was lying on his bed and listening to the commentary. The announcer called out the line ups: For Birmingham: Seaman, Ranson, Roberts, Wright, Hagan, Kuhl, Bremner, Rees, Kennedy, Dicks, Jones; for Chelsea: Niedzwiecki, Wood, Rougvie, Pates, McLaughlin, Bumstead, Nevin, Spackman, Dixon, McAllister, Murphy.

For ninety minutes Darren was tense, just like all supporters were at this time around the country, either on the terraces or with a radio against their ears. Chelsea needed the win as much as Birmingham did to strengthen their title challenge: they were eight points off Manchester Utd in first place and were determined to keep the pressure on them, Liverpool and West Ham, in second and third places respectively.

The first half ended with Darren's team one-nil down, thanks to a Hagan own goal. It was looking bad, but Darren hadn't given up hope, even though Chelsea's nippy Scottish winger, Pat Nevin, was running them ragged with his dribbling.

"What's the score, Daz?" his old man said, popping his head round the door.

"Dayn't even ask me."

The second half began brightly for the home team, with Julian Dicks coming close on one occasion with a sweet left footer. Birmingham was setting the pace, but without a goal it was all for nothing. Faith was restored in the eighty-first minute when Platnauer put one in the back of the net to level the score. Darren jumped up, fists in the air. Seven minutes later, however, and with the final whistle looming, the trickster Nevin scored, deflating Darren and the whole Bluenose nation.

They'd lost two-one. Another match without a point. Things were looking bad.

Darren went downstairs.

"We lost, dad."

"Yeah, I know."

"That Saunders has to go... That bastard Nevin... I'll kill the little Scotch cunt... I hate Scottish people."

"Saunders has to go and so do most of them players like, but dayn't be slaggin' off Nevin – he's pure class, son."

"It's gonna kick off now outside the ground big time, that's for sure."

Final Score was about to start on *Grandstand* and Darren was on the settee with his feet up.

"Wanna cuppa, Daz?" his dad asked.

"Yeah, go on then."

Len Martin's distinctive voice read out the results from the day's matches:

Birmingham City 1 – 2 Chelsea
Coventry City 1 – 3 Everton
Liverpool 1 – 1 Newcastle Utd
Luton Town 0 – 0 West Ham Utd
Manchester Utd 0 – 1 Arsenal
Sheffield Wednesday 3 – 2 Manchester City
Tottenham Hotspur 2 – 0 Ipswich Town

Birmingham City was still third from bottom on seventeen points. Ipswich had lost to Spurs and was two points behind them. West Brom, at the bottom, was playing the following day at home to Watford, but Darren wasn't really worried about the Baggies anyway.

"One of ya 'football' mates, was it?" Darren's mom asked him and the dinner table.

"What of it?"

"Didn't I tell ya, Leslie, about them hooligans he has for mates down there?"

His old man looked on, indifferent as usual.

"Just leave it out, mom."

"And what - see me only child go to hospital time and time again?"

"It was a one off."

"A one off, yeah, a one off all right – the next time I'll find ya in a coffin."

"Leave it out, love. Daz's told ya what happened."

After tea Darren went upstairs to his bedroom. He wanted to be alone. It'd been a hard few days and he was tired.

Although he knew in some strange way he'd deserved to get a smack, he couldn't believe Danny had actually done it. Bang, flash and he was gone, on the deck and sparked out. Danny was a hard cunt – all the talk was true.

He heard footsteps coming up the stairs that didn't belong to either his mom or dad.

"All right, mate?" Nobby said.

"Ah, come in, mate," Darren replied cheerfully.

"Jesus, what a night."

"Ya tellin' me."

"He lamped ya well hard. Have ya still got a headache?"

"Nah, it's all right now like," Darren said, rubbing his head just to check.

"Can't believe he did it."

"He's a cunt."

They talked. Nobby was still trying to persuade him about The Smiths concert, but Darren was having none of it. He'd see them in the future – there was all the time in the world for that, and he wasn't in a rush. It was more embarrassing than anything else, though: he'd lost a tooth and his face was swollen. When he'd first met Lynsey, she'd said to him how handsome he was. He couldn't say that about himself now.

As he was talking to Nobby, Darren had an epiphany, a vision of pure elucidation – it wasn't obvious at first, because it was something that had been with him since he could remember: Football was at the route of all his troubles, and no matter how much he loved it, it was the case. His problems with Lynsey and her family; doing badly at school; the agony caused by being a Birmingham City supporter; and finally, the previous night's action in The Bantam.

But he wanted to fight all that, and momentarily he returned to that summer day fifteen years before, to the day he'd fallen in love with the game. It was just another ordinary date for many – even for most of the supporters on the terraces of St Andrews – but not for him. That day had been the beginning of his football adventure. Little did he know at the time that the date, 15th August 1970, would start everything.

Since he could remember, from August to May, Birmingham City had been the tipping point for his weekends.

But why? This was the question he was now asking himself.

"It's a proper fuck up, Nob."

"What?"

"Everythin' – this football lark, ya know?"

"Nah." His best mate was at a loss to what he meant "I think he hit ya too hard."

"I'm serious – it's all bin a kick in the teeth."

"Ya mean *literally*, I suppose?" Nobby said, smirking.

Darren smiled, then opened his mouth, revealing the black hole made by his missing tooth.

"Are ya goin' to the dentist with that or not?" Nobby continued.

"Yeah, mate, I can really see the NHS bein' able to fix this for me."

"Are ya gonna do summat about Danny?"

"What d'ya mean?" he replied, putting his little pinky in the hole. It was painful.

"Are ya gonna get the cunt?"

Of course Darren wanted to, but actions spoke louder than words.

"We'll see."

"That means 'no', does it?"

"But what d'ya expect me to do?" he replied, irritated. "Fight him all on me tod? Have ya sin the size of him?"

"Go on then, bottle it."

He knew Nobby had a point, though he believed it senseless to have a go at Danny – what for, to have the same happen again? It was impossible he now had three enemies - hiring a bounty hunter like Boba Fett from *Stars Wars* seemed a better idea than going it alone.

"It's okay for *you* – ya dayn't have a care in the world."

"And what's that supposed to mean?" asked Nobby.

"Ya know all right."

Nobby looked at Darren viciously, before saying:

"Ya dayn't even know, ya fuckin' prat... who's livin' it up all cushty and shit with their mom and dad, heh?"

"I am, I know... but what's the problem?"

"There aiyn't no problem other than ya givin' me the bullshit."

"How?"

"By sayin' I have an easy life – how do I have it easy, Daz?"

"Ya do."

"I live alone, *remember*? I have to do everythin' meself – iron, cook – all them things that I fuckin' detest."

Darren looked at his mate's grey sweater: wrinkled to the max and with visible stains – from food, probably – down the front of it.

"I can tell ya do all that – and ya better tell ya old lady to iron ya shirt, know what I mean like?"

Sarcasm, it was always the perfect retort, and beat violence hands down.

Nobby left, leaving a little bad blood between them, which was okay for Darren because he knew everything would be okay in the end.

Darren was making enemies more successfully than a Communist guest at a dinner party at Senator Joseph McCarthy's home, and he was well aware he couldn't make any more if he wanted a violence-free life.

38: Erin Go Bragh

None of the doctors could explain Lynsey's condition to her family. They were flummoxed in a word. She was weak now and there was no sign of her coming out of the coma. Whatever it was, though, her family refused to give up and with their faith in God they believed she would pull through. Only Christy had problems. All the medical-speak the doctors had subjected him to over the weeks had brought him into the depths of melancholia.

Nobody wanted to speak over the dinner table, but Christy more so than anyone else. His bad dreams had become more frequent, and so, too, had the regularity of his sleep, down on some days to one or two hours, which had made everyday functioning difficult. Work had become unbearable as well, and most of the time if he wasn't moping around the house he was down the pub – but not his local, no - there'd have been too much cause for conversation down there, and that was the last thing he wanted. It was usually a pub where nobody knew him, sometimes in Sparkbrook, at other times in Balsall Heath, anywhere really where he'd be left alone to drink and think about how much his life was fragmenting.

"Eat up, Christy," his wife said. He looked at her coldly. "It'll do yer no good just starin' at it, like... Yer haven't even touched yer spuds."

"I'm not hungry, woman."

"But yer haven't eaten a thing."

"Would yer ever give yer mouth a rest and shut up."

"Eat somethin' and I will."

"Feck off, and leave me alone."

He got up and left the kitchen.

Their relationship was becoming more and more strained by the day. Her husband had always been a very strong man – in both a mental and a physical sense – and his recent introspection, untypical for a country man from Kerry known for their garrulousness, distressed her.

"Just leave him, mom," Owen said a second after he'd gone.

"But he's hardly said a word to me in three weeks – what d'yer expect? I'm sufferin' as well, yer know."

"It's just his way of dealin' with it."

"Well, I wish it wasn't.

Every night they were usually at the hospital, though tonight was an exception. They needed a break to do their minds some good. Christy had gone to bed straight after dinner – they were sleeping separately now – and Owen and Noel were downstairs watching telly in the living room. Teresa had gone to visit a neighbour. Thursdays were usually good on the television but neither brother was paying any attention to *Top of the Pops*.

In the Moriarty home – like the Achesons' – the television was an integral part of life, and created the atmosphere in their three-bedroom semi-detached: whether you were watching it or not wasn't important, but it was important that it was switched on at least, otherwise the living room would be a gloomy place and people would have to do the unthinkable: talk to each other.

In the past the two brothers had got along, but not anymore. Now they clearly had different agendas.

"Turn over," Owen ordered his brother.

"I was in here first, fuck off."

Noel had put him straight or so he thought.

"Gis the remote."

"Piss off."

"Go on."

"Spin on it."

Noel knew about Owen's temper, because his face had been at the end of Owen's fist on numerous occasions, and now he was testing him again, seeing whether he could crank him up, partly to soothe his own frustrations at his sister's ordeal. He'd expected a smack, though it didn't come.

"Stop actin' the goat," Owen said, his tone soft and genteel, unlike the usual expletives of a Brummie tradesman.

"Here, have the thing. I'm goin' upstairs," Noel said.

The two brothers were sharing Owen's room now on a temporary basis, since their dad was sleeping in Noel's room.

Owen was still thinking about Darren. It was a constant. He'd been trying to get rid of him from his thoughts, but it had been impossible, and he'd given up. In some way – even at great pain to himself – he wanted some comeback.

Every complex, every expression of hatred, had its root in something, and Owen's had stemmed from 1974 and the *Birmingham Pub Bombings*. It'd been a shock to the whole city with twenty one innocent people killed and countless injured. The later conviction of the six Irishmen of the bombings, known as *The Birmingham Six*, created a backlash for the Irish community in Birmingham that was still being felt in small ripples eleven years after it had happened. Immediately after the bombings any person with an Irish accent had been at risk to verbal and physical attack. A man in Yardley had once confronted Christy in December 1974, not long after the bombings. He'd been doing a job on a house next door for a Jewish couple.

"Ya doin' the roof, aiyn't ya?" the bloke asked. He was in his forties, big and stocky and covered in tattoos.

"Yea', big job 'tis to."

"Ya a Paddy, aiyn't ya?"

"Irish if that's what yer mean?"

"Nah, ya a fuckin' potato-eatin' Mick," the big man said.

Christy had never been one to shy away from a potential fight, particularly with your bully-types, but he'd wanted to get the job done and over with as quickly as possible as the couple were paying him good money and Christmas was approaching, so Christy just ignored him.

Later, inside with Mr and Mrs Lieberman, a childless pair in their fifties originally from Czechoslovakia, Christy had spoken about their jingoistic neighbour.

"Don't mind him, Mr Moriarty, we've had it from that family for the last ten years," Mr Lieberman said.

"Don't exaggerate, Avi," his wife put in.

"No, Mr Forest's specific: he doesn't like foreigners," Mr Lieberman poured more tea into Christy's cup. "It's up to him, really, but I do feel sorrow for him – hate, it's such a bad thing."

Although he'd experienced the racism from the English first hand in the late 1940s and 1950s, Christy had taken it all in his stride – then there had been work to be had in England, more so than in his hometown of Glencar, County Kerry, so he'd tolerated it. But with Mr Forest, something had changed in him, and he couldn't understand why or how a man could judge another human being on the way they spoke or from where they were born.

"It's over the bombings," Mrs Lieberman said.

"That's what I was thinkin' like."

"It's a witch hunt, that's all I know, like with us during the War... Remember, dear?" Mr Lieberman said

"Avi, you're doing it again – *exaggerating.*"

"I blame the papers," Mr Lieberman went on in his good but heavily-accented English. "The British press have been able to say what they like and it's damaged the image of the Irish in this country."

"And what – it's *my* fault?" said Christy.

"It seems according to Mr Forest and many other English people it is, Mr Moriarty," Mrs Lieberman said.

Back when Christy had been a young man in Ireland, he'd been naïve about all things political. An avid Gaelic footballer who'd had dreams of representing The Kingdom in the GAA, he'd always been more interested in that and a pint than what the politicians in Dublin had had to say.

"Well, Mr and Mrs Lieberman, I'll tell yer now like, the fella's lucky I was in a good mood, otherwise I'd have boxed his ears off."

It hadn't been just the Irish born who'd caught the flack following on from the bombings, but their children too. One incident, germane and at the root of Owen's enmity to all things English, had occurred on the first day of school, 1975. He'd been in his fifth and final year.

It was lunchtime, and the pupils were in the playground messing around. A new boy had started, a boy Owen would never forget.

"Ya that Irish cunt who thinks he's hard, aiyn't ya?"

Owen had no idea how the lad had got the information but he was offended, and unlike his old man showed no reluctance to shy away from any encounter.

"Yeah, and proud to be."

Owen hit the new boy with such a smack that he fell to the ground, only for the lad to get up a second later. The best scrap the school had seen in a generation had started. By the end of it, though, Owen and the other boy were outside the headmaster's office, waiting their turn to see him.

The new pupil was no more than two minutes in there, and came out with a smile bigger than Esther Rantzen's minus the teeth.

Owen went in with confidence, expecting much of the same, a small slap on the wrist and a lecture. The headmaster, however, was new and out to prove a few things to his young charge.

"Come in, Moriarty," Mr Collingwood said, who was sitting behind his desk.

The comp was a Church of England, an unusual choice for an Irish-Catholic family to send their children to – but that was what they'd done with the two boys. Lynsey had been a different case: Christy had wanted her to keep her innocence – something that would've been difficult in a mixed-sex school. She'd ended up attending a Catholic all-girls in Edgbaston.

Owen walked in, sucking on his swollen lip he'd got from a wicked left jab."

"Sit down, Moriarty.

The schoolboy sat down, the collar hanging off his white school shirt and a hole at the knee of his black trousers.

"So, we seem to have got ourselves in a bit of bother, haven't we?" Mr Collingwood said in a patronizing headmasterly tone. He was forty-two – still young for the position - and was determined to rule with an iron hand.

"Yeah, sir?" Owen answered with all the compliance the man in front of him deserved.

"Sit down, boy."

The pupil did as he was told.

"So tell me, Moriarty, this fight, what was it over?"

"He called me a name, sir."

"What name?"

"He swore, sir."

"Go on, I don't mind, tell me?"

"He called me a 'cunt', sir... an 'Irish cunt'."

The headmaster stood up in silence, walked around the desk and came within a few inches of his pupil.

"Is that so?"

"Yeah."

"You mean he started the fight?"

"Yeah, sir."

"Which means he threw the first punch?"

"Yeah, sir."

Mr Collingwood walked back to his chair and sat down again. He put his feet on the table and hands behind his head in true American style. Owen was shocked. Headmasters were supposed to be formal, and this was certainly out of character. Mr Templeton, the former headmaster, had never acted like that.

"Your family's Irish, isn't it?"

"Yeah, sir."

"Catholic?"

"Yeah, sir."

The headmaster sighed. He had something on his mind, something that wouldn't stay where it should have. Yes, he had an opinion.

"Do you know anything about the Troubles, boy?"

"Ya mean in Northern Ireland, sir?"

"Yes."

"Well yeah, a little, sir?"

"So what can you tell me, Moriarty?"

"Many have bin killed there, sir."

"Since 1969?"

"Nah, much further back than that, sir."

"How far back?"

"Since the Seventeenth century, sir... the Plantations and all that."

"You know your history, Moriarty."

"Thank ya, sir."

Mr Collingwood laughed, then said:

"Okay, I'll make this quick, as there's no point pissing around... My brother, Captain Jeffrey Freeman Collingwood, was seriously injured three years ago from an IRA bomb – lost the sight in his left eye and half his right leg was blown off... He's in Malvern now, living with my parents, an invalid..."

"I'm sorry about that, sir," Owen said, nervous now.

"And *so* your kind should be."

All the while Mr Collingwood's mood was calm, expressing no discontent, which made it all the more disturbing for the pupil.

"I'm sorry, sir."

"It's all because of you Fenians that my brother's suffering now – and what of all the poor mothers and fathers who've lost sons to combat at checkpoints and from bombs... What do you think of that, Moriarty?" Owen remained silent.

"Ah, you can't, can you? You shouldn't be here, any of you... You take British people's jobs and still expect favours from us... You bomb our cities and think everything's okay when really it isn't... Yes, and you'd probably use many arguments against it, saying we took over your country and we're the occupiers and things like that... But it isn't true, you know... We went there to civilise you. Yes, that and nothing else. We were doing a good job too... You're all so fucking ungrateful."

He understood the historical context of everything the headmaster was saying, because Owen did read and he knew about the history of his parents' homeland.

"Have I done summat wrong, sir?" Owen asked, politely but coyly, respect for his headmaster still in check.

"Fighting for one thing, fighting – and on the first day of school too," Mr Collingwood replied, strangely changing back to the original subject as if nothing had happened.

"But he started it."

"He said you did."

"He's a liar then."

"It doesn't matter – I know what your kind are like... trouble."

"Nah, sir, it wasn't me!" Owen said, his voice raised from frustration.

"Yes, I'll have to suspend you... I can't have such behaviour becoming part and parcel of this school."

"It aiyn't fair, sir."

"You're suspended for a week... Get out of my sight, you *Irish* bastard."

It wasn't so much the suspension that hurt, but the abuse. He'd never forgotten that. Mr Collingwood had planted Owen's seeds of hate.

Ten years later nothing had changed. Owen's target, for reasons he knew, was Darren now.

Christy's mental condition was worrying Noel. He'd always been a great support to his mom and dad, and like Owen, was a good brother to his sister. Quiet as a kid, he'd tended to be forgotten about. He liked this, though. In the shadows, Mr Anonymous. He was four years younger than Owen, and had received none of the fallout from the bombings his older brother had got. Maybe it had been because back when it had happened, he'd been a first year, more interested in conkers and marbles than the politics of Ireland, unlike Owen and his books on Irish history. His chip on his shoulder was considerably smaller than his older brother's too, and he'd always felt great in the city of his birth. Owen's ten years of hurt brought on by his dad's experiences and the Mr Collingwood episode had seen to that.

The next morning Teresa and Christy went to the hospital alone. Owen and Noel had to work, but would join them later in the day. There would be no time for Christmas celebrations, no tree and presents – these were distractions to the real important thing: Lynscy and her well being.

39: Fight of the Century

Darren spent all Sunday at home, wrapping presents and lazing around. Christmas Day was just three days away. His holiday would start from Christmas Eve, and continue until the 2nd of January.

Christmas Eve was usually great in The Bantam, with a special mood; however, Darren was still only thinking about Lynsey and his struggling team. He wanted more than anything to give her the present he'd bought her, though he'd left the wrapping in the caring hands of his mom. He'd wanted to wrap it properly, with care, with none of the slapdash wham-bam-how's-ya-man kind of wrapping, and his skill with a pair of scissors and sellotape was minimal. Looking at it on the bed, the small gift nearly brought a tear to his eye. He was sure she'd love it.

Forest was next and maybe a first win in ages. Saunders was already on his ninth and final life and in need of help – if not from Santa, then at least from Brian Clough and his boys. Forest was mid-table and just going with the flow, not threatening anyone but not bowing down to the likes of Birmingham and the other cannon fodder at the bottom, either.

A win, that was all Darren wanted.

He was in two minds whether to go. His two brothers-in-arms for matchdays, Mickey and Danny, were off the scene, and if he wanted to go he'd have to go alone or find someone to tag along with. It was a good job Nobby was still up for the crack.

Monday morning came with a fresh round of snow on the ground, and as Darren headed for work, anticipation too. He had a doctor's note, so everything was sorted on that front, he hoped. But with the neurotic Yam Yam he was never sure. He'd already sacked John on a whim, so it was only a matter of time before he could find himself on the dole and his arse without any trousers again too.

"Mornin', Daz," Sid said.

Darren still looked pasty-faced and the remnants of a black eye visible.

"All right, Sid.

The gaffer wasn't in.

"So what happened to ya, mate?"

Darren told him all the details over a morning cuppa. The gaffer strolled in after ten.

"Me office, now," Yam Yam ordered.

Darren walked in, note in his back pocket and fingers crossed.

"All right, Dave."

"Sit down, Daz."

Darren sat down.

After all the niceties, the gaffer got down to the nitty-gritty.

"So, what dow yow think I should dow about this difficult situation?"

Darren pulled the sick note from his pocket.

"Here, it's off the doctor like – just in case ya think I'm takin' the piss and pullin' a fast one on ya." He handed it to Yam Yam.

"And yow think yow okay with this, ahr, that yow *secure*?"

"It's all sorted, boss."

"A doctor 'Melvin'," Yam Yam said, examining the slip of paper carefully.

"I dayn't remember the bloke's name."

"So what yow tellin' me is yow could be makin' all this up?"

"Fuck me, Dave, look at me face – does it look like it?"

"Whatever the case, yow on yow last warnin'... Get outta me sight. Ask Sid what yow should dow... Ahr, a few mowtas need crushin' down and I'm sure he could dow with a hand."

He'd survived - it was one massive reprieve, kingsize.

Sid was on the crane, picking up a white 1966 Ford Cortina, ready to condemn it to the crusher.

"Hey, Sid, what d'ya want me to do!" Darren shouted up to Sid in the cabin; the rattling noise coming from the crane's huge grab as it gripped the car's metal body caused such a racket that Sid was oblivious to Darren's shouts. He tried again, but this time retreating away a bit, so Sid would be able to see him. Darren began waving his arms up and down like a lunatic with chicken wings in an attempt to get his work mate's attention. After a minute of these desperate gesticulations and screams, Darren caught Sid's eye, and Sid immediately turned off the crane.

"What?" Sid asked, opening the door and popping his head out of the claustrophobic cab.

"The gaffer said ya'd get me on a job... he said I had to come to ya."

"Err, yeah, there are some bumpers standin' over by the crusher that have already bin stripped from the cars – on the left-hand side. Sort 'em out, will ya: the rusty ones leave - the good ones, well, give 'em to Dave and he'll have to sort 'em out himself."

The day was going slowly with none of the atmosphere of the year before, when Darren had been doing some casual at the Royal Mail Central Post Office in town to deal with the pre-Christmas rush. What a time that'd been: sorting letters and packages by address with a group of morons and career dolites whose only goal was to have a laugh – it'd been a miracle anyone had received their Christmas cards at all in the end.

Back then he'd not a care in the world and he'd enjoyed himself. He'd had a few full-time jobs but most of the work he'd had since he'd left school had been casual – cash in hand stuff, the best sort in Darren's opinion. The job in the scrapyard was a different world, a world of holiday pay and taxes and *responsibility* – yes, that sad word to all the young men in their twenties. And though he was happy to have a job, he'd always enjoyed the freedom that casual offered: he could go in whenever he liked – as long as he never took the piss – and he could still sign on too. But now, being a respectable working man, paying taxes to a government he hated, Darren had to toe the line. Idleness wasn't an option, particularly if he wanted to keep his job.

At one, Darren and Sid went to the chippy for lunch. They both ordered fish and chips.

"Plenty of vinegar on mine, Stavros," Sid said.

"Hey, come on, Sid me man, as if I didn't know – gis how long dis bloke's bin me customer for?" Stavros, an overweight forty-something Greek-Cypriot who'd have fit perfectly into an Italian-heavy role in any American gangster film, said to Darren.

"Nah, how long?"

"Since 1975 – since I opened this bloody racket."

Stavros's English was heavy on the accent and annoying at best, though that'd never stopped him from being popular with the factory workers in the area. He was also an out-and-out racist, hating all the Asians who'd flooded Sparkbrook with their curry houses and giving him a run for his money in competition. A lot of his discontent he kept to himself, but on some occasions – especially with such a long-standing and trusted customer as Sid was - he'd start with a xenophobic diatribe that would've made any National Front party member proud:

"Ya see, Sid, since all the Pakis have moved in, nobody wants to eat me fish and chip the way they used to – it's all curries and baltis now and all the shit they make, know what I mean, mate? What's happenin' to the traditional British Friday evenin' meal? There's a new Paki just moved in on the Ladypool Road... He's opened up and all of a sudden he has queues of people outside his shop at all times of the fuckin' evenin'... Ya know, it's one of them balti houses – an unlicensed shop where ya just bring ya lager in with ya."

"Give 'em what the people want, I say," Darren put in suddenly "Someone from way back said it, I think. Ya gotta give the people what they want... And anyway, I bloody love me curries."

Stavros wasn't impressed by his customer's openness.

"And what's that supposed to mean?" Stavros asked.

The chips were still sizzling in the fryer, so it was either leave now and go hungry or face the full wrath of the Greek.

Darren decided to risk it – how worse could it be from what he was already going through?

"Things change, people now like curries – like meself... Ya know, it's like McDonald's and Wimpey and stuff... In twenty years' time nobody'll be eatin' Yorkshire puddin' and ya fryups."

"Yeah, mate, and it's an injustice, know what I mean?"

"Come on, lads," Sid commented with a laugh, trying to diffuse any bad feelings. "It dayn't matter. Food's fuckin' food."

They took their grub and headed back to the yard.

"Where are ya goin' for Chrimbo?" Darren asked Sid. He'd made a hole at the top of his vinegar-soaked bag and was picking out the piping hot chips one by one with his fingers. "Jesus, these are fuckin' hot cunts."

"Dunno, mate," Sid answered sadly. "Me kids dayn't want me round their mother's, so I suppose I'll be spendin' it on me tod."

"Why's that, mate?"

"Since the divorce the family's bin against me – all of 'em."

"Why's that?"

"They blame me for it."

"For what?"

"Our divorce."

"And was it ya fault?"

"Ya a nosey fucker, aiyn't ya?"

They were nearing the yard and Darren had almost eaten his chips and most of the cod fillet.

"Sorry, mate," Darren said, burping.

"Dirty bastard," responded Sid.

They walked through the gates and towards the office. As they stepped closer, they could make out the squeaky cries of what sounded like the gaffer, and breaking them, thumping noises and another bloke's voice shouting. Suspicious, Darren rushed in, with Sid casually behind. The door flung open and it was like a scene from a police raid. Unbelievably, John was on top of Yam Yam and beating the living shit out of him.

"What the fuck are ya doin'?!" Darren cried out, reaching for the attacker and trying to grab his left wrist. John's clenched fist was weighing down on the defenceless Black Country man.

"Fuck off, Daz, it aiyn't ya business."

Moulded dry saliva was coming out of John's mouth. He looked like a knackered racehorse after the Grand National; his eyes, bloodshot and bulging, clearly showed the injustice his ex-gaffer had dealt him. Moving away from Yam Yam, it was clear he'd really gone to town on him – Yam Yam's face was one bloody mess.

"Help me," Yam Yam whimpered with the last of his energy.

John tried to kick him in the stomach but Darren got in the way and he took the full blow on the shoulder. Darren gave out a yell of pain and shouted to Sid for help; in shock, and with his lunch getting cold, Sid said in a panic:

"What d'ya want me to do?"

Darren and John were now on the floor, rolling to and fro and fully engaged. They knocked over the bin and the coat stand. In desperation, Sid threw his bag of fish and chips, still wrapped up, at John; however, he missed by a mile, and socked Darren in the face with a direct hit.

"Not me, ya cunt!" Darren screamed, panting now... Get him off me or call the Old fuckin' Bill, will ya?"

Sid, flapping his hands up and down around like Stan Laurel in a crisis, froze.

"What should I do, what should I do?!" he cried.

"Do summat, I dunno," Darren replied, his face reddening from suffocation. John had the advantage and had him in a strong headlock. The attacker's grunting and groaning was an obvious tell-tell of his anger. John was capable of anything, it seemed. Knowing Darren was in danger, Sid jumped on John with all the power his age would allow, breaking the deadly grip John had had. While all this was going on, Yam Yam was cowering by the wall close to his desk. They began laying into John with all they had: one punch, two punches; John fought back bravely, screaming all the time in a mad fit of rage:

"It aiyn't fair! It aiyn't fair! I have child support to pay and I can't now coz of *you*!"

John tried once more to get to the gaffer, but Darren was having none of it.

"Sid, phone the Old Bill, will ya?"

They were both locked together and going nowhere, totally exhausted.

Sid grabbed the phone and began dialling.

OPERATOR: West Midland's Police, emergency.

SID: Yeah.

OPERATOR: What's the problem, sir?

SID: Me gaffer's bein' (heavy breathing) attacked by an ex-worker.

OPERATOR: Is he injured?

SID: Yeah (heavy breathing). He's lyin' in the corner and me workmate's on top of him.

OPERATOR: Is the attacker being restrained?

SID: Me mate's tryin' (heavy breathing). John's goin' psycho here.

OPERATOR: What's the address, sir?

Sid told the operator the address.

OPERATOR: Okay, sir, we'll send a unit straight over.

SID: Make it choppy like.

Darren was still struggling to hold him down.

"Hey... Sid... come... and help... me, will... ya?!" Darren shouted, panting.

Sid went over to help, his lungs now bursting.

"Dave... help... us!" they both cried, while John was wriggling and spitting like a man possessed, exhausting the last of his energy. Yam Yam, face bloodied, had his hands up against his ears and was clearly traumatized. Darren called out again but it was no good – Yam Yam was glued to the spot. They struggled on until John had run out of steam.

"Let me go, Daz... What, ya... on the fuckin'... gaffer's side... now, are... ya?"

"Why... did ya... do... it?" Darren asked, breathless.

"He was... takin' the piss... I've got... things to pay, ya know that... If I dayn't pay me child support I'm fucked... and I'll end up in the nick, d'ya hear... me?"

Two coppers arrived and arrested John. A few minutes later an ambulance came to take Yam Yam to the hospital, followed by another police unit to question Darren and Sid. The first unit took John to the cop shop, not without a struggle.

Darren had got a few cuts and bruises, but nothing for which he had to go the hospital for. After a constable had asked him a few questions, Sid closed up the yard early and they both went home.

Darren's face, sensitive to the touch, felt like it had been stung by a hive of bees. Looking in the mirror was no fun, either – he wouldn't be pulling any birds this Christmas, even if he wanted to - Jaws from the James Bond films would've had more chance than him – no, *Bagpuss*, for that matter.

40: On the Scrounge Again

Darren's old lady nearly collapsed when she saw him: once had been terrible but the second time was a complete shock.

"Darren, love, what happened to ya?"

He didn't want such pampering – well, from Lynsey it would've been okay.

"Nothin', I fell over."

"Over me dead body did ya... Is that all ya can do... get into fights and stuff?"

"Mom, nothin' happened, okay."

"Was it that Danny again?"

"Dayn't worry about it."

"Dayn't worry about it – how can I not... Ya me only child."

"I'm goin' up to me room," he said.

Darren began to walk up the stairs.

"Oh, ya'll have to make yaself summat to eat tonight – I'm startin' the cookin' for Christmas."

"Who's comin' for dinner?" he asked on the landing.

"That's a bit of a stupid question, aiyn't it... Ya aunt and uncle as usual."

"So, the same old borin' Christmas, then?"

"How's Lynsey, love?" his mom asked after a moment.

He went into his room, sighing – Darren didn't want to answer that question. He kicked off his trainers and lay down on the bed, next to Lynsey's still undelivered present. He closed his eyes, only to open them a moment later. Bored, he switched on the radio. Paul McCartney's *Wonderful Christmastime* shrieked out, making Darren all the more depressed. *How was it wonderful? No, it wasn't – it was shit in fact.* He'd never been lower – or not since Birmingham had last been relegated from the First Division.

He went downstairs.

"Mom, can ya do us a favour?"

"What is it, love?"

"But I dunno if it's a big ask at the minute with all ya doin' for Christmas?"

"Ya know ya goin' to ask me, so just ask me." She had her hand in a bowl and was kneading some stuffing mix. "Come on, what is it?"

"Can ya bring Lynsey's present to her parents' house?"

"What for? Ya can't do it yaself?"

"Nah."

"Well nah, not really - Ya can see I've got a lot on."

"It'd only be droppin' it off like – five minutes tops."

"I knew summat was goin' on with ya and her family... So what is it, what's all the trouble about?"

"Will ya do it or not?"

"Ya'll have to tell me everythin' first."

"Tell ya what?"

"Darren, son, dayn't come all innocent with me – ya know what I'm talkin' about."

He sighed, before saying:

"Okay, I'll ask dad then." He came back a second later from the living room. "Okay, I'll tell ya, but ya have to promise to deliver it *today*."

Darren couldn't remember when he'd been so open and honest with his mom. He was a little embarrassed, truth be told, but he didn't have a choice, and in the end it all came out, his gob free-flowing.

"I'll do it later, okay?" she said after he'd finished.

With that out of the way, Darren moved on to his next problem: he was out of pocket – he hadn't worked a week in hand since the gaffer had taken him on full-time, and didn't expect he'd get any holiday pay. By his calculations, Yam Yam owed him four days' money: the Monday, Tuesday and Wednesday of the previous week before his unlucky visit to A&E, and the day he'd already done. If Yam Yam wanted to dock him half a day's wages for his late show up the week before on the Monday, he could live with that – but he wanted his dough. Only problem, he had no contact with the gaffer.

"Mom, I need another favour?" Darren said, thinking she'd be full of the Christmas spirit.

"What now?" she asked, sighing and stuffing the turkey.

"Can ya lend us some money till I go back to work on Monday?"

"What, ya aiyn't bin paid?"

"Nah. I'll get me Christmas money when I get back and I'm skint."

"Okay, that twenty can be part of ya Christmas present... Take the thirty quid that's in me purse over there... I can't, me hands are fulla stuffin'."

Darren took the money.

"Thanks, mom, ya a life saver."

"But remember, ya owe me housekeep too."

How could he ever forget that?

The phone rang.

Darren picked it up.

"All right, mate, it's Nob... Are ya comin' out tonight or what?"

"Nah, I wanna save for tomorra."

"Come on, ya borin' cunt, just for a couple?"

"It's always 'just for a couple'... What about ya savin' and stuff – gone with the wind, has it?"

Darren wasn't down there for long – just long enough to tell Nobby and the rest of the pub what had happened to him and for Tina and a few of the other birds to take the piss out of his missing tooth.

He got up late on Christmas Eve. His mom and dad had already gone to do some last-minute shopping and deliver Lynsey's present. He had the whole day to himself until the evening, when there'd be plenty of drinking to do.

41: One of the Three Wise Men

She approached the door with caution, holding the tiny present in her hand. Her finger pressed the doorbell. Next to it, on the brick wall, hung a wooden placard which read: *cead mile failte,* though she had no idea what it meant. The figure of a human form, blurred through the misted glass of the front door, came towards her from the hallway. It was a man. He opened the door.

"Hello," he said. It was Noel.

"Err, hello, I'm Darren's mom."

"What d'ya want?" he responded coldly.

She showed him the present.

"I'm deliverin' Lynsey's present from Darren."

"What, he couldn't deliver it himself?"

"He didn't wanna... He told me everythin', ya know?"

Noel just looked at her, indignation clearly visible on his face.

"Ya better come in."

She looked back at her husband, who was sitting in the car, and signalled to him she was going inside.

"I dayn't wanna trouble ya," she said.

"Don't worry, there's nobody else in: me parents are at the hospital again and me brother's workin'."

"I'm so sorry to hear about ya sister. She's such a lovely girl."

"*We know...* It's just a pity ya son dayn't think the same."

"Listen, are ya Noel or Owen?" she asked, embarrassed.

"Noel."

"Well listen, Noel, I aiyn't come here to make trouble, I've come coz me son asked me to."

"Yeah, for the present."

"D'ya know how worried about everythin' he's bin?"

"Hah, that's a joke... Worried, Darren – I doubt it."

She raised her voice a level.

"That's where ya wrong."

"If ya precious son had even bin bothered about me sister, he woulda bin at the hospital day in and day out like we've bin."

"Have ya heard of work?" she retorted in a scolding manner.

"So, I have to work too and it's never stopped me."

"Let's get to the point, Noel... I know everythin' that's bin goin' on... He tells me ya father and brother have always had summat against him and he dayn't know why."

"Oh, no, he should know all right."

"Well, whatever it is he's me only child and I'll always defend him... I dayn't wanna argue with ya, it's just as far as I can see the problem's from ya family's side – ya brother in particular."

"If that's how ya feel about it."

"And it's a shame poor Lynsey is in the middle of all this and aiyn't got no clue what's goin' on."

"Ya dayn't need to patronize us, Mrs Acheson, we know the score."

"Anyway, this is why I came." She put the present on the dinner table. "Merry Christmas," she then added, before walking out silently.

42: A Lesson: North-of-the-Border Style

Back at home, Darren was watching *The Wizard of Oz,* a staple for Christmas on the telly, and all these years later, the wicked witch of the North still scared the shit out of him. It was similar to when a lunatic bunch of Walsall hooligans had steamed him and a couple of his mates after an FA Cup third-round away tie back in January '83 outside Fellow's Park and all the way to Aldridge on foot. That experience - close to home and one of his first real tastes of the casual culture and violence that went with it - had stayed with him along with the first time away to West Ham. The replay, in contrast - a one-nil win on a freezing Tuesday evening in Birmingham - had seen him and a couple of his terrace mates get their own back on some Yam Yams in the City Centre. It hadn't been anything too brutal: just a light kick in before they scarpered for their lives back to Walsall. It'd been a buzz, though.

Yes, but she was still there on the screen with here rank green skin, big fuck-off nose and coterie of mad flying monkeys.

At six Darren was out of the house and in the pub. Even this early it was rammed, with most of the locals up for it big time, smiles on their mugs and wearing an assortment of barmy party hats that most had probably got by opening their Christmas cracker box a day early. It wasn't New Year's Eve, but you'd have thought it was judging by the manic way people were hugging and kissing each other. Bagpuss was working as usual, as well as Tina and a new bloke from Scotland called Malcolm. His duty was to help serve between the busy Lounge and the quieter Smoking Room, just for an extra pair of hands.

Charlie, glued to his stool as always, had a face on him longer than an UB40 application form.

"Merry Christmas, Charlie... What's up, mate?" Darren asked.

"Ya dayn't wanna know, but Merry Christmas anyway," he replied, grimacing.

"Try me?"

"I got a terrible pain in me arsehole – I stuck me finger up there earlier and I can feel a few lumps... I tried to have a look with a small mirror too, but it was impossible to get it up the crack and see what was up there at the same time, ya know what I mean."

"Sounds like piles to me."

"Yeah, and it's fuckin' murder."

"Have ya sin a doctor yet?"

"What the fuck do I wanna go and see one of them for?"

"Well, ya wanna go and get *ya arse* straight down there, mate."

"Was it hurtin' last night? Ya seemed all right then?"

"This mornin' it started like."

"Anyway, Nobby told me before ya came in that ya had a bitta trouble at work yesterday... Fuck me, Daz, ya aiyn't very lucky at the minute, are ya?"

"Yeah, a bloke was sacked – a bloke I went to school with – he went ballistic on the gaffer, beat him up and everythin'."

"Is the gaffer all right?"

"Aiyn't gotta clue, Charlie mate."

"I heard ya steamed into him?"

"Well, ya have to, dayn't ya?"

Darren moved over to Bagpuss.

"That's a bitta bad luck, aiyn't it?" Bagpuss said.

"What, ya heard?"

"Listen, get the tooth sorted out, mate – ya look a right cunt."

"Thanks, Arth," Darren said sarcastically. His confidence was already low and he didn't need it to go any lower.

"Another scrap, hey? What are ya sayin' to these people?"

"Dayn't worry about it – I can look after meself."

"Yeah, but ya face has sin better days, aiyn't it?"

"All right, Arth mate, leave it out."

"How's the misses?" Bagpuss asked after a second.

Darren didn't want to answer that question:

"How's the new bloke?" Darren asked.

"Ah, he's all right. He was in the Bar last night... He's from Scotland. His name's Malcolm."

"Where's he from?"

"*Scotland*, like I said."

"*Nah*, the city, ya cunt?"

"Glasgow, I think."

"So he's hardcore then?"

"What d'ya mean?"

"Is he a Hun?"

Bagpuss shook his head as he didn't understand.

"Ya what?"

"Is he Rangers?"

"Oh... dunno... I aiyn't asked him."

"Okay. I'll ask him meself later."

"Are ya goin' down to the Forest game on Boxin' Day?" Bagpuss asked.

"I wanna – ya fancy comin' down, Arth?"

"Nah, I'll think I'll deaf that one," he replied with a snigger.

Darren took out his fags and crashed.

"Mickey aiyn't bin in here, has he?" asked Darren.

"Not since it happened, nah."

"I wanna give him a ring but I dayn't have his number."

"He saved ya fuckin' skin, mate – jumped in, ya see. Danny woulda pulverized ya otherwise."

"Have ya got his number?"

"His *your* mate, Daz, how am I supposed to have it, ya daft sod," Bagpuss said, rolling his eyes.

"Dayn't remember nothin', other than sayin' summat to him and then darkness – it's fuckin' weird, ya know."

"Well, I tell ya one thing, that Dunford bloke'll never come in this gaff again while I'm runnin' it."

"Are ya serious?"

"Fuck, yeah."

"That's fair enough," Charlie said, raising his glass.

"Merry Christmas anyway, Arth," Darren then announced.

Darren swayed over to Tina, who was busy serving. She looked as sexy as ever.

"Merry Christmas, Tina love," he said, before pecking her on the cheek.

Interested in the new barman, Darren shifted over to him.

"All right, mate. Name's Darren. Merry Christmas."

"Ahrite, Merry Christmas. Neme's Malcolm, pleased ta meet ya."

They shook hands.

"Nice, aiyn't she," Darren commented.

"Aye."

"Needs to be rightly shagged if ya ask me, yeah, Malcolm?" The question embarrassed the barman and he kept his mouth shut. "Nice, aiyn't she?" Darren asked again.

"Aye, she's a bint, but canna git ya anythin'?" asked Malcolm.

"Nah, I'm sorted thanks," Darren said, lifting his concealed pint.

"Ya Scotch, aiyn't ya?"

"Aye right, ah'mno." Malcolm's said.

"But the gaffer told me ya was." Darren's was surprised – his accent was enough of a give away.

"Aye, but ah'mno definitely not *Scotch,* and I cannie agree with ya there, son."

"Hold on then, mate... If ya aiyn't Scotch, what are ya?"

"*Scot-tish.*"

"I know, that's what I said."

"Naw, yir sed ahm 'Scotch', not Scottish," Malcolm replied with a healthy measure of sarcasm.

"And is there a difference?"

Malcolm rolled his eyes – another ignorant English twat to deal with.

"Scotch is for scotch egg, mate – the thing yir eat. Ahm Scottish – there's a big difference."

"All right, sorry about that, mate." Darren downed his pint in one and ordered another. He was determined to get shit-faced drunk. "So anyway, Malcolm, what side of the coin d'ya roll with?"

"Wit?"

"D'ya support Rangers or Celtic?"

Malcolm laughed. He'd been asked the question a few times before in England and was surprised how fascinated the English were with the Old Firm.

"That's a wee bit personal new, aye?"

"Nah, I'm just askin'... It interests me."

Darren was cautious at this point: he didn't need another smack in the gob.

"Maybe ah dannae even like football."

"Come on, what Jock dayn't like footy?"

"We got rugby and golf and shanty and other sports, ya know?"

"Ya havin' a laugh, aiyn't ya?" said Darren, disbelief etched all over his face. "Are ya tellin' me ya dayn't like football?"

"Naw, I like football."

"And what team d'ya support?"

"Partick Thistle."

"Ya takin' the piss now, aiyn't ya?"

"Naw."

"What division are they in now?"

"The First... Now, son, ya a wee baw juggler but ah waz just takin' the piss." Malcolm replied, laughing. It was a cutting laugh – full of all the mockery that was always North of the Border.

"Rangers then?"

"Gow way, mate."

"Celtic?"

"Too fuckin' right there, son."

Great, another Irish cunt, Darren thought. He walked off, his anger fuelled some more.

It was one after another of the crap Christmas songs that everybody said they hated but when they were on everybody danced to them. Nobby was talking to a couple of young girls – no more than eighteen – over by the fruit machines, so Darren made his way over to them, expecting at least five minutes of decent entertainment.

"Whot's his problem, Arthur?" Malcolm asked.

"Who?"

"Thet there radge in the red tracksuit top."

"Oh, Darren."

"Aye."

"Nah, he's sound."

"Cannae be dealin' with his bastart kind. Bit nosy if ya ask me."

"What, was he borin' ya about football? He's as bad as me, he is," Bagpuss said with a giggle.

"Aye, we're playin' Rangers on New Year's Day – the big one," Malcolm said, pulling a pint.

"So ya a Celtic fan then are ya?" asked Bagpuss, curiously.

"Aye."

"D'ya think ya'll win?"

"We cannae lose, Arthur. We lost to Dundee Utd yesterday an nuw we're in fifth fuckin' place. It's either us or Aberdeen again this yahr – I cannae see Rangers dain' anythin'."

"And ya aiyn't gonna go home for it?"

"Wanst they goat a few in 'em, they goes pure aff their heid... and ya goatta git the fuck ootae there cause a the Barnie...I wouldna gow tae see that there game if ya paid me... It's too risky, Arth, ya with me? And anywey, the girlfriend'd kill me. She wannae gow to a club on New Year's Eve in the City Centre."

"Ah, ya'll have a right crack there. Which club are ya goin' to?"

"Huvny idea."

"Where are ya livin', Malc?"

"Yardley Wood."

"Bit of a trek, aiyn't it... for work, I mean?"

"Naw, it's not tay bad... What, it's a mile or too awey."

"So, the Old Firm derby, is it as intense as they all say?"

"Cannae be barnie in there."

"I heard it's a right atmosphere."

"Aye."

"And what d'ya think of the Second City derby here in *Burmingham*?" Bagpuss announced, pride filling every word.

"The Second City derby... Thet's the Villa-Blues one, aye?"

"Blues-Villa, Malcolm, Blues-Villa... B is before V in the alphabet, remember... And look," Bagpuss pointed to all the Blues memorabilia at the back of the bar. "that's the other reason why."

"Ah'mno really inta Blue, Arth," Malcolm said, sniggering.

Meanwhile Darren was doing a Nobby and downing them like the world was about to end. Everybody was enjoying themselves, and Darren too. He wanted to forget.

"And our derby, how does it compare to yours?"

"Well I cannae say it can compare at all in all respect, Arth."

"Why's that?"

"Ya cannae compare the Glasgow derby. Ya can forget all the rest... the Liverpool-Man Utd, Barcelona-Real and River-Boca – anybody who knows anythin' abhut football knows the Old Firm has it all."

"But ya wanna see over here in September, in town – there was a right fuckin' clash... The Old Bill everywhere like."

"To tell ya the truth, Arth, an withut spoilin' anythin' for ya, ah'mno really interested in all that barnie and stuff, get me? Ah'ma a kinda normal sort, ya know?"

"Yeah, I suppose."

"But ahm talkin' abhut everythin' in general, naw just the footy – cause I know it's not always better than doown 'ere in England and on the Continent."

"And who's ya favourite Celtic player of all time, Malc?"

"Ouer Danny McGrain."

"Why's that?"

"Just a great all-roond defender and dedicated man of the club – naw bad gain for a Protestant, aye? And ya see, Arthur, ah never bin one for Sectarianism and stuff."

A customer rang the bell in the Smoking Room.

"Shall I get that one, boss?" Malcolm said, smiling.

"Well, that's what I pay ya for, ya silly sod."

Malcolm walked through to the adjoining bar of the Smoking Room to serve the thirsty punter.

The jars were sliding down Darren too smoothly. Nobby had a small quarter pint bottle of vodka in his pocket and was lacing his own and Darren's lager with it.

"Gis another one there, Tina love – and get yaself one," Darren said flirtingly.

Darren was getting paranoid now: Malcolm was giving Tina more than the eye and it had started to piss him off. The two girls – sixth formers from an all-girls school in Solihull as it turned out – had irritated him so much with their middle- class pithiness and think-it intellectual supremacy, that in the end he could take no more and he just walked away. In desperation, Darren moved like a snake in Charlie's direction, who as usual was alone.

"How's the arsehole, Charlie?"

"*Fuck off*," he replied. Charlie was in no mood for a laugh.

"Have ya sin that cunt?" Darren said to Charlie.

"Which one?"

"The barman, Malcolm."

"What about him?"

"He'll have his hands down her knickers next."

Charlie's only concern was the excruciating pain up his back passage.

Whistles went up, followed by a round of applause: Nobby had his tongue down one of the girl's throats.

"Hey, Daz, have a word, mate." Bagpuss said.

"I know, I can't take him anywhere," answered Darren.

"Come here a sec," Bagpuss then said.

Darren stepped away from Charlie and approached the gaffer, who was leaning on the bar.

"What?"

"What's goin' on with ya mate John then – will he get a prison sentence?"

"Dunno."

"Ah, he'll get one for sure."

"To tell ya the truth the gaffer deserved everythin' he got."

"Why's that?"

"Ah, it's a long story."

Darren's eyes had locked in on Malcolm with Tina in the Smoking Room. The barman now had his hand around Tina's in what seemed like an amorous embrace.

Fucker, Darren thought, before spitting it out loudly:

"Fucker." Though only as loud as Charlie and two lads, unknown to Darren, could hear.

"Ya what, mate?" one of them, an emaciated Jimmy Somerville lookalike wearing a parka ten sizes too big for him, growled.

"*Sorry?*" replied Darren, aggressively and ready for combat.

"Got a problem, have ya? Ya startin'?" the second snarled, stockier than the first but equally pathetic in his donkey jacket.

"Fuck off, ya cunts," Darren said. Their look matched their courage, and as soon as they realised Darren was up for it, they backed off.

Tina had blown him out to some skirt wearing Fenian fuck and he wasn't going to take it. Malcolm looked harmless enough - not like some of those dicey bastards he'd seen on the BBC in documentaries about the council estates of Glasgow. He reckoned he wouldn't cause him any trouble, and if he did, he'd have the whole pub behind him in a flash. No, he'd just give him the verbals at first, he thought, just to crank him up a bit.

Tina came back from the Smoking Room, a huge smile on her face.

"Ya okay there?" Darren asked her.

"Yeah, fine."

Carrying some ashtrays he'd just cleaned out the back, Malcolm came through.

"Just put 'em on all the tables, Malc – thanks," Bagpuss said, elbows on the bar. The new barman did as he was told, chatting to the locals as he did it, the odd handshake here and kiss there on the way. All the while Darren stared at him.

Bastard. He comes down here to live with his bird and all the while he's game for a bitta skirt, he thought, sucking on his fag and guzzling his lager.

And then Mickey walked in. Bagpuss spotted him straight off. Their eyes met. He walked over to Bagpuss. Darren, still tracking Malcolm, was oblivious to the fact.

"All right, Arth," Mickey said. "Merry Christmas, mate."

They shook hands.

It'd been nearly a week since the incident with Danny.

"So how's our Danny?" Bagpuss asked.

"And before ya ask - I'm sorry, I'm truly sorry, mate," Mickey said remorsefully.

Mickey had tried to stop Danny, but it had all happened way too quickly for him to do anything. While Darren was sparked out on the deck, Mickey had pulled the incensed Danny away from him.

Malcolm had returned behind the bar – it was then Darren noticed Mickey's presence: there was a split second of tension, only broken by Mickey's calming words:

"I'm sorry, mate."

"Well, it wasn't *your* fault, was it?" Darren said.

"Here, let me get the pints in."

Mickey bought the round and they talked: it had turned out that Danny had been arrested during the Chelsea match for throwing a dangerous object onto the pitch, intended for the head of the Chelsea keeper, Niedzwiecki, and was still in custody. He'd have been a free man hadn't it been for his ranting in the cell – fuelled by a skin full of Breakers – that he'd been one of the top boys involved in May's riot against Leeds. That had been enough for the bigwigs on Steelhouse Lane, and he'd subsequently been arrested on charges of football-related violence and disturbing the peace.

"... and ya know what, lads," Mickey said to Bagpuss, Darren and Charlie, laughing as he was saying it, "at the time of the riot he was in Drayton Manor with his cousin, the thick cunt."

A cackle went up.

"Ya dayn't press charges, did ya?" Bagpuss asked Darren.

"Nah, fuck it – I aiyn't no grass."

Darren was pouring the pints down his neck, watching Tina with Malcolm.

"Well, I tell ya what, it's the end of football in this country," Charlie said, his face twisted from pain. "We'll have no European football now and the terraces are just a mess. If ya ask me, the police need to take a harder line on the yobs."

"Yeah, ya gotta point there..." Bagpuss said.

Darren had distanced himself from their conversation as the jealousy he was feeling had built up to an unimaginable level.

"I thought ya face woulda cleared up a bit more than it has, Daz?" Mickey said. He didn't know about Darren's other incident with John.

Darren had gone over to Malcolm again.

"Hey, Malcolm, so what about ya Scottish football then?"

The barman had been in conversation with a couple at the far end of the bar.

"Whit?" he replied, upset at the interruption.

It was getting loud now; everybody had had way too much to drink except for Darren, who'd gone even way beyond that.

"Can I talk to ya for a minute?"

"Ahright." He turned to Darren. "Whit is it?"

"Have ya got summat goin' on with Tina?"

"Sorry, mate?"

"She's just a bit of a dabble for ya, is she?"

"Wit ya say, ya numpty? It's none of ya business." This time Malcolm turned aggressive.

"Yeah, it's the dabble ya want – aiyn't ya ashamed of yaself? Ya gotta bird at home."

Malcolm moved away from Darren as a customer was at the bar twiddling his thumbs.

"I'll be with ya just now," Malcolm called out. "If ya'll excuse me, please." Malcolm then said to Darren, before going over to serve the man.

All the time Darren's eyes were like a periscope, watching Malcolm. Tina, sensing something was wrong, approached Darren:

"Did ya say summat to Malcolm?"

"What d'ya mean?" he replied like a child whose hand had just been caught in the sweetbox.

"Ya givin' him grief, aiyn't ya?"

Malcolm had served a couple of people.

"Hey, ya league's... shit, mate," Darren said as Malcolm approached.

"Listen tey him," Malcolm said sarcastically to Tina.

"The Scotch league's shit and fulla shit players."

"Tina, d'ya know this numpty?"

If he wanted to enrage Malcolm, Darren was going the right way about it.

"Unfortunately, yeah," she replied, a single giggle, sharp and cutting, right into Darren's delicate ego.

"Yeah, the football's crap... I mean, come on, man, how's it ya play each other four times? And another thing..." He was stumbling over his words now, "ya only got two decent teams, and they even aiyn't no good, really... Who can win it... I mean... It's just Celtic and Rangers and the other teams are a complete waste of everybody's time... They might as well play in the fuckin' Conference down here... Berwick Rangers, Morton, Dunfermline – fuck all them."

"So wit ahbut Aberdeen and Dundee Utd over the last few seasons, son, they dannae count?"

"Dayn't call me 'son', all right?"

"But it's true, aye?" Malcolm's rejoinder was wounding.

"I dayn't care, but it's a crap league."

In any pub across the Tollcross Park area of east Glasgow, that would've been goodnight Vienna for Darren. You could push things only so far up there before you found yourself on the wrong end of a Glasgow Kiss. But Malcolm was in England, and he'd have to be careful.

"That's ya opinion, son," Malcolm said.

"Dayn't call me 'son', ya cunt... I aiyn't ya son."

"Calm it, Darren, ya twat," Tina warned in her squeaky voice.

The gaffer heard what was going on and strolled over John Wayne-like to control the situation.

"Hey, ladies, ladies, what the hell's goin' on here?"

"Darren's had too much to drink and he's actin' a prick," Tina said.

"Aye, too much brew en him, Arthur – he's steamin'," Malcolm added.

"Ya what, ya Irish cunt," Darren yelled. He then went for Malcolm, swinging with a right punch.

The Scot managed to protect himself before countering with a left-handed tornado of a jab – which hit his attacker directly on the jaw: Darren went flying backwards, landing on the beer-soaked manky carpet, only for the enraged Malcolm to follow him, jumping over the bar quickly. The crazy Jock then proceeded to hit the helpless Brummie with a dozen combination punches. Darren managed to keep his arms up to his face, deflecting some of them away. It was clear Malcolm knew how to look after himself.

The whole place erupted as Nobby and Mickey became involved, jumping on Malcolm and pulling him off their mate. Bagpuss was having kittens.

"Get out, get out, all of ya!"

Half a dozen locals got mixed into it too as they grabbed the two fighting dogs and dragged them outside.

"Hold on, dinnae do that ta me, it wasn't *mae* fault," Malcolm protested. It didn't matter, though, the gaffer had had enough:

"Ya sacked, mate. Get the fuck outta here."

"And me?" Darren asked as Nobby, Mickey and two other blokes grabbed a leg and an arm each. "I'm all right, aiyn't I, Arth?"

"*Ya barred.*"

"I'll fuck ya up, Bagpuss, I swear it," Darren threatened. It was plain the alcohol was talking now.

Considering the beating he'd got, Darren wasn't in such bad shape at all: a sore chin and a grazed cheek from where Malcolm had caught him with his Claddagh ring.

Irony pervaded.

However, that was no consolation for his old lady.

"Me son, me son, what have they done to ya again?" she moaned, tears in her eyes.

"Leave it out, will ya. Nothin' happened, all right?"

But a mother was a mother and some things never changed.

"How many times is this now? Are ya here to spoil me Christmas?"

43: Christmastime, Mistletoe and Wine

Darren was as pissed as the most pissed newt, which was very pissed even for the standards of Richard Burton, so the moment his head hit the pillow, he dropped off and didn't wake up until late on Christmas Day morning. When he did trundle out of his hole, he didn't even open his presents: he didn't want to get inundated once again with a mountain of socks and pants and another bottle of that awful Old Spice. And it wasn't as if he usually got a lot of presents anyway: one or – if he was lucky – two off his parents, one from his aunt and uncle and that was about it. Not a good aggregate really.

"Ya can help me now if ya like?" his mom asked.

"With what?" he answered, head spinning with pain and yawning.

"Stir the apple sauce mix."

"Where's dad?"

"Oh, yeah, ya can give him a hand movin' the table into the living room - Vera and Des will be here at two, so ya both better get ya arses into gear."

He didn't want to – it was too much like hard work and Christmas was supposed to be a holiday, but if he wanted his dinner on time, he'd have to do something.

The 25th was the same every year in the Acheson home – four or five hours spent round the table, eating until everybody was bursting to the seams and talking about nothing that was interesting.

Futility.

And then there was the Queen's speech, that cornerstone of British cultural life that anyone who had an ounce of honesty within them knew was a complete waste of the taxpayers' money – everybody always seemed to watch it, though.

Darren wasn't allowed to eat anything. Mom's orders: she was too busy in the kitchen and it was out of bounds.

After he'd made the apple sauce, Darren helped his dad move the table in to the living room ready for the mighty feast.

Darren went upstairs to have a bath and to get ready for dinner. Usually he'd take something in to read with him, like when he was having a dump. It could be anything really: *Shoot*, *Match*, an old *Sports Argus* – whatever was lying around. Today was different, though. He brought in his Panini *Football '85* sticker album.

Baths were always a great source of inspiration. Whenever he had a problem lying in the tub for half an hour would usually sort it out. He'd started collecting the sticker albums with the first edition *Football '78* when he'd been a fourteen-year-old. He'd filled them all: '78, '79, '80, '81, '82, *Espana '82* - the World Cup edition - '83 and '84. 1985's edition was another matter. He was getting a bit old for them now, and the little problem was it cost 10p a pack – 10p he'd have rather put towards the next packet of fags or a lager down the pub or entry into a match.

Darren was in the steaming hot bubble-filled water, the album in his hands, and he was carefully perusing its pages, trying to keep water splashes away. All the albums he had stashed away in his bottom draw, and he only took them out from time to time. When he did, memories of his schooldays came flooding back.

He was disappointed as he flicked through it: there were so many empty spaces without stickers. The Birmingham City page was the most embarrassing of all, as Julian Dicks was the sole contribution. Most of the big name players and teams were missing and he'd only got the silver foil badges of half a dozen teams – and they were none to shout from the roof about:

Huddersfield Town and Leeds in the Second Division, Heart of Midlothian and Morton in the Scottish Premier. There were no First Division badges to brag of. He had the Everton team photo and that was about it. All in all it wasn't much to look at, and if he'd shown it to any boy of school-age in the playground, they would've taken the piss out of him no doubt. He still had a massive swop pile from all seven previous albums and he'd often wondered how much pocket money and wages he'd wasted over those seven glorious years buying them.

From the calming effects of the steam and aroma of the bubbles, Darren drifted off to the memories of school and swopping with his mates. The break time ritual of sifting through their piles quicker than a Las Vegas croupier. The declarations of 'got' or 'need' were common playground parlance. The foil badges were worth two or three times the normal ones – much like the big gobbies were to your ordinary small marbles.

Yes, they were the days.

He threw the album on the floor next to the bath, sighed, then closed his eyes and fell asleep, only for his dad to wake him up a few minutes later by knocking on the bathroom door:

"Daz, get out, I need a shit."

"What's the time?"

"Half one. Vera and Dave will be here in a minute."

"All right, gis a sec."

His aunt and uncle arrived promptly at two. It had been different in the past when the whole family had gone to Cynthia's mom and dad's, but once they'd passed away – incidentally within two months of each other – they had all decided to go to Cynthia's instead. Things weren't the same now, though – even uncle Des's jokes had become lamer, though it was always good to talk to him about St Andrews and the nostalgia connected to it.

Today would be no exception.

"Darren, dear," his aunt exclaimed, hugging him.

"All right, Vera," he replied. He was watching *Top of the Pops* and didn't like the disturbance.

"And ya can turn that off for starters... Where's ya bloody tooth gone?" his aunt asked.

"Long story... I got into a fight," he answered, turning off the telly.

"Ya jokin'... Have ya sin this, love?" Vera said to her husband.

"Fuck me, Daz, whoever he was he caught ya good, didn't he?"

If Darren's old man was the chalk, then his uncle Des was the cheese – or should it have been fire and ice? Yes, that was more fitting. Mrs Acheson's brother always had something to say and thought he was an expert on everything. Not that it pissed his brother-in-law off; Leslie had actually got used to it over the years and his passive nature was suitable to taking a back seat.

Christmas dinner was at half past three and the two women were in the kitchen working hard with all the last minute preparations; the boys, meanwhile, had settled comfortably and Leslie had opened a bottle of cherry – a family tradition at this time of year. Darren had switched the telly back on and caught the back end of *Top of the Pops*, disappointed that Shakin' Stevens had made it to number one.

"So, Daz, Leslie tells me ya found yaself in quite some trouble the last couple of weeks: Fights, hospital visits, that kinda thing."

"Ah, nothin' I can't handle." Darren knocked back the small glass of cherry in one. "Got another one of 'em, dad?"

Leslie filled his own glass and theirs too. Darren threw it back again, now in half the time.

"Ya wanna watch it there, son," his uncle said, before looking at his watch, "it aiyn't even three yet."

"Pour us another."

It was almost three and time for the Queen's Speech.

"The Queen's on now," Des said.

"I dunno why ya so interested in that every time. Year after year... What's the fascination, Des?" Leslie asked.

The Queen began her speech:

'Looking at the morning newspapers, listening to the radio and watching television...'

"Whatever's that woman talkin' about?" Leslie asked.

"What matters, lads, what matters," Des answered enthusiastically.

"Well if she really appreciates all them people and what they do, why dayn't she give up some of her wealth to 'em... and to me for that matter?" said Darren.

Only his uncle Des was for it all. Although no Royalist, he appreciated what the Family did for the country and the prestige it gave Britain around the world. He was atypical for your average Brummie blue-collar worker.

Leslie wanted to go on with his tirade, but then realised it'd get him nothing other than lecture for the next couple of hours and no peace, so he decided to keep his mouth shut.

They all sat down to dinner. Each took a cracker and they proceeded to pull them: Crack! Crack! Crack! Crack! They put on their paper thin coloured hats. The table was full of food: two meats: turkey and pork, carrots, roasters, peas, Yorkshire pud, mash and sage and onion stuffing. The gravy was in the boat, thick and aromatic.

"Okay, everyone, ya can tuck in now," Cynthia announced.

They got stuck in and within twenty minutes everybody was stuffed of stuffing and everything else.

"So, Daz, how's the bird," his uncle asked. "I heard she's sick?"

Des was known for being a little insensitive at times.

"Sick, she's *more* than a bit sick, Des."

Darren didn't want to talk about it. So much so that he hadn't even asked his mom the day before how she'd got on delivering the present.

"I'll put the telly on again," Leslie said, changing the conversation.

On BBC One the Children's Royal Variety Performance was on.

"Check in the *Radio Times*, love," Cynthia said to her husband.

"Yeah, go on, Les – I aiyn't watchin' this pile of crap. Every bleedin' year it's the same," Des said.

Leslie picked up the *Radio Times*. On the front cover were Del Boy, Rodney and in a Santa costume, Uncle Albert.

"*All Creatures Great and Small's* on in an hour – oh, but at half seven it's *Only Fools and Horses...* after that *The Two Ronnies* at nine..."

"What's on BBC Two, Les?" Vera asked.

"*Citizen Kane.*"

"Well I'm watchin' *Only Fools and Horses*," Darren exclaimed.

His uncle started a conversation about football, and in particular a funny anecdote about his brother-in-law at St Andrews in the 1950s:

"Remember, Les, the game against the Vile at home in '58, just before Christmas when we beat 'em four-one... They were relegated that season, but that aiyn't what's important... Remember when we got off the bus on Garrison Lane on the way to the ground and ya lost ya shoe – got caught in the door or summat, didn't it? And the bus driver – the cunt – just drove off – remember?"

"Hard to forget that," said Leslie, rolling his eyes in embarrassment.

Darren started laughing: he'd never heard the story before.

"Yeah, and that wasn't the only thing... We thought we'd have a quick pint before too... Well, ya can imagine, the place was packed and the fuckin' smoke was everywhere – ya couldn't breathe – so what did ya old man go and do, Daz? He only took his jacket off... it was hot, ya know. Remember, Les?"

"Yeah, I left it on the chair and went for a slash. When I got back the bastard had disappeared: some cunt had nicked it... What were ya doin', Des? Ya couldn't even look after me coat." Leslie smiled. It was rare for his dad to smile. "So there I was, without a shoe and a coat and it was bleedin' brass monkeys outside... Well, ya can imagine how it was in the ground – people were lookin' at me and there I was all blue in the face from the cold and lookin' a right twat with a shoe missin' and no bleedin' coat... It was a good job we won..."

"Remember the Tower Ballroom, Des?"

"Ah, that was a good night."

"What was that about the Tower Ballroom?" Cynthia and Vera asked at the same time.

"It was nothin', ladies – summat to be kept between us lads," Des replied, a big obnoxious smile glued to his mug.

There was silence during *All Creatures Great and Small.* On one or two occasions, though, Vera tried to extricate some information from Darren about Lynsey, but Darren was having none of it and shrugged off her questions.

The men downed the sherry and then started on the bottle of whisky uncle Des had got from his gaffer at work as a Christmas present. He worked at Rover, too, but in a different section to his brother-in-law.

"How come I didn't get one of 'em?" Leslie asked, referring to the whisky.

"I thought everybody got one in the plant."

"Well I didn't."

"Sshh, will ya three be quiet," Cynthia said. They were watching *Hi-de-Hi* and the men were disturbing them.

They went into the kitchen and parked themselves down on the breakfast table.

"I'm only havin' one shot," Des declared. "I've gotta drive home."

"Vera can drive," Darren said.

"Nah, I dayn't wanna – last Christmas was a riot, remember? I had a hangover and didn't make the game against Grimsby on Boxin' Day."

"Yeah, me too," Darren said. "I was round Nobby's and we had a bit of a session... Stayed in bed the whole day at his."

"Maybe we'll go down tomorra together?" his uncle asked after a moment.

Leslie opened the whisky, got three glasses from the cupboard and poured it into them.

"With *you*?" Darren asked.

"Yeah, why not?"

"Are ya serious?"

"Yeah, I mean how long's it bin? I think ya were a nipper the last time I took ya."

"Nah, Des, I was sixteen... It was a League Cup match against Exeter."

"Then that gives ya all the more reason to come with me."

"Nah, I'm goin' down with a couple of mates and I wouldn't like ya to get all offended when we start swearin'."

"It wasn't so innocent in our day, was it, *Les?*"

"Nah."

"Yeah, but have ya heard the latest song from the Derby fans: *Cloughy, you're a wanker, you're a wanker... Cloughy, you're a wanker, you're a wanker...*" Darren sang.

"So that's what they're all singin' down at the Baseball Ground now, is it?" Des asked.

"Nah, I dayn't think so, I just made it up." Darren said, laughing.

After they'd twisted his arm to drink a couple, Des began – as always – to yap on about the glory days of his youth. Not for five minutes, not even for one hour – but for two whole hours, so much so that Darren even missed the *Only Fools and Horses* Christmas Special. Des was good competition for Bagpuss in that respect.

"Come on *you*," Des' wife interrupted. "It's time to go home."

"Yeah, and ya'll drive, I hope?" Des said.

Darren and his dad could barely stand up straight or keep their eyes open: the whisky and Des' self-gratifying dialogue had done their damage, and the bottle was also empty anyway.

His aunt and uncle left. Darren went up to his room and fell asleep.

44: Brian Clough and His Merry Men Rob Them

Darren woke up the next day without a hangover surprisingly, and early, at around eight. It was matchday, so there was a certain amount of adrenalin surging through his veins. And there was nothing strange about that, they were his team. It was three juicy points today or bust. Yes, all three counted up and in the bag. He'd give all the beatings they'd got and a lot more for the chance to climb that little bit higher up the table towards the Vile scum, to grab their dirty claret-and-blue arses and drag them down to the bottom and the gloom of relegation.

On paper, Aston Villa was as bad or good – depending on how you wanted to look at it – as his own team. Most of the '81 League Championship side and the '82 European Cup winners had moved on or had retired, and now they had the likes of Tony Dorigo and Paul Birch in the ranks, as well as a crap manager in Graham Turner and a 'has been' Andy Gray – no, they weren't world-beaters anymore. Three points, that was all. Not too much to ask, really.

Before all that, though, there was the small job of beating Forest, a team on the up again after their halcyon days in the late 1970s.

He expected Mickey to call and they'd both go down the match together, but the phone didn't ring. Darren left at half-one: enough time for a couple of swift ones in a pub near the ground.

Lynsey was still there, mind you. He wanted to see her, but the coward started communicating with him again, trying to talk him into the sensible option. What was it, though, the 'sensible' option? Darren wasn't sure. He couldn't believe it: he was bottling it against her dad and brother when now he was entering the coliseum like a gladiator in ancient Rome, where at any time both to and from the ground there was a good chance of meeting up with some aggro. And it wasn't as if he had never seen some of the top lads like Big Max mix it with the top boys from other firms. To Darren, Big Max was the stuff of legend. One of the founders of the Apex Crew, he certainly knew how to kick it off and there were many a time he'd left a trail of blood and proper mayhem across the country. Darren had seen him in action a few times – even once bashing in a little Scouser. He thought Big Max was probably on the run now from the Old Bill - or worse still, in the nick, like half-soaked Danny, though at least Big Max had a reputation.

The journey to the ground was always game for a laugh. Darren got on the bus in Kings Heath and as it got closer and closer to the City Centre, more and more supporters got on too, but they were mostly your old blokes in flat caps and scarf-wearing teenagers.

Half a mile from the ground he got off and walked down the Coventry Road. The street was crowded with rowdy types together with the normal supporters.

Darren went into a pub jam-packed and after a long wait bought himself two pints, which he drank quickly.

Coppers, one or two on horseback, the rest on foot, stood by nervously next to the mobile burger bars and a vendor selling hats, scarves and pennants. In amongst all this, was a splattering of red from the away supporters. The Old Bill had everything under control, just like at West Ham it seemed.

Darren paid his two-fifty entrance and fifty pence for a matchday programme and went through the creaky turnstile. St Andrews was a wreck of a place and in need of a lick of paint – no, not that, it needed condemning, though Darren and the other Birmingham City faithful knew it would never happen.

He was standing in the corner of the Tilton Road End and the Spion Kop, and from where he was standing, reckoned there were no more than ten thousand – maybe less. The Kop had a few in it, but the Main Stand was practically empty – a sure sign of Birmingham's league position and recent poor performances. Years before, when his uncle Des, Bagpuss and Sid had been regulars, the ground had been rammed every Saturday - but now the club's perennial yo-yo status and the hooligans had seen away with all that.

Forest, to their credit, had brought a few with them and they were cooped up in the Railway End's lower tier singing their hearts out.

At kickoff the usual chants started but today it was obvious they were strained and the fans were becoming disenchanted. The match against Chelsea had been louder, Darren thought, and it surprised him as they were playing a Midland rival.

Boos and aahs were coming out from the back of the Kop and also the occasional scream of 'nigger' when Forest's flying winger, Franz Carr, was on the ball. Darren looked behind him, surprised. There was a group of about ten white lads responsible. He scanned his surroundings. There were some blacks in the stand, but they either failed to hear the chants or were too scared to say anything. There was no sign of the Zulus – things were looking bad for the club now that even their hooligans were abandoning them. The racist chants went on. One bloke, fair play - fat and in his fifties - had the bottle to say something to them:

"Will ya shut the fuck up?!"

They were young and naïve – and probably drunk. They kept their mouths shut from then on.

The coppers on the pitch were all smiling, and Darren thought they must have been fresh from their Christmas blowjobs from their girlfriends and wives.

The Forest supporters - buoyed by their team's early surges forward and the Dutchman Johnny Metgod's howitzer free kicks - started singing Christmas carols and a hopeless rendition of Slade's *Merry Xmas Everybody,* which enraged the Bluenoses even more.

Cigarette smoke and beer fused with the cold afternoon winter air and, together with the rusty smell of St Andrews, produced an unpleasant antiquated whiff around the ground.

It was apparent Cloughy's boys were well up for it. The well-built Stuart Pearce at left back – a summer buy from Coventry City – was industrious in defence alongside Neil Webb in midfield. Up front, the manager's son, Nigel Clough, was causing endless havoc to the beleaguered City defenders: Bremner was having a nightmare. The merry men from Sherwood Forest were making Ron Saunders and his team look like a Sunday league side, and a bad one at that. Darren had little hope of the lads getting a shot on target, never mind a goal and the three points.

Dissolute cries from the home supporters became louder and louder as the match wore on. The Trentsiders were dominating in all areas of the pitch, especially up front. Peter Davenport threaded a through ball to Franz Carr, but the player's shot was in no way equal to his pace to get there. Darren knew they'd score sooner or later.

He couldn't watch, knowing what was coming, though something inside him – masochism, probably – forced him to endure it. Standing together behind the club, they all knew what Darren knew – about the hopelessness of it all. But they would never mention it on the terrace to the bloke next to them. You could criticise the players and the board no end – somehow that was okay, but never the team itself, which was everything: the history, the tradition, the songs, the crest – all that.

And as Forest passed the ball around – not quite Samba style, but something verging on it – Darren realised his team was in deep trouble - it was only a matter of time before Forest scored. The only thing to look forward to was the tannoy announcement at the end of the match – *had the Villa won or not?*

It was all too predictable – they'd lost one-nil and the moans went up as the whistle blew. But there was something to wait for: the scores rose up from the speakers, reaching to every part of the ground: The Villa had lost away to Leicester, and the screams and laughs that followed were as good a Christmas present as any Bluenose could've wished for. Adding to the joy, the Albion had succumbed to Luton at the Hawthorns.

Leaving the ground with a mixture of sadness and joy, Darren went to a nearby newsagent where he waited for the delivery of the *Sports Argus*. He bought a copy, then caught the bus to Kings Heath, flicking through the paper as he did but not exactly reading it.

He went to a local pub – one his dad used from time to time. The Bantam was out of bounds – for the time being, anyway.

Darren ordered a pint and sat down, turned the paper to the back and looked at the First Division table:

	P	W	D	L	F	A	PTS
...15. Manchester City	23	6	7	10	27	32	25
16. Leicester City	23	6	7	10	31	41	25
17. Coventry City	23	6	6	11	27	35	24
18. Oxford United	23	5	8	10	35	46	23
19. Aston Villa	23	5	7	11	27	36	22
20. Ipswich Town	23	5	3	15	18	37	18
21. Birmingham City	22	5	2	15	13	32	17
22. West Bromwich Albion	23	2	5	16	20	55	11

It was tight in the basement with five Midlands clubs in the bottom eight. The Manchester City game was a must win. The

Villa had the Albion and the best result for Birmingham would be a draw.

And then Darren smirked as he saw they had a game in hand on the rest of them – it wasn't much, but it was something.

He had another few pints and then went home, thinking all the way about Manchester. The Sky-Blue half of the city wasn't United but he was sure they'd put up a fight – enough for the eleven twats Saunders was putting out every Saturday, anyway. That was two days away, and before all that he wanted to pop into the yard and get his wages off the gaffer. That would give him the cash for the trip up north. His only worry now was to find a couple of lads to go with. Travelling alone didn't really appeal to him at all. He'd been a few times in the past and had been bored shitless.

It was after ten when he got home. His mom and dad were already sleeping. The stresses of the day had taken it out of him and he went straight to bed.

45: Doctor Yam Yam and Mr Hyde

The next morning Darren went to the yard. There was no guarantee the gaffer would be there, but he wanted to try his luck.

"All right, Dave."

"Oh, it's yow," Yam Yam said.

"I'm here about me wages."

"Thought as much." He walked over to the kettle, filled it up and switched it on. "Yow wanna cuppa tae?"

"Go on then."

"Sow, how much do I owe yow?"

"Four days."

Yam Yam took out a wod of notes from the breast pocket of his coat and began counting:

Ten... thirty... forty... and there's... a hundred." He handed it to him.

"What's that for?" Darren asked, surprised.

"Let's just say it's a thank yow in some way."

The gaffer made a brew and they sat down.

"What about John, Dave?"

"What about him?"

"Is he still in the nick?"

"Dunno – he's yow mate. I'll see the cunt in court, whateva happens."

The gaffer was serious.

Darren felt for John – he had to. They'd spent years together at school, but now he knew he had a job, and the more he sucked up to Yam Yam the better it would be for him in the end. Maybe there'd be more money coming his way in the future too.

"So, what d'ya wanna do to him?"

"Ahr, I'll have the cunt done good and propa."

The topic of conversation changed.

"How was Chrimbo, Daz?"

"Ah... the usual."

"The Blues ay strugglin' a bit."

"Ya tellin' me," Darren said, tutting.

"Who are yow playin' tomorra?"

"Man. City away."

"That aiyn't gonna be easy."

Darren noticed the gaffer's usual vindictiveness and aggression missing: now he was friendlier, warmer.

"Well, it's a must win for us."

"I say that every time the lads play but it dayn't never work."

Yes, Darren had to look at the bigger picture: Wolves were at the foot of Division Three and precariously sliding to oblivion. Their best days had long gone and Yam Yam had more to cry about than his own team. Maybe things weren't so bad.

"Keep ya head up, Dave."

"I'll have tow like. Dunno what's gowin tow happen to us... Them tow Welsh clubs, Cardiff and Swansea, ay just above us... Welsh sheep shaggers, yow believe it?"

Darren still had another week off. The gaffer expected them back on the second of January. With some dough in his pocket he went home in high-spirits.

On the way home Darren thought about Lynsey. How had her Christmas been? What state was she in? He could go right down to the hospital if he wanted to. Darren pondered it for a while as the bus got closer to home, before deciding that was what he would do. He'd buy some flowers and walk in there with his head up high. *What was he ashamed of?* He'd always been faithful, and it was her family's problem if they didn't like him.

He went to a florist's and bought a bunch of tulips. With the flowers under his arm he got on the bus to the City Centre. From there he'd buy her a nice box of chocolates in Marks & Spencer.

"What are the best chocolates ya got?" he asked a shop-assistant. The shop was packed as the sales had started.

"I dunno – just look at the prices... The most expensive ones are probably the best," she said, obviously tired and overworked from the Christmas rush.

That was no help then.

He saw a box for a fiver from Belgium and bought them.

Armed with his gifts Darren was confident Lynsey would be pleased to see him.

He got on the bus to the hospital

46: Another Lecture on the Nature of Morality

Nobby's Christmas had been nothing special, spent with a family that didn't seem to like him. The feeling was mutual, however.

There was a knock on the door.

"All right, Daz," Nobby said.

They went through to Nobby's living room and sat down.

"So how are ya, mate?" Darren said.

"What have ya got there?" Nobby asked, referring to the flowers and chocolates in his hands.

"Ah, these – for the old lady."

"What, is it her birthday or summat? Nah, dayn't tell me – ya forget her pressie for Chrimbo?" The shame stopped Darren from telling the truth. "Well, anyway, it kicked off big time, didn't it?" Nobby asked.

"Wasn't *my* fault, Nob, ya know that?"

"What did ya say to the cunt?"

"Dunno... I can't remember."

"Ya know ya barred now? And another thing, ya called him an Irish cunt, which I aiyn't too happy about... I should give ya a kickin' meself like."

"Well, if Yam Yam wants to act like a cunt, he can... I aiyn't bothered... But about the name callin', I didn't mean it. Dayn't take it the wrong way or nothin', mate."

"All right, ya forgiven, but with an attitude like that he's never gonna let ya back in."

Darren turned the topic to football.

"Rubbish match it was yesterday."

"What, ya lost again?"

"Yeah."

"What was the score?"

"One-nil."

"D'ya wanna cuppa?" Nobby asked.

"Only if ya got some biscuits in."

"Yeah, I should have half a packet of Rich Tea in the cupboard."

"What, ya aiyn't got none of them chocolate digestives?"

Nobby went into the kitchen and put the kettle on.

"So what with him?!" Nobby shouted from the kitchen.

"With who?"

"The Scotch bloke?"

"Ah, he was sacked like... Yeah, gone with the wind, he is."

"Well that's a bitta bad luck, aiyn't it?"

"I couldn't give a flyin' fuck, mate – it aiyn't me problem."

Putting the two mugs of tea on the table, Nobby sat down again.

"What's with Lynsey?"

"I dunno and dayn't ask," Darren replied, his tone indifferent.

"Ya a cunt... Ah, ya a waste of space... Ya got a great lookin' bird there who cares for ya like – ya know... well, too much in *my* opinion, and all ya can do is take the piss."

"I aiyn't gonna argue with ya, mate... What ya say's right, what her fuckin' family says is right... I'm the bad one here, right? It's all my fault, nobody else's... Ya all fuckin' angels."

Nobby put the *Meat is Murder* album on.

"Now this'd sort any problem out," Nobby said.

On the coffee table, stacked high like the Tower of Babel, were dozens and dozens of magazines. Darren sifted through them one by one every time he came by. They were mostly copies of *NME* and other music publications. Beside them – somewhat strategically placed – was Nobby's scrapbook on The Smiths.

"Ya still doin' this thing?"

"Too bloody right I am," Nobby stated proudly.

Darren leafed through the chaotic mess of newspaper cuttings, pictures and subjective scribblings. Although he loved the group no end, he thought it was going a bit too far.

"This is a bit O.T.T, aiyn't it?"

"So's ya stupid fuckin' football albums."

Nobby had cut out a picture of Morrissey dancing on stage and underneath it he'd written the words:

THERE ARE ONLY SO MANY MEN LIKE THIS. UNITE AGAINST THE THATCHER MONOPOLY AND ALL THAT IS BAD IN THIS COUNTRY.

"D'ya like it?" Nobby asked.

"Did ya write it or was it him?"

"It was all me own work."

"True words but ya fucked up... Nah, only jokin'... Yeah, there's a certain amount of imagery that's says everythin' about the band... I like it..."

They started talking about music. Nobby went to the kitchen and brought in two cans. Darren didn't want to drink but Nobby forced him to. For a while the mood was amiable until his mate brought up the subject of Lynsey again.

"I dayn't wanna hear it," Darren said, sighing and rolling his eyes.

"But ya bein' a right cunt."

"So what?"

"Ya wanna fuck her old man and her brothers. Just leave it like, ya know?"

"That's easy for *you* to say."

"Yeah, it is. Go and see her."

"I dayn't wanna."

"Ya got no bollocks, ya know?" said Nobby, sighing.

"Just shut it."

"I can't let it go... I mean, it's about Lynsey but more than that: I wouldn't let two idiots dictate to me about me love life, ya know what I mean?"

His best mate was testing his resolve.

"Nah, Nob, ya wrong on this one."

"Nah, I aiyn't... and I can't let it go."

"I'm goin." Darren got up. "I've had enough."

"Listen, ya me best mate and I dayn't want ya to take nothin' the wrong way, but ya gotta have a bitta spine now, ya know? It aiyn't no good hidin' away from the fuckin' idiots coz ya'll only regret it in the end."

"Shut up."

"I only wanna help."

"Ya can help by keepin' ya trap shut." Darren took a swig from the can. "Ya see them flowers there, well they aiyn't for me old lady – never were, mate. They were supposed to be for Lynsey, ya see. I was at the hospital... well, outside at least. I couldn't go in. I fuckin' bottled it."

"Ya see what I mean?"

"Yeah, but at least I had the bottle to tell ya."

"Ya gotta go, ya gotta go and see her."

"I dunno," Darren began, sitting down, "maybe all this is me own fault. Maybe everythin's bin caused by me own fuckin' laziness and everythin'."

"Just takes a bitta effort, son."

"Her dad's a cunt but I just dunno."

That Joke isn't Funny Anymore began.

"Ah, what a tune. Me favourite," Nobby said.

"What's this song actually about anyway?"

"Suicide. Fuckin' suicide."

"Yeah, it sounds like it... I always feel in a crappy mood after listenin' to it."

"That's just how Stephen wants it, mate, it's just as he wants it."

"Any chance of goin' back home then?" Darren asked after a moment.

"What for?"

"Well ya payin' a bit too much on the rent for this gaff in me opinion."

"Yeah, but it's me own and here I make the fuckin' rules – not the old man."

"So, Christmas was okay? Who was round?" Darren asked.

"Mom, dad, me sisters... Oh, and one of me aunts from Ireland."

"How's Marie?"

Marie was Nobby's nineteen-year-old sister; Darren had had a crush on her for most of his teenage years.

"Ah, she's workin' somewhere in Handsworth or summat for an electrical contractor."

"Doin' what?"

"Receptionist."

"Has she got a boyfriend?"

"Some muppet keeps knockin' on the door for her."

"What's he like?"

"Dunno."

"How's the old lady?" Darren then asked.

"She's always askin' about ya. Ya should go down there for a cuppa and a chat."

"Might do that, son, might do that." Darren looked round the room. "So ya dayn't see yaself ever goin' back?"

"Nah, I've got me freedom here and I love it."

"What about the cookin'?"

"I go down for me dinner – ya dayn't think I'm that fuckin' stupid, d'ya?"

"Yeah, and all ya records are in one piece... Which ones did he break?"

"Nah, it wasn't that he just took the fuckers away – hid 'em under his bed.... He said to me: 'turn that fuckin' queer cunt off!' Angry as fuck like, he was."

"If me old man tried to do that with me record collection, I'd deck the cunt."

"Ya dayn't have a record collection."

"Yeah I do."

"A couple of Smiths albums and Prince's *1999* single's hardly a record collection – ah, and ya got me single *Blue Monday* – I want that cunt back."

"I aiyn't got it."

"I want it back pronto."

"Ah, I'm goin', I'm bein' accused of fuckin' all sorts now," Darren said, getting up.

"Ya won't be down the pub tonight then?" Nobby asked sarcastically, knowing his best mate was barred.

"I'd like to but Bagpuss will only do his nut."

"Ah, he'll have forgotten all about it by now."

"Nah, not him."

"Well, I'll give ya a ring later, all right?"

47: The Forgiven

"Here ya are," Darren said, as he handed his mom the chocolates and flowers.

"What's this all about, Darren?" she asked, shocked.

"I dunno – I just thought it was time."

"Leslie, love, come here quick and see what ya son's bought his mother."

His dad came into the kitchen from the living room.

"What's all the fuss about?" his dad asked.

"Look, love." She thrusted the flowers into her husband's hands. "Put 'em in some water, will ya."

Darren went upstairs and, for the rest of the day, lay on his bed, thinking to himself of everything and nothing and reading football magazines.

His dad woke him up.

"What time is it?" Darren asked.

"Half seven. Nobby's on the phone."

Yawning his mouth off and hungry to boot, Darren went downstairs.

"Yeah, what d'ya want?" Darren asked.

There was a loud racket in the background: voices and music: Nobby was in the pub.

"Get ya arse down here now."

"I can't."

"Dayn't be a wanker, Daz. I've had a word with the gaffer and it's all sorted... Come down."

Darren wasn't sure whether Nobby was joking with him or not.

"Put Bagpuss on..."

"Arthur speakin'. All right, Daz," Bagpuss said after a moment.

"Yeah."

"How are ya, mate?"

"Not too bad."

"Ya'll have to speak up – I can hardly hear ya," Bagpuss said.

"So, I'm allowed back in?" Darren asked awkwardly and after quite a long pause.

"Yeah, of course."

"Sound, mate. Thanks."

Darren changed his clothes, made himself a quick sandwich and went down to the pub. He hadn't expected to see The Bantam for some time – not ever, but for a while at least.

"So, Daz," Bagpuss began, hands on the bar in his habitual pose, "what have ya to say for yaself?"

Darren stood there shitting it. Well, it was more from embarrassment than anything else.

"Yeah, I'm dead sorry... Err, it aiyn't gonna happen again... I was outta order and that, ya know what I mean like?" Darren then looked to his right and left, then scanned the rest of the Lounge. "Where's Tina?"

"She's off tonight."

"I bet she thinks I'm a right twat, dayn't she?"

"Yeah," Bagpuss said, nodding.

"Two pints, please, Arth, and get yaself one in."

"Ah, so it aiyn't 'Bagpuss' now, is it?" the gaffer asked.

Nobby came to the bar.

"Is that mine?" Nobby asked, looking at the two pints.

"That's two forty-eight, please Daz," Bagpuss said.

"So, what about Malcolm, Arth?" Nobby asked.

"Aiyn't sin him – shame, good worker he was, but I can't have me bar staff actin' like they're on the terraces, can I now?"

"Again, I went a bit over the top and I'm sorry," Darren said.

"I'd say a bit more than that, Daz," the gaffer opined.

"Have ya got a new body in yet?"

"Nah, why? D'ya know anyone?"

"Nah," Darren answered.

"What about *you*, Daz?" Nobby said. Darren smiled. Such a statement was mocking. "No offence, Arth, but I couldn't do it... I mean, come on, I love a tot and it'd be a torture more than anythin' else... Can ya imagine me standin' where *you* are and blaggin' the punters? Nah, I wouldn't enjoy it."

Bagpuss raised his eyebrows, thinking how his life would have been if he had taken a more adventurous career route.

"Well, were ya down there yesterday?" Bagpuss then asked after a second of deep contemplation.

"Down where?" Darren asked.

"The match?"

"Awful, Arth, fuckin' awful. They couldn't kick a can of Carling that lot."

"Has to be expected – Forest's on the up anyway... The Vile-Albion game'll be key. I'm prayin' for a draw."

"I think we all are, Arth."

Nobby walked away from them as fifteen seconds of football-speak was enough for him for one day.

"Where's Charlie?" Darren asked.

"Yeah, think it strange meself. Maybe he'll be in later."

"He told me he had summat wrong with his arse so maybe he's at home."

"Oh, the piles – yeah, he was complainin' about that the other night. Yeah, I remember now... Well, anyway," Bagpuss went on, "we need a new manager – that Saunders is fuckin' useless: his tactics are all wrong."

"It aiyn't even that really, Arth... Just look at the players... I mean, come on, they aiyn't performin' at all."

"Ya down there every Saturday, so I suppose ya know what's goin' on."

"I've had enough of it, though – ya know what I mean like? It's all knock it up and high and hope for the best. I thought Saunders was gonna change all that and the magic would rub off on us."

"Ya havin' a laugh, aiyn't ya," Bagpuss said, laughing.

Just then Mickey walked in.

"All right, lads – Daz, ya cunt... Didn't expect to see ya in here."

"Then ya in luck then," Darren replied sarcastically.

"Two pints, please," Mickey said.

The gaffer had his work cut out. He hadn't worked on his own on the bar since he could remember. Service was slow but he was getting there.

"No news on Danny?" Darren asked.

"He's bin released from custody."

"What, he aiyn't goin' down?"

"Nah, he's got a court case in February, I think."

"Have ya sin him then?"

"Yesterday."

"What, he wasn't at the match, was he?"

"Nah, he's banned from goin' to any ground in the country. He had to check in at the cop shop at three."

"Forever like?"

"Nah, just till the court case... Then we'll see what's gonna happen... I saw him yesterday after the match."

"Where?"

"In town."

"Did he say summat about me?"

"He didn't mention ya."

"So, ya were down there yesterday," Darren asked after a moment.

"Yeah."

"What d'ya think?"

"Next question."

"If we dayn't win tomorra it's all over for us."

"There ya go, lads," Bagpuss said, placing the second pint on the bar.

"Cheers, Arth," Mickey said.

"Off to Manchester tomorra, lads?" Bagpuss asked.

"I'm goin' – and *you*, Daz?" Mickey said.

"Who are ya goin' with?" asked Darren.

"Just me and Tony."

"I thought ya said if ya took Tony again ya old man would have ya bollocks?"

"Yeah, he's gotta find out first... And anyway, Tony wants to come."

"I'll come with ya if ya like," Darren said, hoping.

"I was gonna ring ya anyway to find out."

"Well, why didn't ya ring me for the Forest game?"

"Ah, I forgot all about ya, mate... Anyway, I went with a few other lads."

"All right, it dayn't matter... What time's the train tomorra to Manchester?"

"There's a Football Special at ten past eleven. I wanna play it safe tomorra – especially up there. We'll stick with the scarvies for this one."

"Sounds decent to me," Darren said. He was relieved with that. Mickey and his brother wouldn't be looking for a row like the barmy Danny Dunford. Now he could breathe easily.

"Just bought meself a ZX Spectrum-plus, mate?" Mickey said.

"Have ya bought some games?"

"Got a couple free: *Ghostbusters, Codename Mat* and *Bruce Lee*."

"How much did it set ya back?"

"Nearly two hundred quid."

"I was thinkin' about gettin' a Commodore 64 meself, but for that price I think I'll deaf it," Darren said.

"They're a bit expensive at the minute, though. I wanted to get one meself as it's got a loada games – loads more than for Spec."

"Have ya got a joystick?"

"Nah, not yet. I'll have to buy one."

"Dunno how ya use the keys – it's rock hard - when ya used to playin' on the Atari ya would never get the hang of."

"Ya can come round if ya like and have a go..."

48: Monster in the Dark and Back to Me Own Ego

I leave the pub at twenty past eleven on me own like. I'm starvin' and so I go to a nearby chippy. It's about a half a mile from the chippy to me own gaff, so I take a short cut through the rec. The 'rec' aiyn't a rec at all really. There aiyn't no goalposts to play footy and it's fulla dog shit, though I'm fond of the place as I spent loadsa time as a kid playin' Wembley and 'three and ya in' with me mates.

It's dark and a cold wind's blowin'. Usually I dayn't walk this way as it's fulla glue sniffers and scumbags. I'm half-pissed, though, and braver coz of it. It's about seven hundred yards from one end to the other.

About halfway through I notice that someone's behind me. I ignore it and walk on, but after a second I realise the person's walkin' fast like, faster than me, as if tryin' to catch up with me or summat. I ignore it again, and then I stop, and look round. It's a bloke. I stop dead in me tracks. Summat's up.

"Are ya all right there, mate? Can I do summat for ya?" I ask, me heart racin'.

The bloke moves closer to me, yet the darkness hides his face. I move back a bit. The bloke's now a matter of yards away.

"Ya cunt," he says.

"Who are ya and what d'ya want?"

"Ya know who I am."

I know the voice but I can't put it to a face.

"I aiyn't got no money if that's what ya want, and I wouldn't give ya any even if I had," I say, brave like.

"I dayn't want ya money, I wanna piece of *you*."

It's Owen Moriarty.

I put me guard up. I'm gettin' used to it now.

"Okay, Owen, if ya want some, let's go."

Owen walks up to me slow like. Were now face to face and within punchin' distance of each other.

I can see his face clear now and he looks a wreck.

"What's happened to ya?" I ask.

"Wouldn't ya like to know?" he replies.

"So ya've come to finish me off, have ya? Did ya old man put ya up to it?"

"Ya dunno nothin', d'ya?"

"What are ya on about?"

"Nah, ya really dayn't," Owen says, like he has no strength left in him and he's almost dead of emotion.

"Let's get it over with if we have to," I say.

"Ya dunno what's happened, d'ya?"

"What?"

Summat awful – a feelin' of gloom, if ya like – comes over me. Owen aiyn't come here for a fight. He's here to tell me summat, summat which I aiyn't gonna like.

"I'm surprised ya dunno."

"What are ya goin' on about... Is it to do with Lynsey?"

"Yeah, it's to do with Lynsey... Well, ya could ask us if we had a good Christmas, but I dayn't think it'd do no good... Ya could also ask us if we still think there's any fuckin' hope in all this when there aiyn't... And ya could ask another question about why the fuck I'm here in the freezin' fuckin' cold talkin' to the nob who wrecked me sister's life-"

"Stop pissin' around and tell me, will ya?" I say, interruptin'. "What's happened?"

"She's gone, ya fuckin' bastard. She aiyn't no longer with us..."

And then me mouth goes dry quick and it feels like the whole weight of all and everythin' in the world's on me. I feel weak and wanna lie down where I am, though I dayn't coz I know the grass's wet.

"*She's what?*" I then ask, not believin' what the cunt's sayin'.

"She died on Christmas Day."

Owen walks up to me and knees me right in the stomach. I fall to the ground in agony and he attacks me again with a succession of kicks, swearin' at me as he's doin it.

The pain's the least of it. I dayn't believe what Owen's said and I have me doubts.

He's already gone at this point, so I pull meself up and start walkin' - and then I walk some more, till I practically wander the whole of Kings Heath and most of South Birmingham.

I get home early the next mornin' when the paper boys deliverin' the papers. I go straight up to me room and stay there till me old lady comes in.

"Mornin', love. What time d'ya get in from the pub?"

I keep me trap shut.

"Well, I'm doin' a fry so come down in twenty minutes, all right?"

Me eyes are fixed on the ceilin' and nothin' else. All outside noises aiyn't got no relevance. Me stomach's bruised as fuck and I'm in pain.

Me old lady sighs and takes it as a sign I've got another hangover.

Maybe Owen's lyin'? Maybe he did it just to piss me off and get me to bite, I think to meself. But then it can't be – what sick fucker would say his own sister's dead? I have to find out for meself one way or another. I get dressed and shoot outta the door.

49: Somebody up There Loves Ya, Lynz

"Ya've gotta patient... Lynsey Moriarty," I say to the receptionist at the hospital.

She looks through some files.

"Who are you, sir?"

"I'm her boyfriend."

The woman's face freezes and she seems uncomfortable.

"Err, excuse me, sir... But don't you know... what's happened?"

That's enough and I leave. I dayn't wanna hear the words again like from Owen. So he wasn't lyin' - Lynsey passed away and I dayn't even say goodbye to her.

I leave the hospital and go home. Me breakfast's in the oven but I dayn't wanna eat it. I go up to me room and, knowin' I'm alone, I cry. This is gonna take some time to sink in. What about her funeral, I think, as I'm lyin' on me bed – will Lynsey's parents invite me? I guess that's a silly fuckin' question. I think about stickin' some tunes on, but not The Smiths – I dayn't wanna commit fuckin' suicide... But hold on like, maybe then I could join Lynsey... I'll have to think about that one.

Time's tickin' and I know I have to meet Mickey at New Street at eleven. I look at me watch, before turnin' over and fallin' asleep, only to wake up an hour later more depressed than before. Suicide – or the thought of it like – is still on me mind.

Nah, I aiyn't gonna bother - Mickey and his brother will be goin' alone. They'll be okay, though – they'll be travellin' with a sound lot and they'll be no trouble that way. There's only one thing for me to do now coz all in all the hope for anythin' else has gone. I'm quite at odds to everythin' except this.

Lynsey was such a great girl and now she's gone I dunno what I'm gonna do. Did she get her present? There's other things, too, but they aiyn't that important.

I get up from the bed and go out, not sayin' a word to me parents. The bus comes straight away and, with me pockets fulla dough, I'm ready for anythin'.

Manchester City and First Division survival – huh, what's that now compared to the depression that's fallen on me like a fuckin' brick from the sky?

50: Into the Lion's Den

The suicidal thoughts have disappeared and there are already a few Albion supporters walkin' round harmless like, lookin' for a place to wet their tongues before the derby. The Vile, mind ya, aiyn't out yet, but they will be soon. This match aiyn't famous for its clashes between rival supporters. That aiyn't to say they aiyn't never happened like, but comparin' 'em to the Blues-Villa games they're basically like a Disneyland picnic.

I decide to walk from town to the ground. I dayn't really know the way, ya see, but who gives a fuck. I aiyn't gotta clue about this side of the city really, so I suppose it's like an adventure or summat – I can feel the hatred cryin' out within me fuckin' body as I pass Aston University – for me, this is the dividin' line between 'us' and 'them'. It's about two miles to Vile Park down the Lichfield Road. This is the first time I've ever bin down enemy territory voluntary like. For work, yeah, loadsa times, but I always try not to look outta the window, that way none of the stink and filth from Aston, Erdington and Kingstanding infects me.

She's still in me thoughts with every brave step I take towards enemy turf. The crowds are thickenin' now like a Sunday gravy heatin' in the pot after the two miles I've covered from town. And yeah, she's dead - now it's startin' to sink in.

I stop off for the first time in me life at a Villa pub and, without thinkin' too much about it coz I'm gaspin' for a pint, I drink the Devil's cup. It tastes different here – there's summat strange about it. The pub dayn't smell too clever and the banter's worse still. I leave the pigsty quickly and walk on, all the time tryin' to spot the bloke I'm lookin' for. I aiyn't got no idea what he looks like other than he's a big fucker, though amongst the teemin' thousands of a West Midland's derby it'd be easier findin' an honest Pikey. The banter – mainly piss-takin' outta me team – fuels me hatred more and more and I wanna explode there and then.

Nah, it aiyn't the right place. Checkin' me watch I guess it's time to make a move to the ground as it's half two.

I walk towards the biggest kop in the country – or so the Vile faithful think, anyway. Me one visit to the place, a one-nil defeat back in '83, turned out to be a runnin' battle outside the ground, which happened to be equally uncomfortin' inside: two thousand of us there were, squashed in the North Stand's away pen and above us, in the stand's upper tier, some Villa cunts were throwin' bottles down at us and any other stuff they could lay their hands on.

One thing I have to admit, though – even if I dayn't like to – Vile Park's light years ahead of me own team's ground in terms of comfort and the grand fuckin' stage. One of the oldest and noblest ladies of all English grounds, it makes St Andrews look like summat destroyed in Beirut.

The price of admission turns out a bit more expensive than at St Andrews and I dayn't wanna pay it. I dayn't take a programme, either, though I know at home we're short of bog roll and soon regret not buyin' one.

The Holte End – or the Arseholte End as I like to call it – is fillin' up quickly with more and more slimy north Birmingham bastards. The chants from the hardcore at the back are becomin' louder and louder and they aiyn't targeted at the home team's opponents, West Bromwich Albion – nah, the truth is the Vile dayn't give a flyin' fuck about them cunts from the Black Country – it's *my* team, 'Small Heath FC' as they like to call us, which draws all their hate and attention.

I look round at the scum. Here they are, the dregs of the Second City, givin' it the blag coz they feel safe in their numbers. Yeah, they can be like that, knowin' most of the Zulus are keepin' a low profile or are in the nick. Who are the fuckin' Steamers and the Villa Youth anyway? Go on, sing some more, that's all ya can do. I'd love it, yeah I'd love it now to have a bomb and finish ya all fuckin' off.

Lookin' around at every bloke close to me, I'm sure none of 'em are *him* – they all lack the size.

Up the steps I go, up towards where all the noise is comin' from. All the time I have me eye on every supporter I pass, tryin' to remember the face. But it dayn't do no good: it's only his hulkin' size and the sound of his voice. I climb further up till I can't go no higher. Here I am: in the home of the Villa hardcore, and if I'm gonna find him, it's gonna be here.

There's a stranger on their turf and a few suspicious gazes go out after me. One bloke, black and in his thirties, pays real attention to me. He walks over casual like, squeezin' in between his own crew and says above the roar of the crowd:

"Dunno ya, mate. Fuck off down there where ya came from."

It would be easier to give the arrogant dick a slap there and then, to sorta embarrass him, but I aiyn't in the mood just yet and I slowly go back down again, though all the while keepin' one eye open for the bloke I'm lookin' for.

I stop halfway down and stand next to a bearded bloke wearin' a donkey jacket and a claret and blue scarf.

"Shit, aiyn't it?" the bloke says, not directly at me but I hear it anyway.

"Yeah," I reply.

"As long as them cunts lose today, I aiyn't bothered about nothin' else and I'll be all right."

I know exactly who the muppet's talkin' about, and it aiyn't the Baggies.

Me thoughts for a moment go wild as in me imagination I slash the oldtimer in the neck with a stanley, stampin' on his fuckin' head, flattenin' it to a pulp and spittin' on him for good measure.

Havin' enough of the stupid Villa cunt, another has the nerve to speak to me.

"Gotta light, mate?" he asks. I duly oblige. "Tight so far, aiyn't it?" the bloke continues.

"Yeah, whatever," I say, eyes rollin'.

A Villa player then goes close and an 'ooooh' erupts from all four sides of the ground.

"Fuck, that was close!" the bloke next to me shouts "Come on, Villa! Come on Walters, ya cunt! He's always doin' that – it's over fuckin' excitement with him all the time like. He did the same a couple of times against the fuckin' Blues in September, remember?"

I smile.

Another 'ooooh' rises up along with a loada 'fucks'. The Albion nearly score, but like it's bin with 'em the whole season, they fail to capitalise on the chance. The Baggies supporters who've bothered to make the trip are pissed off, naturally, and their faint cries die down as quick.

The memory of the previous night returns in flashes and with it I'm unable to figure out why I'm in the Holte End at Vile Park. Summat's wrong. Lynsey's face keeps appearin' in front of me eyes and then she disappears. I again find meself surrounded by scumbags and me purpose on the earth's clear to me again.

There's a roar – somebody's scored. The home team, probably, though I can't be sure. Me emotions and feelers are only on one bloke and one bloke only.

I go down to the right corner at the front of the Holte, next to the Witton Stand, sit down on the concrete steps and smoke. There aiyn't no people here and it's possible to stretch out a bit. A boy – no more than eleven – walks up to me from the fence.

"Gis a fag, mate?"

"Nah."

"Oh, go on?"

"Nah. Fuck off ya little cunt." I blow smoke in the boy's face.

"Ya fuckin' twat," the boy answers, before leggin' it.

For it's Aston Villa, Aston Villa FC
For we are the greatest team
The world has ever seen...!

Nah, I've had enough with all this singin' and everythin' else. I throw me fag on the floor and get up, furious. Next there are a couple of anti-Blues chants, and they get louder as I get higher. I wanna take a chance again, but this time from the other side, so I slalom me way in and out. A few years back, this little movement woulda bin impossible, as the ground – especially the Holte End – was packed out like match after match, so I'm lucky.

You're shit... aah, comes from the Vile faithful after the Baggies keeper, Tony Godden, takes a goal kick. What the Villa wouldn't do for it to be Seaman instead, the Blues shot stopper. They're still pissed off with the three-nil defeat they suffered at home in September against us, and wanna get their revenge sweet like.

The whistle blows for half-time and in the Holte End the crowd quickly disappears to the lower depths of the stinky bogs and the pie stalls.

The tannoy announces the scores from around the country. I'm so wrapped up in me own world in search of the bloke, I dayn't even hear how we're gettin' on at Man. City.

I get meself a good spot at the back, a sound place as anywhere to find him. There are quite a few shady characters stood around, similar in look to the ones at St Andrews, but at least I know the faces there and feel safe. Most of 'em, judgin' by their clobber, are the team's casuals, I reckon – the 'famous' fuckin' Villa Youth. I listen carefully to the bollocks comin' outta their gobs and it dayn't impress me. I'm becomin' more angry and frustrated. One bloke, lookin' good in a blue Ralph Lauren jacket that looks the dog's bollocks with his perm, stares at me over his open programme that he's pretendin' to read.

"All right, mate," he says in a friendly tone.

Not bein' that badly dressed meself, I fit in no problem in that respect. But it's me face – nobody knows it up here and it's a problem.

"Not too bad. And yaself?"

The Villa casual crashes his fags. I keep it tight-lipped as the bloke fires questions at me quicker than a western gunslinger, one question's summat about Steve Hodge's transfer, I think, but I dayn't take that much fuckin' notice.

"I aiyn't sin ya up here before – usually down there, are ya?" he asks.

"Yeah, summat like that."

Supporters start returnin' from the lower levels. The casual goes back to his place. Two burly types, not hooligans by the way they're dressed but lookin' hard enough anyway, walk towards me.

"Ya in our place, mate," the bigger of the two says.

"Sorry, I didn't know it had ya name on it."

Both are pissed off at me sarcasm.

"I'd fuck off if I were *you*," the smaller one warns, "before I give ya a slap."

Not yet, not yet, I'm saying to meself, bitin' me bottom lip.

"Sorry lads," I say.

I move away without sayin' another word to 'em.

The second half kicks off and once again I find meself down the botton of the Holte with all the kiddies. I've just realised it's dark now and the massive floodlights are shinin' their light to every corner of the ground, and the chants are resonating downwards, liftin' the spirits of the Villa players.

I wanna know where the bloke's hidin', but the seconds are tickin' away and there's less than forty minutes till the final whistle and a mass exodus outta the ground.

Me thoughts return to the past – the very recent past – when me bird was still alive.

Suicide.

Nah, I need to cry, I need it. The tears come naturally like and after 'em the sobs of a little fuckin' boy, hands in face and muffled.

"Fuck me, mate, it aiyn't that bad yet," a middle-aged scarfy says, standin' next to me. "We'll get a point outta this one at least, ya'll see."

I look up at the bloke through teary eyes that are reddenin' and gaze at him, then say:

"I dayn't give a fuck, mate, all right?"

The bloke huffs and distances himself from me, and I'm now lookin' up to the back of the Holte End again, tryin' to distinguish through the thousands of tiny pink faces the bloke I wanna deck good and propa. There's a lotta irritation as I search – desperation, if ya like. I aiyn't got nothin' else to live for but revenge and wanna see it through. From all the people in the ground, I reckon only meself and the coppers round the perimeter of the pitch dayn't give a fuck what's happenin' in the match.

A player skies the ball well over the crossbar and it lands in the Holte End: hundreds of hands go up in a vain attempt to catch it. A lucky bloke does and an applause breaks out before he throws the white Mitre ball back down to a sea of hands and back onto the pitch and the keeper.

I wanna wander up one more time, but this time I wanna go up from a different way, so just to avoid any of the characters I've already bumped into.

The one thing that tortures me is the *face* – how can I remember it? Months have passed since then and it all happened too quick like. The bastard's face has completely vanished from me mind. I've got a few excuses, I know, but it dayn't console me now: a few too many tots for one thing and the booza was also a dark place. And yeah, I legged it for me life, so that didn't help. The fucker's mug, though, that's everythin' and I dayn't remember it.

I look to the pitch. Screams. Garth Crooks shoots towards goal after a beautiful cross comes in from the left-hand side, but somehow the ugly Nigel Spink – Chinny as I like to call him – palms it away for a corner kick. The set piece comes to nothin', yet this dayn't stop the Vile faithful from voicin' their disapproval at the pathetic markin' of the ex-Spur's man. I get back to what's at hand.

A few days ago I woulda pissed meself seein' this on *Match of the Day*, laughin' with the lads about seein' Graham Turner on the sidelines pullin' his hair out at his side's crappy football; but now, bein' a witness to it first hand in their own cathedral, I dayn't actually give a shit. Nah, the bloke, hooligan of all hooligans, harder than all in Brum, is up there somewhere, enjoyin' himself, givin' it the lash and the bash with the lads, waitin' for another Saturday night on the razzle in town. He can have his fun if he wants, at least for a bit anyway.

I start walkin' up the steps again, in and out and body weavin', tryin' to avoid the hot and fiery fag ends every supporter seems to be holdin' in their hands. Are they weapons? Are they tryin' to burn the fuck outta me? Do they know already who's infiltrated their inner sanctum? As I climb up, gawpin' into the face of every pasty-faced supporter as I do, I try to relive that night again. One clue would be enough – otherwise there's no way I'll be able to spot him. I go back down to the front and wait for the final whistle.

It's the end of the match and all the players shake hands. It's a one-one draw and even-stevens. Most of the crowd rushes out at this point so as to be the first ones on the number 7 or 11 buses and the trains; some stay to find out the results from the rest of the day's matches. Unluckily the Blues have lost again, three-one to Man. City, and when the tannoy announces it the remainin' supporters shout fuckin' jubilantly: a late Christmas present, I suppose.

A gloom crashes over me, crashes and crashes again into me mind and with it Lynsey's face. Either she's alive or she just finds it funny as fuck to scare the shit outta me.

The ground's almost empty now. Above, the floodlights illuminate the pitch. Scattered round me on the floor are fag ends, polystyrene chip containers, silver foil pie trays and crushed cans of lager. Pound-an-hour cleaners – here coz it's an honour to serve their club this way and they get in for fuck all – pick up the rubbish. One, a man in his sixties, moves towards me, back bent and carryin' a black plastic bag in one hand.

"Ya'll have to leave now, son – we're cleanin'," he says. "Ya in me way."

I'm lookin directly at the floodlight in the corner of the North and Trinity Road stands, and it's makin' me vision blurred. In the light, I can still see Lynsey. The cleaner repeats himself, but this time louder so I hear him - it aiyn't no good: I'm somewhere else like, spaced out and dreamin', though I know the bloke's beside me. He kicks me in the thigh gently.

"What?" I ask.

"Get up. Ya in me way."

"That's *your* problem." I take out a fag and start smokin'. The cleaner tutts, nods his head - coz he's pissed off - and trundles away up the concrete steps.

The floodlights are still a fascination. I wanna keep on seein' her face, so I stare up once more, hopin' to see it. But it aiyn't no good – whatever was there a second ago's fucked off now. I make me way outta the now empty ground. Outside supporters are in small groups chattin', but most are already on the way home. The Old Bill still has a presence, though.

51: The Final Whistle

I walk to Witton Road and wait for the number 7 bus into town. By the time I get there it's after seven, and the place is already startin' to come alive with ya Saturday night revellers. I get meself a fish and chips as I'm starvin'. The queue's dead long and I have to wait twenty minutes to get served, and the chips turn out to be fuckin' horrible and all hard. Luckily, the chippy's right next to the pub on Corporation Street where everythin' kicked off in the summer. I try to get in:

"Sorry, mate," the bouncer says, "ya wearin' trainers. Not on the weekend."

I look at him as if the big bastard's nobody.

"What d'ya mean?"

"No trainers."

"Ah, come on, mate," I beg.

"Rules are rules."

"Listen, I just wanna check if somebody's in there like, that's all – I swear, nothin' else. I dayn't wanna try no funny business."

"Quickly then," the bouncer says.

The pub's one of the best in town, though it aiyn't really a pub but a wine bar. The term 'wine bar' is all the rage now. The gaffer actually wanted to attract a different kind of person to his place – yuppies like, in a word. They've got dough to burn and wanna spend as much of it as possible. The only problem is the football crowd has taken over, and the professionals and well-to-do types only really use the place at a lunchtime and for an hour after work, so really it's 'as ya were'.

I walk in and look round. The place is big and it's got loadsa hidden corners. It's quite busy already. I look hard into every face. Behind me is the bouncer, watchin' me closely.

The night's comin' back to me now. I remember where I was when it all kicked off. We were sittin' by the bogs on two stools near the end of the bar. The group the bloke belonged to – summat like seven or eight in number – was along the bar, creatin' a wall.

The bouncer's still lookin' at me suspicious like. He's gettin' annoyed at me now as there aiyn't no sign of the bastard.

"Just a minute, mate, all right?" I say.

"Who are ya lookin' for?" he asks.

"A mate."

"Well he aiyn't here, it looks like. Can ya leave?"

I start to walk out, frustrated. As I do, the door opens, and a group of blokes walks in.

Sometimes miracles do happen.

Among all the natter, I distinguish one voice that I've heard before – or at least I think I've heard before. I look at the bloke. Without a doubt it's him. Me heart starts poundin' faster and faster, and I've got butterflies in me stomach.

"Listen, mate," I say to the bouncer, "if I go home and change, will ya let me in later?"

"I dayn't care. It's just no trainers."

I rush outta the place and catch the bus home. Me adrenalin's at an all-time high and I smoke a shit loada fags on the bus. When I get home, I dayn't even say a word to me mom and dad, who are sittin' down in the living room and watchin' telly.

I take off me jeans and trainers and put on a grey pair of Farah's and a pair of brogues – now I look the dog's bollock's. Who'd give me the red card now?

"Is that *you*, Darren?" me old lady shouts, as I'm slammin' the front door behind me.

I have to wait ages for the bus back into town, and I'm worried the bloke has already done one and left when I do get there.

"All right, mate?"

There's another bouncer on the door.

"Ya can't come in," he says, holdin' his hand up.

"Why?"

"Ya just can't come in."

"Where's ya mate gone?" I ask.

"Which 'mate'?"

"The other bouncer?"

"He's on his break."

"Well he said I could come in."

"What are ya talkin' about?"

"I was here earlier," I say, now pissed off.

"I dayn't care. Ya can't come in."

"Ya havin' a laugh."

"Nah, I aiyn't."

"Go and get him for me."

"Fuck off," he says to me.

"Ya can't do it – there's someone in there I've gotta meet."

"*Who?*"

"It aiyn't ya business."

"Everythin's *my* business – I work here."

"Come on, dayn't be arsey."

"Nah, ya aiyn't gettin' in."

"Then I'll wait for ya mate to come back."

"Ya do that then."

Ten minutes go by and his mate returns from his break.

I hear 'em talkin' to each other as they're lookin' over at me. I'm over the other side of the road, next to The Crown pub. Seein' the two bouncers talkin', I cross the road.

"Did he tell ya?" I ask the one bouncer who was bein' a cunt with me.

They let me in.

The place is busy, though it aiyn't like some of the pubs in town on a Saturday night.

I look round. There aiyn't no sign of the bloke. Where is he? Has he left already? I get meself a pint in. A minute later the bloke I'm lookin' for comes outta the bogs. He goes up to a group of men. They're all in their thirties and forties and look pretty hard, not the sort to fuck with. I wanna know what they are talkin' about, so I move towards 'em – not too closely, mind ya, but close enough to hear 'em.

I'm surprised, the bloke aiyn't that big, but it's definitely him.

"Fuckin' hell, Mel, I dayn't believe that today..."

"Me too – that fuckin' manager needs shootin'..."

It's ya usual pub banter, and nothin' I aiyn't heard before.

I'm sure it's him by his voice. The bloke has a squeaky one, ya see, and different from the resta the blokes he's with. I stare at him and feel angry. Me anger and nerves are buildin' up slowly. I wanna do summat there and then but know if I do, I'll be fuckin' run over by the cunts as they'll all pile in. I wanna bide me time. A couple of pints will do it, and I aiyn't gonna over do it in any way.

A couple of the blokes go over to a few birds sat round a table by the window. By their look, these are ya posh sort - highly unlikely to be impressed by a couple of lager-fuelled football louts.

"How are ya, ladies?" I hear one ask, swayin' backwards and forwards and obviously the worse for drink.

The birds turn towards each other in an attempt to ignore his come on.

Another bloke from the group, well-dressed and with a handsome face, approaches 'em.

"Come on, girls, dayn't treat me mate like that."

They look at him and laugh.

Then the *bloke* comes over, wantin' to get in on the action.

"Have a word, Tim," one of his mates says.

So, his name's Tim. Tim. Timothy. Yeah, it dayn't sound very hard. In fact, it's such an ordinary name, I laugh. Tim, a Villa hardman. I dayn't believe it. Rocket, Bozza, Cuddles, Delford – now they're hard names, names that'd put the fear into anyone. But Tim? Well, not in my *book*, not at all. His one savin' grace is that at least he looks the part in his designer gear.

"Go on, Tim," the handsome one says, "have a go.

"Hello, ladies. How are ya, all right?"

They look at him all pissed off like. If they're gonna pull tonight, it definitely aiyn't gonna be with *Tim*.

With his manhead and three chins hangin' down, a real beer belly loaded to the max with pies and pints and a dozen tattoos - one on his forearm: VILLA FOREVER that'd embarrass even the most dedicated Hell's Angel - who coulda blamed the birds?

He introduces himself but it aiyn't no good. They'd rather sleep with Ken Dodd than talk to Tim.

The birds get up and, holdin' hands like a loada Amazonian lesbians, go to the ladies' bogs.

"Oh, I'd love to be one of them fuckin' toilet seats in there. I bet they've got a lovely fannies," I hear Tim say, sorta loudish.

The resta the group come over and they begin singin' Villa songs over Spandau Ballet's *Gold*. One of the barmen, pissed off at this, goes out to the bouncer by the door.

"Have a word with them dicks, Terry, will ya?" he asks.

Terry's a big cunt and he aiyn't the kind to mess with.

"Sorry, lads, ya'll have to pipe it down here, I think, or ya'll have to leave... Know what I mean?"

They shut up straight away.

I still have one ear on what they're sayin', especially what Tim's sayin':

"I dayn't believe that, Tone, ya takin' the piss, aiyn't ya," Tim says.

"Nah I aiyn't, mate. I swear he robbed me fuckin' blind."

"What d'ya do to him?"

"What d'ya think?"

"Dunno?"

"Forget it, ya thick twat..."

The more he speaks though, the more I start thinkin' it aiyn't the bloke who gave me a good kick in. He's too – well, too summat and I dunno what it is. Tim dayn't seem the kind who could lead a mob on the terraces, that's all, and though he's big, he aiyn't *that* big.

I start to have me doubts. The night it happened, I was well pissed, but the voice matches what I heard on the night: It's squeaky and a bit irritatin'.

What's goin' on? Now I'm in two minds whether to fuck everythin' and just lay into the cunt. Just as I'm about to do it, Lynsey starts talkin' to me again. Maybe I'm possessed or summat. She tells me to wait – wait coz waitin' will be the cure for everythin'. I dunno if it's really her or it's just me and I wanna bottle it.

The three birds return from the bogs.

"Back are we, girls?" Tim says, laughin'. He's ya jovial sort, up for the crack and a clown for his mates and it's gettin' harder and harder for me to picture him mixin' it on a Saturday afternoon at Vile Park. His face's too soft lookin'. But as they say, looks can be deceptive.

"What's the difference between a Bluenose and a pillar?" one from the group says. A loada 'dunnos' follow. "A pillar knows what it means to support summat."

A couple of laughs go out, but nothin' too loud.

There are another couple more lame jokes of that nature which I dayn't find at all funny – not like Tim, coz Tim's in his element now. What could be better for him than this?

I go to the bar and buy meself another pint. The group's still rowdy and annoyin' the birds at the table. Tim has his eyes firmly fixed on one of the bird's perty breasts, but there's probably more chance of Jimmy Hill winnin' sexiest man on telly award 1985 than Tim gettin' his end away with this tasty prize.

"What d'ya do, love?" he asks.

"Fuck off, ya fat cunt," she replies in her posh accent.

"Where ya from, love – fuckin' Harborne?"

"Piss off, ya knob."

I laugh. A piss is callin' so I head to the bogs.

There can't be more of a contrast between the bogs here to the ones in The Bantam: These are done out elegant and dayn't smell of a tramp's kegs. The urinals are spotless with no pools of piss below 'em – not like at The Bantam, where the floor reminds me of the film *Singing in the Rain*.

I drain the main vein and go up to the sink and wash me hands. I dunno why I even wash 'em, coz usually I never do. I stare at the big mirror in front of me, not likin' what I see but acceptin' it fully. A bloke walks in and stares at me.

"All right, mate?" he says.

I'm always a bit suspicious of blokes like that. I dunno him for Charlie and I'm wonderin' what he wants. I dayn't return the greetin' and I leave with a smarmy look on me face.

Back in the bar a loada people have come in. A couple of nice birds too, but that's the last thing on me mind.

Tim's still there, though almost immediately I notice summat aiyn't quite right. I'm sure Tim was wearin' a green Fila shirt but now he's wearin' a red Slazenger one, and when I look at his neck and arms all the tattoos have disappeared.

"All right, Jim," the handsome bloke says, who just minutes before was callin' him 'Tim'.

I thought his name's Tim, not *Jim*. Jim? How can *Tim* be *Jim* in a matter of minutes, when *Tim* aiyn't *Jim*. Maybe I misheard 'em and it's really Jim and it aiyn't Tim. Nah, I'm sure his name's Tim.

Somebody's spiked me drink or summat, otherwise Lynsey's really havin' a laugh somewhere.

"Jimbo, couldn't be no tighter at the bottom, could it?" another asks 'Jim' from the group.

"We'll be all right, ya'll see."

"Fuckin' three-one, though – how d'ya explain that?"

"It's a setback, only a setback. That cunt Saunders is goin' soon and everythin' will be sorted..."

What's goin' on? Tim or Jim, the Blues or Villa?

"Did ya spike me drink or summat, mate?" I ask the barman who last served me.

I rush to the bogs and splash me face, comin' out a few minutes later. What I see when I return is unbelievable but explains everythin':

There are two Tims or Jims or whoever the fuck they are. Yeah, right in the flesh and before me eyes. They're the same size and build and are smilin' at each other like tweedle-Dum and Tweedle-Dee.

I've had enough of all this voodoo shit and I go straight up to 'em.

"All right, lads. I'm Darren Acheson."

They look at me. It aiyn't usual – even in a city-centre booza on a Saturday night when everybody's outta their tree – to just introduce yaself like that, but that's what I do.

"Ya dayn't remember me, d'ya?" I ask.

"Nah," they both say at the same time.

"One of ya gave me a decent kick in a few months back, remember?"

They're puzzled like.

"What the fuck are ya on, mate?" Jim says, laughin'.

"I aiyn't on nothin' but the floor."

"Then fuck off," Jim says.

"Ya twins, yeah?"

"Fuck me, Tim, he's a right observant cunt, aiyn't he?"

"Yeah, he is."

"So ya dayn't remember which of ya it was givin' it the verbals with me and me mate then?"

They're both thinkin' now – bein' twins and all and telepathic like – that I'm game for a laugh. They fancy the crank up as they're gettin' fuck all from the fanny in the place.

"What's ya name again, mate?" Jim asks.

"Darren."

"So, Darren, what makes ya think me and me brother here did ya over?"

"Nah, only one of ya did."

"Ya've got some fuckin' bottle, son," Jim continues. "I mean, look at us – how many strong are we tonight-"

"There are seven of us, Jim," Tim comments.

"Seven of us, ya see. We could easily bash ya in if we wanted and ya'd know no better."

"Yeah, but are ya gonna?"

"That depends – nah, it's a Saturday night... I fuckin' rate ya, though, big time."

Though they're twins, Jim's evil lookin' and I fear it's all gonna end badly.

"Are ya a Villa supporter?" Tim asks me.

"Everythin' all right, lads?" their mate – the one with the handsome face – asks, who's come over from where the resta the group's standin'.

"Nah bother, Steve," Jim says. "How are ya gettin' on with that fanny over there?"

"It's in the bag, mate," Steve says, smilin'.

"What's ya name again?" Jim then asks me.

"Darren."

"Steve, this is Darren."

"All right, Darren. I'm Steve."

We shake hands and that's that, and he traps back over to where he was.

"So, Darren, where was I? Oh, yeah, so are ya a Villa supporter?"

"Nah."

Tim smiles and looks at his brother.

"*Blues*?" Tim asks.

"Yeah."

The ugly lookin' twins turn to each other again in a way that only twins can – no words are needed. Everythin' is through the eyes which hides the message.

"Ya hear that, Timothy boy... He's one of me own."

"So ya a Bluenose?" Tim asks.

I have me fists clenched in me pockets ready for blows.

"Ya see, Tim, at least some of us have half a brain in this City... Let me get ya a pint, son?" Jim then says, his tone now friendlier than a minute ago.

A bit lost for words at what's goin' on, I accept.

Jim goes to the bar and I'm left alone with Tim.

"What's all this about one of us batterin' ya then, Darren?"

"I dunno... I coulda bin confused or summat... I aiyn't sure," I answer, embarrassed.

"Ah, it dayn't matter now anyway – let bygones be bygones, that's what I say."

"So, Tim, ya a Villa fan?"

"Too fuckin' right I am."

"And ya brother's a Bluenose?"

"Yeah, the fuckin' muppet... But they say there's one in every family."

"So tell me if ya can, coz maybe it's just me, coz maybe I'm just a little fucked up or summat, but how... I mean, how can one of ya be Villa and the other Blues... It just dayn't make no sense to me?"

"It's a long fuckin' story... we were born four minutes apart in 1947... Our old man's an Albion supporter who's followed 'em since we can remember. We were brought up in the Great Barr area of Birmingham, ya see, and we remember most of all our old man goin' off on his tod on a Saturday to the Hawthorns without us to watch the Baggies. At the time we didn't have a clue what he was doin', as we were probably still in nappies. It was only later that we sussed what it was all about. Sometimes we'd go down the rec with him to play footy, but he wasn't really interested then in playin' with us... He was always pissed up, ya know what I mean like? Well, anyway, to cut a long story short, we went for different teams just to piss him off a bit, ya know, for the way he neglected us as babbies."

Jim comes back from the bar.

"There ya go, ladies," he says, handin' us our pints. Jim then goes back to the bar to fetch his own. As he's comin' back, though, Culture Club's *Church of the Poison Mind* fades away and a beat that I know, oh so well, replaces it. The rapid percussion hits Jim and instantly he makes eye contact with me, then he starts movin' his hips to the rhythm and swayin' in all directions. Jeff Lynn's finely tuned vocal chords begin doin' their work:

Sun is shinin' in the sky
There aiyn't a cloud in sight...

And basically that's it. I dayn't believe it really – believe that such a thing could happen: that two brothers could support different teams and still be okay about it. I just found out that it's possible, and that football's just a game in the end. The next time I'm in The Bantam Cock, with Mickey, Nobby and Bagpuss, I'm gonna tell 'em how it really is.

I laugh to meself on the way home from the pub. It's late and all I can hear are screams and shouts from both men and women who've had too much to drink. A lotta the noises are football related – ya know, the usual bullshit. Yesterday I think

I woulda done the same like, maybe not to such a degree, but a little anyway. But now, after hearin' Tim and Jim's story, I doubt it.

And as for Birmingham City and visits to St Andrews? Yeah, I'll still be goin' down – for ya team's always ya team, aiyn't it? I'll be there on the terraces givin' it loads, but only for the sake of the eleven shitty players on the pitch. I just wish we could win a few matches, I aiyn't askin' for the Championship or a cup. Maybe '86 is gonna be our year.

Hooliganism and the Zulus – well, that's another thing. I'd be lyin' to meself if I ever thought I was part of that scene anyway, coz I never have bin, though that aiyn't to say I never glorified it to some extent. But not no more. Nah, that's all gone.

And Lynsey, yeah, Lynsey's always gonna be there. Maybe all this shit has bin a test for me or summat. Maybe Lynsey lived in a way for *my* fuckin' change, and if it's true, then she's done a right good job there – thanks, darlin'.

An honest review – however good or bad – would be appreciated on the platform where you purchased the book. Thank you.

Don't miss out!

Click the button below and you can sign up to receive emails whenever James Dargan publishes a new book. There's no charge and no obligation.

Sign Me Up!

https://books2read.com/r/B-A-PIH-PXZ

BOOKS 2 READ

Connecting independent readers to independent writers.

About the Author

James Dargan was born in Birmingham, England, in 1974. Coming from an Irish background, he frequently writes about that experience. As well as England, he has also lived in the United States, Ireland, and - for the best part of fifteen years - in Warsaw, Poland, his home from home from home.

Printed in Great Britain
by Amazon